Wealthy &

WICKED

A Novel By

CHRIS RENEE

Wealthy & WICKED

A Novel By

CHRIS RENEE

Life Changing Books in conjunction with Power Play Media
Published by Life Changing Books
P.O. Box 423 Brandywine, MD 20613

Library of Congress Cataloging-in-Publication Data;

www.lifechangingbooks.net
13 Digit: 978-1934230336
10 Digit: 1-934230332

Copyright © 2012

Acknowledgements

First and foremost, I have to thank God. His wonderful gift of his son Jesus, saved me before I even knew that I was lost. I know that my Grandmother is sitting beside You, watching where I'm headed. I'm forever grateful!

Mommy, Daddy, Reese, and TJ, I can't find enough words to thank y'all for standing by me. I know at one point you probably wondered where I was going in life. I'm happy that I'm on a path that I hope will make you guys proud. Your unrelenting love for me has given me a great appreciation of self.

Bradon, MaKayla, Tayler and Kalia, you bring me joy! Having the four of you is something that I'm so proud of. I can be at my best or worst and you guys still find genuine worth in me. As long as the blood pumps through my veins, you all are loved!

Mark, I truly can't thank another soul for making me the woman that I am. You've taught me so much about life and human beings. I'm grateful for this experience. Everything happens for a reason, I'm confident in that.

Tam, Leandrewski, Ebby, JB, Tanya, Keia, and Kisha, I know that I have gotten on all of your last nerves with writing over the years. You've read the rough drafts, listened to me cry and supported me like crazy. The greatest thing is that you have never complained, at least not to me (lol).

The Barnett and Kendle family. There are way too many to name but you each play a major part of my life. Ride or die type of love that I wouldn't change for nothing in the world. If I have forgotten anyone, charge it to my mind and not my heart!

It was your love of Zora Neale Hurston that made me want to become a writer. When you became a journalist, I knew that I wanted to follow in your footsteps. Thank you Kim!

Tressa, I can't imagine this book taking place without you. Thanks from the bottom of my heart for the phone calls, emails and encouragement. I can't count how many times just talking to you has wiped away any sign of discouragement.

To those who supported me from the first blog I started, I give a big tremendous, THANK YOU! Before I believed in myself, you all encouraged my love of story telling. Without your support, I would be nothing.

Lastly, thanks to everyone on the LCB team. Leslie Allen, Tasha, all the test readers and anyone else who helped with the project. To the LCB authors, Miss KP, Kendall Banks, J. Tremble, Tonya Ridley, Jackie D. CJ Hudson, Carla Pennington, Danette Majette, Mike Warren, Ericka Williams, VegasClarke and anyone else I failed to mention. Thanks for welcoming me to the family.

To all the readers, I really hope you enjoy this novel as much as I enjoyed writing it.

Love,
Chris Renee

Dedication

This book is dedicated to my mother, Sharon Barnett. I sat with you, I cried for you, I was strong for you but you were stronger. You never complained, always a smile. You screamed, MOVE MOUNTAIN. Cancer is no match for you. I'm happy my mommy is such a fighter; I can't imagine life without you.

Prologue

My eyes opened wide to the sight of the white ceiling. The bright lights caused a temporary fog as I tried to shake away the numbing pain that exploded in my brain.

"Well, it looks like my patient is awake," the voice said from the other side of the room. I tried to turn my head towards it but I had no strength left in my body.

"What do you mean patient? Where am I?" I couldn't remember much of anything before this moment. I tried my hardest to figure out how she had gotten me in this position.

"You're my patient. And in very good hands." She walked towards me with a long needle in her hand and a sinister smile on her face. I panicked!

"I swear, if you don't let me up from here."

"If I don't let you up, then what?"

"Then, I'll…"

"You won't be doing a damn thing, sweetie. I'm running this show." She laughed at my futile attempt to untie myself.

"This shit isn't funny." I continued to tug at the burlap ropes that had my arms confined to the bottom of the heating pipes.

"This isn't supposed to be funny. Well, maybe it is for me, but I'm sure you won't find any humor in this at all."

"Why are you doing this?"

"Because bitches like you deserve to lose every now and then. Now, open those legs up wide so I can take what belongs to me."

My heart rate accelerated as the liquid in the needle shot through my arm. I wanted to fight but whatever she pumped my veins with had rendered me paralyzed. "Please, stop! I don't have anything of yours. I swear it's not what you think. Please, just let me explain." Tears flew from the corners of my eyes as she continued to laugh at me. I had to admit, I had done some pretty foul things in my life but I couldn't think of any that would make someone want to do me in like this.

"I'm over wanting to hear an explanation from you. At the end of the day, you did what you did and now you must pay." Her voice took on a stern mother's tone.

"Don't do this, please. I'm begging you! I'll do whatever you want, just let me go." My pleas fell on deaf ears as she started to hum a nursery song. One I'd never heard…it seemed more sadistic than anything.

"For reasons unknown to me, you keep landing on top," she spat. "So, it's only natural that I take matters into my own hands," she whispered in my ear as I began to lose consciousness. "That's right, Tracey, take a deep breath. You never deserved to carry this precious gift, not someone as trifling as you."

Quickly, she started the tedious process of taking what she thought should've been hers in the first place. All I could do was cry and hope like hell that someone would save me. As the cramps rapidly shot through my stomach, I realized that she had come to take my baby.

Chapter 1

As my driver stopped in front of my building, I was in an excellent mood. I hopped out of the back of the Suburban with a conceited smile and rocking a brand new Diane Von Furstenberg dress. My feet felt great from a fresh pedicure and I was wearing the hell out of a nice pair of peep toe Prada pumps. They may've been last season, but for two grand, I rocked them like they were brand new. I decided to give weave a rest, so my own natural hair-do was cropped short to frame my face.

It was evident that my new trainer had been working my body to death, because I heard more than a few cat calls as I walked towards my office. Thanks to all the extra toning, my invisible waistline had caused my ass to sit perfectly upon my back. This gave men extra incentive to all beg for a chance to be with me.

Feeling myself, I used the sidewalk as my personal runway. As all eyes turned towards me I served up a heavy dose of fierceness. Those boys could look and want, but there was no way in hell I would even consider being with a construction worker.

Kanye West's *Gold Digger* played in my head, and I strutted hard to the beat. Days like these were the best, and I knew that it could only get better. Some might even consider me one of the luckiest girls in town. I had what the have-nots wanted. I was who the nobodies wanted to be. More importantly, I was who they never could be. I, Tracey Robbins was the *it girl* of St. Louis.

Yes, life was real good and with this upcoming meeting in a few weeks, it would only get better. I was ready to take over St. Louis and move out of my parent's shadow. It was time for a new storm and Hurricane Tracey was about to run rampant through downtown. It felt good knowing that in a short while, I would be the talk of the town, and not just the gossip section.

My magazine, *Totally Chic*, had really begun to take off. I wasn't the least bit surprised; I knew that this would all be possible back when I was fifteen. Most people wanted to be a lawyer or doctor, but I always knew that some form of journalism would be the only life for me. After years of serious grinding, I was finally starting to see the fruits of my labor.

I was easily on the fast track of the backwards Oprah plan. Starting with owning my magazine company, I hoped to be on television by the time I was thirty-five. I could see myself now, screaming to my audience, "YOU GET A CAR! AND YOU GET A CAR! AND THEY GET A CAR!" Everyone would fall out, cry and worship me just like they did the Mighty O. I felt my big break coming and I was excited as hell.

I was so caught up in my own thoughts of greatness, I barely noticed the men working on the sidewalk. At the last moment, I stepped onto the cobblestoned strip they were working on, and pranced towards the entrance way. I winked at the workers and put some extra swing in my hips for their enjoyment. I twisted so hard my left heel got stuck between the bricks, causing me to tumble down in the middle of the block.

"Shit!" I screamed out loud in pure agony.

"Damn, baby, you ok?" one of the construction workers exclaimed while springing into action, helping me to remove my shoe and my body from the old, tattered cobblestone street.

"I'm fine, thank you." I angrily snatched my shoe from his hand, distorting my face after getting a good look at his disgusting teeth.

His dirty ass hands were smudging the satin on my pumps. His friend shook his head in disgust.

"Man, leave that stuck up ass bitch alone. Stank ass!" he shouted.

He made no secret of his hatred for me. He had tried multiple times to step to me. Each rejection made him more bitter. But I was used to that type of treatment from those beneath me. My reputation was clear. I'd been labeled a mini celebrity in St. Louis... always in the spotlight for treating people like the bottom of my shoe. Those who deserved it, of course.

"You sure you ok, you took a nasty spill right there." Yuck mouth was dead set on making sure I was fine.

I would be a lot better if he would get out of my face.

"You don't have to pretend to be concerned. You people are all the same. What are you waiting for, a tip?" I pulled ten dollars out of my ostrich Yves Saint Laurent bag and shoved it in his hand.

"Wow, did you really just say, you people? I don't want your damn money. Yeah, you fine and all, but you ain't the shit like you think." He threw the money on the ground and walked back over to his project of kicking up dust.

I contemplated picking the ten dollar bill up, but wanted them to know money that small didn't mean squat to me. I felt the sting in my knee and tried to ignore the bright red blood that spurted from the tiny slits. I wasn't that hurt, but my ego had been snatched down several notches. My mood had instantly gone from great to sour.

What part of the game was this? Could a sister feel good without making a damn fool out of herself? I wondered how the universe could turn on me so fast. I was so pissed at myself for wrecking my new Mercedes truck the previous week. Had I not done that, I would've entered my building through the parking garage and wouldn't have fallen in the street.

I wobbled into my office building and barely waved at the old pot belly security guard at the front desk. I wasn't in the mood for his blatant old man flirting. Every day, for the past year he made it his business to cop a free stare when I walked past, but today he barely glanced my way. I guess the little pop tart standing in front of him had his eyes occupied.

I mean really, who wouldn't look at her? I had to catch myself from catching whiplash. She made me double take so hard. Her skirt barely reached the bottom of her behind, and her low cut shirt could've been in a Got Milk ad. It was just that tight. Dare I say it, but I thought I could see the outline of her nipples.

The cattiness within, made me want to tap her shoulder and tell her that the strip club was a few blocks over. However, I was raised to never be rude. Besides, who was I to knock another sister, even if she looked like she belonged on Playboy.com?

"Good morning, Kurt," I called out to the old security guard.

He'd pissed me off by not showing me more attention. How dare he ignore me for the likes of trash? He could've easily passed as Old Otis off the TV show, *Martin* with his thick glasses, bucked teeth, and musty smell.

"Tracey! So glad you came in my dear. You saved me a trip. I was just on my way up to your office. This is your new assistant Shanice." Kurt always screamed when he talked. His hearing aid was set higher than normal.

"I'm sorry, Kurt. I must've heard you incorrectly." Maybe I had fallen harder than I thought I did. Obviously my mind had entered into a state of delusion.

"This is your new assistant! The temp service just sent her over this morning. I was keeping her company for ya!" Kurt longingly eyed the young lady as if he only needed just one taste of her to live.

*My new what, m*y mind screamed.

This had to be a joke, right? I swear, the employment agencies weren't worth a damn. I specifically asked for a professional assistant, not a professional call girl. What in the hell was I supposed to do with this hoochie momma? Heads would be rolling after I got done chewing out whatever S.O.B sent her my way.

"I was just in the process of taking down her information for her ID card. Soon as we get through with her picture, I'll send her right up!" Kurt yelled as usual.

"Nice to meet you, ah, what's your name again?" I asked, while giving her a once over for the millionth glance.

This time, I made sure she could see my look of disgust. I didn't want to come off rude, but seriously, I didn't know how to deal with people of her caliber.

"Shanice, my name is Shanice. I just wanna tell you it's such an honor to work for you. I just love, love, love your newspaper. It's so hip, so chic, so high fashion. You the bomb.com, for real girl....my role model." She flipped her hair back and forth and excitedly screamed while she talked.

"Ok, thanks, I guess. Have you ever worked as a secretary before?" I highly doubted that she worked anywhere other than the strip club in East Saint Louis.

"Yeah, girl, I done worked some of everywhere. I've done a little bit of this and that." She handed me her resume and I couldn't help but notice her acrylic nails with chipped polish.

"Ok, so you've worked before. But just what do you know about fashion?" I barely skimmed her resume awaiting her response.

"Oh, I know bunches about fashion. I be styling hella people for they pictures and stuff." She popped her gum and looked at me as if I should know who she was.

"Hella people? Who is that? I've certainly never heard of them. Are they a new rap group or something?" I ran through my mental rolodex and knew that whoever these people were, they must have been nobodies because I didn't know them.

"Girl nawl, that's hella funny. When I say hella, I mean like a lot. You from St. Louis and you ain't never heard nobody say, hella?" Shanice laughed at the look of confusion on my face.

"I'm sorry sweetie, I don't speak hood terminology. I'm a six figure type of lady. You know…money in the bank." I started snapping my fingers real crazy like, hoping she got the picture. This girl was nuts if she thought I was down with speaking like an idiot.

"Well, anyway. When they told me I was gone be working with you, I was like, helllllll nawl! It's like God just knew how much I loved you, and sent me right your way." Shanice eagerly talked and sung my highest praise.

If her outfit wasn't enough, the smacking of her tongue, and popping that gum while she talked, drove my first nerve insane.

"Shanice sweetie, don't let me interrupt your little groupie moment that you're having here, but I don't run a newspaper. It is a magazine and you should've been here thirty minutes ago."

"I know but…"

"My office opens at 8:30 a.m., and I specifically requested the arrival time of 8:00 a.m. That would give you a jump start to make sure my day goes smoothly." I paused and swung my neck just like my mother for the dramatic effect. I didn't want to hear any of her excuses.

I wanted to let this Shanice child know, that I was the one always in control. She couldn't just waltz in here whenever she felt like it. Rules were made for people like her to follow.

"Girllllll, lemme explain, I can tell you what happened."

"I don't give a damn what happened. The one thing I can't tolerate is tardiness. The second is ghetto people, and finally blonde hair on a woman with a chocolate skin tone. You're in violation of all three." I was in full bitch mode; someone had to pay for me making a fool out of myself out there in the street.

"Hold up, I just got my hair did last night. Ain't nothing wrong with my hair." Shanice looked offended as if her hair really looked good.

Miss Shanice had life twisted if she assumed that I would make this easy for her. I couldn't possibly be her role model. You would never see Tracey Simone Robbins dressed in anything so hoochie, nor would I ever admit knowing someone like her.

"If you think for one second I'm your role model, then you would know that I wouldn't condone this outfit you have on. I don't have time for the back and forth with you."

"But I'm only trying to tell you what happened, dang." Shanice folded her arms and pouted like a child.

"Are you in or out?" I had grown tired of her already.

I looked her up and down and shook my head. Her shoes were bedazzled out with several studs missing from them. The way they were peeling, I could tell they were cheap, fake leather. As short as her dress was, she didn't even have the decency to wear stockings. The nerve of these people from the ghetto!

My mother would murder me for sure if I ever thought of dressing so 'improper' as she would call it. The daughter of Dr. Robert Timothy Robbins would never disgrace her family's name by associating with someone like Shanice. I knew people were supposed to dream big, but she was borderline delusional.

"I'm in, but you gone have to talk to me betta. That's all I know," she said while she rolled her eyes at me.

"Shanice, this is my place of business and that means I can do whatever the hell I want. Now, if I do decide to hire you, you will follow my attendance guidelines. Understand?" I stared at her waiting for her to admit that she comprehended."

She just shook her head.

"And just so you know, I fired the last assistant who couldn't do her job the week before Christmas. And guess what Shanice?" I paused. "She ended up in a homeless shelter and I didn't lose two minutes of sleep about it!"

"Dang, I'm sorry for being late, but my baby daddy ain't come home last night, so I had to find someone to keep my babies. It's hella hard trying to do all this on my own. I'm doing the best I can, and I would think another black woman like you would appreciate that." Her attitude came through loud and clear.

"I don't know *you* to appreciate anything that *you* do. I could try to appreciate you a little if you were dressed properly."

"How I dress or my hair, has nothing to do with my ability to handle this job. You just like the rest of them wanna-be uppity people, put me down to make yourself feel big. I don't take junk from nobody, not even you!" Shanice rolled her neck a little too hard and flipped her ten dollar bag of yaki weave over her shoulder again.

This exposed a really big tattoo on her neck that read "Lil Chris." I assumed that would be the baby daddy that she spoke of. Her attitude told me that she couldn't catch a break. Of course she was looking to me, her "role model" to give her one. Maybe it was the flamboyant, ghetto mind frame that she tooted around that was blocking her.

"Didn't Shanice!" I corrected her, because ain't, was a word I'd never been allowed to say. I didn't personally know anyone illiterate enough to say it. I felt like I was in the middle of a Maury Povich episode.

"Didn't what, Tracey?" she asked with a confused look on her face.

"Your baby daddy *didn't* come home last night. Ain't, has never been a word in any dictionary, other than the urban one. You only get one chance with me, Shanice. You're already skating on thin ice."

There were thousands of people in St. Louis. Why was she sent here for me to save? Ugh! I hated having to do the right thing. Of course, I knew that charity work was a part of my role as a socialite, but I still hated doing it!

"Ok, Boss," she said with a huge smile.

"Consider this as a friendly warning. Show up on time and start reading books to better your English." Once again I gave her a harsh glare.

"Ok, I promise I'll do everything that you saying, I swear I'm going to work hella hard."

I glared at her again. She'd only been here for five minutes and that *hella* word had worked my nerves more than her little cheap outfit did. If Shanice was anything like me, that look scared the hell out of her. Hopefully, she would take it seriously. I was serious when it came to my business. Hell would turn into a sheet of ice before I let her mess this up for me.

"Be sure that you make yourself an appointment with my hair dresser, Shuronda and my stylist, Mario."

"I sure will, I'll call as soon as I get to your office." I noticed the gleam in her eyes and assumed it was because she'd never had a makeover before.

"Their numbers as well as any other pertinent information is on the electronic file on your desk. My former assistant has left you a sheet with all the passwords you'll need to access every record."

"Ok, Boss. I promise for Lord, I will do my best," she said.

"Shanice, please don't show up to my office dressed in this manner again. Not only do you represent yourself, you represent me and my company as well. And I hope you have your baby sitter situation taken care of. It will not be used as an excuse to be late or absent." I screamed more orders at her as I walked away from the security guard's desk towards the elevator.

I was not as heartless as I would've liked, especially not like my mother. The fact that she had babies tugged at my heart a little. God should bless me for even talking to her for more than five minutes. I looked back just in time to see Shanice jumping up and down excitedly.

My mother would just have to understand, that keeping Shanice around was a good idea. I could help develop her into the woman that she should be. A little project has never hurt me before. I was actually excited, that I would have my very own Eliza Doolittle.

Plus she might be able to help me in other ways than just being my assistant. Just wait until the local media heard how I took in the welfare mom and gave her a chance when no one else would. Sounded like a win/win situation for me. I opened my phone and dialed the number to the St. Louis American newspaper. When I heard the recording come on, I quickly disguised my voice.

"Hello, I have a tip that I think would be a great feature story. Local philanthropist and business woman, Tracey Robbins just saw a young prostitute on the street. Out of the kindness of her heart she took her in, cleaned her up and gave her a job as a secretary. Ms. Robbins prides herself on helping out those less fortunate." I hung up the phone pleased with myself. I may have fabricated a tiny bit, but who was keeping tabs on little white lies?

I was floating on cloud nine as I entered the elevator. A young woman with her hat covering her face rushed off and bumped into me so hard, I almost fell for the second time in one day.

"Excuse the hell out of you! You should watch where you're going." I yelled like I owned her.

"Bitch, you the one who should be careful," she said, taking two steps backwards and stepped into my path.

Nervously, I tried to make some space between the two of us. I hadn't planned on her coming off so roughly. She was bolder than the people I was used to communing with. "Look, I don't have any money on me. Take my bag, but please don't hurt me. You can get about two grand for it," I stammered as I imagined her big masculine arm choking me to death. I closed my eyes and pushed my bag towards her.

"It won't be me who hurts you. You ever heard of Karma? You reap what you sow, you pretty young thing." She laughed loudly at my discomfort.

I opened my eyes just in time to see her walking away. Something about the laugh still had me shook. It was actually more of a cackle than laughter. The energy that I felt from her rocked me to my core. Who was she speaking of? Who wanted to hurt me?

Before I could open my mouth to call security, she blew a kiss at me and quickly sped off. I stood still trying to catch my breath before deciding to push the number ten. As soon as the elevator stopped at my floor, I ran in my office and locked the door. I was going to have to get a new office, this building was turning into the slums.

Chapter 2 ─────────────

As long as I could remember we lived at 5642 Disturbia Lane. The street name sounded a little horror movie-ish, but the neighborhood was anything but. Life in West County, St. Louis was far different from the tales in the urban areas. There were no drive-by shootings, robberies, or random home invasions. With well-manicured lawns, mini mansions, and Olympic size swimming pools in our backyards; we were living the American dream.

I was never allowed to tell anyone that I was adopted, not even my best friend, Christian. She and I were more like sisters, since her dad worked at the hospital with my father, and our moms were real close frenemies. They were the real Desperate Housewives, and this was long before the sitcom. One moment they would be in truce mode and speaking ill of the other wives together. The next moment they would stop speaking to each other and go back into war mode. Everyone was a casualty of war then, including the kids and husbands.

As one would expect, Christian and I grew up in a forced competition that neither of us wanted to compete in. From musicals, pageants, dance recitals, plays, and horse riding...anything you could name, our mothers forced us to participate. Our homes were even rivals, each one vying for the attention of having the best kept yard.

Christian and I were the only two black girls in a land of the rich and the white. Naturally she and I would've been friends even if our parents didn't care for each other. Our bond was sealed based on the fact that we both thought our mothers were certified lu-lu's, and our fathers were our Knights in shining armor. I truly loved Christian, I guess that's why I broke my promise to my mother and told her I was adopted. She was sworn to secrecy in a blood sister ceremony that was held on our 10th birthdays, which were a week apart. Nineteen years later, she was still the best friend a girl could ever have. It was no wonder Christian was the first person I called to complain about the Shanice debacle.

"God Christian, I wish you could see the little hoochie momma that the employment agency sent me this morning. She is a complete embarrassment to the black race to say the least. Those cheap shoes and horrible outfit, almost made me have a heart attack."

"That's horrible!"

"Tell me about it," I rambled on giving her the details. I leaned back in my chair and looked out the windows towards the St. Louis Arch and Mississippi River thinking about Shanice and the crazy day I'd had thus far. I'd chosen the location based on the scenery just for days like the one I was having. Sometimes I wished I could float like the river tides. My nerves had been wrecked ever since I set eyes on Shanice. Talking to Christian always helped put things into a brighter perspective. Calling her the sister I never had was truly an understatement.

"Girl, you should forget that charitable lost cause. I would've sent her ass packing on first sight. I can't believe it's late afternoon and you still have her working there. Didn't you say that you could see her thong?" Christian seemed almost as devastated as I was. That's what I love about her.

"Yeah, I could. It was really sad to see, just disgusting as hell."

"And you said she had cheap glue in her weave? You know you can smell that stuff when women sweat."

"What do you mean you can smell it?" I laughed at the thought of her hair smelling from sweat.

"You're laughing, but I'm so serious. She must be from the projects." Christian paused. "Tracey, do you feel safe around her?" Her voice was slightly above a whisper. I assumed that her husband was still home.

He was an ignorant, conceited, jealous, womanizer and couldn't stand her gossiping on the phone with me. In fact, he hated her talking to me, and did everything in his power to show me. That put Christian in an awkward position, but she had thus far, kept the war from breaking out. To his dismay, I was the maid of honor in their wedding. He fought tooth and nail for that not to happen, but Christian made it clear that kicking me out of the wedding party wasn't going to happen. As payback, he at times forbade her to talk to me. He was a controlling prick like that.

"Safe! Girl, please, what do I look like to you? I will have her ass locked up the first time she tries anything. I may look all girly, but I'm tough as hell and can easily kick some ass."

I continued to watch the door to see if Shanice had returned from her not so glamorous make over. I know she didn't really think I was going to have my team go all out on her for free.

I advised them to go to the nearest Target for clothes, and dye that hideous blonde hair black. I wasn't even sure she would be here that long. Plus, I was the queen around these parts, and there wasn't enough room for two.

"Ok Tracey, I get it, you're real tough." Christian couldn't stop herself from chuckling at my outburst.

Ever since the age of fifteen, I'd taken on an, I don't play persona. We both laughed because I'd never had a fair fight, but talked a good game like I'd fought wolves before.

"Look Trae, why don't we meet up at the Jazz Loft later on for happy hour? I have these new Gucci shoes that I'm dying to wear, and I need a drink or seven." Christian always wanted a drink. It was her favorite past time other than shopping.

"I don't know. I have some things I need to take care of here at the office." I'd been working hard most of the day but knew I had a major deadline approaching. Yet the thought of a margarita sounded like an excellent idea as well.

"Please friend. I don't want to go by myself. Chuck has football practice later and I'm sure he'll be nowhere to be found when it's over."

I thought about her comment. My heart went out to her. Chuck played for the local professional football team. With his kind of money he bought her just about everything imaginable. That was more than likely to make up for his whoremonger activities. I had no problem going out with Christian, even though her wardrobe rivaled the celebrities. There really was no jealousy there. We were almost in the same boat, except she was married and I was working on getting a ring.

"That's fine with me. You just make sure the warden, better known as your husband, lets you out the house tonight. Even though you say he's barely there, he loves for you to stay at home waiting on his simple ass." I shook my head because I didn't understand her situation.

"I'm not in the mood to discuss my personal life today, heffa. For your information, Chuck and I are doing just fine. In fact, he bought me some beautiful earrings when he got back in town last night." I could hear the smile in her voice, but I knew that it was fake. She'd been miserable with him for the longest.

"That's good to hear, I hope he can keep it up. While I'm talking about having drinks, let me call Anthony first and see if he plans on coming over."

"Girl, I laugh every time you mention his name. Boring, with a capital B. You'll never be faithful to him."

"I know, but I'm working on it. I've devoted a lot of time to our relationship." I was slightly offended that she had so little faith in me.

"Yeah ok, I know you've been creeping with somebody this week and last week, too…hint hint. You can't just be doing him. Not Freaky Tracey."

I chose to ignore where Christian was trying to take the conversation. I still hadn't told her who I went to Vegas with. She would never know considering I dealt with so many men. In the past I really struggled with being satisfied with just one man and often found myself in serious trouble because of my addiction to variety.

"Anyway, I haven't heard from Anthony in a couple of days and Lord knows I could use one of his massages. We haven't seen each other in a while."

"Oh, I would love to hear all about that but I gotta go. I promised Chuck's mother I would take her shopping. You know how she hates to wait," Christian said through gritted teeth.

"Ugh, bye child. I'll see you tonight."

I hung up the phone and instantly thought of the problems I would have with Mother if I didn't find out what was wrong with Anthony. I knew she would be pissed if I ruined another potential marriage. Anthony wasn't the first guy who almost had me down the aisle. I seriously thought he and I were doing well, but lately he'd been rather distant. Mother would kill me for sure this time. Once she got on my nerves, she would never get off.

From my first day of conception, I had it hard. At least that was what Mother told me. When I say Mother, I was speaking of my adopted parent. I was born to a teenage mom who could barely take care of herself. I was immediately given up for adoption at the hospital and landed into the arms of Gertrude Robbins. It used to bother me that my birth mom didn't want to hold onto me. Even if we had to struggle, I still was hers. The fact that she could have a baby and give it up without thinking of the consequences angered the hell out of me. Then I flipped the coin and thought about life in the ghetto. I'm sure I wouldn't have adapted to that environment very well.

Mother never lets me forget how lucky I am that she picked me out of all the little girls in the adoption agency. Daily she reminded me of what I could've been or what she thought I would be. She couldn't have kids due to some bad home abortion back in the late 60's. After being asked countless times by her snobby family and friends when she would have a baby, she decided to secretly adopt.

To save herself the embarrassment of not being able to carry, she went away on an extended missionary assignment. She announced that she was expecting before she left. Several months later, she returned home acting like she'd conceived the most beautiful baby girl this side of the Mississippi River. People always complimented us, saying how we looked just alike. It always made me laugh.

Everyone praised her for being a doting loving mother. However, nothing could've been further from the truth. Privately she treated me like shit. As if it was my fault she couldn't have children. Constant reminders, snide remarks about how my nose was too big, and how there must've been a fat gene inside my body angered me to the core.

I had come to the conclusion that, Gertrude Robbins was happy being the mother of someone she chose. It would always make her superior to me. She wanted me to believe, it was because of her that I breathe. Thank God my adopted father was the complete opposite. He always showed me unconditional love and helped build my self-esteem.

Being the daughter of a surgeon and a pageant mother, I grew up rather glitzy. There were always balls and charity events that we attended. Every summer we would vacation in a different country. Fourth of July was spent in the Lake of the Ozarks with the mayor of St. Louis and his family. On holidays we rubbed elbows with politicians, musicians, doctors, lawyers, and anyone else with money attached to their name. I smiled thinking of all the wonderful parties, clothes, and gifts I'd been given over the years. Life had been wonderful to me and I planned on taking advantage of it always.

A loud knock on my door scared me half to death. I thought about the young woman from earlier and quietly crept to the door. I still couldn't figure out what her problem was and the thought of her coming back to harm me gave me the chills. I turned the knob to the door slowly, heart beating and all just as the person pushed their way in. We both screamed, probably scaring the other tenants on my floor.

"Shanice! What in the hell are you doing creeping?" I was beyond annoyed that she'd damn near frightened me into a heart attack.

"Me, creeping? Hell, you the one barely turning the knob all hella slow. I mean, super slow."

I smiled at her attempt to correct her language.

Shanice looked like a completely different person. The three hour make-over she'd just experienced, made a huge difference. A little bit of modest makeup, new clothes, and a hair-do had never looked so good. I almost couldn't tell she came from the slums. Everything about her was actually perfect for someone like her.

"Thank you for correcting yourself and you actually look a lot better than earlier," I applauded.

Behind her was some guy who looked like he had one hundred pound weights in his back pockets. His pants were sagged below his behind and exposed his Calvin Klein boxer briefs. Thank God they were clean.

"Damn, Shanice, why you ain't tell me you had fine chicks like this working at your new gig? Shoot, a player could get used to this. This one right here is good to go baby!" Mr. Bound for jail said as he walked around me slowly.

He was right on the back of my neck and I could smell the marijuana as it turned the corner of my nose. He looked me in my eyes and just stared. Even though they were bloodshot red, something about him made me nervous.

"Excuse you sir, I don't work with…" I started to say, but he cut me off.

"I mean, I really could get used to a sista like you, all fine and old and shit. You just what I need, an older woman to teach me some old tricks. I normally like 'em younger, but I could do thirty-five or so. They say being a cougar is the new in thing anyway." He licked his lips and grabbed what would've been his crotch area, if it wasn't sagging at his knees.

"If you don't get your little dusty ass out of my office, I'll call the police." I was beyond pissed that he even had the nerve to stand in my presence.

I wanted to slap his face. How dare he call me old? I was only twenty-nine, and knew I looked damn good. Thanks to years of expensive facials, I didn't even look close to thirty. How dare that country, ghetto hoodlum try and insult me? Gouging his eyes out with a pen and cursing him like a sailor would have done him some justice.

"Damn, and you mean. I swear, you just how I like 'em. Look at you looking all cute in your work pants. Lil yellow ass, I been wanting a red bone." Once again he made a circle around me. Obviously, he was insane to say the least.

My mind screamed for me to pick up the phone and call for help, but for some reason I just stood still with my mouth closed like a mute. I wanted to say something, but my words were caught in my throat.

"Who are you?" I asked. Not because I was interested, but more because I couldn't believe he had the nerve to stand in my presence.

I should've walked away, but I was deathly afraid they would see my knees wobble. Whoever that ignorant little soul was, I found myself oddly attracted to him. He was the most gorgeous man I'd ever laid eyes on.

"I'm sorry, Tracey, where are my manners? This is my play brother, Tez. Don't pay him no mind, he always playing all the time. He been talking before he thinks since he was little," Shanice said as she punched him in the arm, probably harder than he thought she would.

He grabbed his bruised arm and pushed her back. I was still stuck on the fact, that grown-ups still called each other play brother and sister. Everyone knew that was code for, we have slept or was currently sleeping together.

"And why is he here, Shanice?"

"He picked me up from the shop and came in to see what I

do here cuz I just went on and on about you and how I love this place. Tez, this is my boss, Tracey."

"Yo boss? Daaaaamn, what a nigga gotta do to get a job here?" he asked.

"Goodbye Tez," Shanice quickly uttered. "And don't forget to come back and get me. Be here at five o'clock sharp to pick me up please."

"Shiddddd, why don't I just stay a couple hours 'til you get off."

Shanice hadn't been here long, but it was obvious she could tell I was pissed. She knew getting him out of there was the best thing for her and him. "Uhhh, I think you making my boss mad Tez."

"Shanice, my patience is wearing thin. Introductions are completely unnecessary. I would like for your "play brother" to leave immediately. And I hope you fully understand, personal company is not allowed in my office." I rolled my eyes at him and gave Shanice a hard, stern look.

This was exactly why I didn't want to hire her. I knew she would poison my air with ghetto energy.

He nodded his head at her as if he got the message that she and I sent. He then looked at me, winked his eye, and again licked his lips. Before I could flick him off like I wanted to, he Kool Moe Dee'd his too large attire out the office door. Something about that little boy screamed sexy and dangerous! Thank God I would never have to see his face again. I turned towards Shanice and tried my hardest not to go off on her too bad.

"This is the first and last time that personal company will be allowed at my office. If I haven't made myself clear and this mistake happens again, please feel free to dismiss yourself from my presence." I spoke to her harsher than necessary. Her kind didn't seem to understand pleasant talk.

"I got you Boss. I'll never let you down again. You can believe that." Shanice sat down and started rearranging some things on her desk. I almost nodded my head in approval, then she popped that gum again. The poor child really knew how to work my damn nerves.

"Oh, this package was sitting on the side of the water cooler when I first got here. I forgot to give it to you." When she handed me a big blue Tiffany box, I smiled in anticipation.

I loved receiving surprises, I wanted to clap my hands I was so happy. I grabbed the box and started to open it. I considered going in my office, but wanted Shanice to see how I had it like that. The box was so big it had to contain more than one item.

"See, Shanice. This is something you can learn from me. Sophisticated women get jewelry. Hoochie mammas get kids," I condescendingly told her as I finally pried the box open.

My smile quickly turned to a horrid frown as the large box contained two dead snakes with a piece of paper attached. I screamed as Shanice snatched the paper that laid on top of them. She didn't even seem fazed as she read the note.

WHEN YOU CUT THE GRASS LOW,
THEM MOTHERFUCKING SNAKES WILL SHOW

"Where did this box come from?" I angrily yelled at Shanice.

"I don't know, but this is hella crazy!"

"Who would do this sick shit to me?" I shouted.

"You know Boss, I may be a hoochie mamma, but ain't nobody out there in the world pissed enough at me to send me something like this," she softly spoke. There was pity in her eyes as she threw the box away.

"Just sit down and do what I'm paying you for." I sneered at her.

I looked around for the candid camera crew. Someone had to be playing some sort of sick joke on me.

Chapter 3

By the time I got out the office later that night and made it to The Loft Nightclub, Christian was already seated and had ordered for the both of us. She had a pitcher of margaritas on the table for me, as she drank her usual, apple martinis. The place was rather empty, but it was still early. Around 11 o'clock, the walls would be sweating. The chicken wings at The Loft consisted of everything good in the world. The wait for food was close to thirty minutes every time we came, so I was ecstatic that Christian had already ordered.

St. Louis was in the height of the gentrification movement and I loved it. Before the white people moved back downtown for the cheap buildings, the area was almost deserted and severely impoverished. There were no stores or pretty lights in the middle of Washington Boulevard. The area had previously only known crime, drugs, and the homeless. The same hood clubs lined the streets, and it was a good chance you would not make it out of there alive. Back in high school we ditched one day and snuck downtown. I was in for the biggest culture shock of my life. It was the only time I saw drug addicts and homeless people up close.

Thank God those horrible days were over. Me and my girls could eat and drink until our hearts were content. My body was calling tequila and I was hoping it would answer. Christian had her sleeves rolled up and her chubby face was covered with buffalo sauce. The girl had no shame in her game when it came to eating.

"Hey girl," she sang out to me, while we air kissed. I was sure she was already on her second drink because her naturally, golden colored eyes were slightly glazed.

"What you know good hooker? How's the music tonight and why you order so much food?" I sat in my seat and looked down at her feet.

She was working the hell out of a pair of nude colored Gucci pumps. I'd never seen them before, so I assumed they were the ones she spoke of earlier. You never know with her indecisive mind though.

"Not much. I just needed to get out the house. The music is great. Rhoda G. is on the saxophone tonight."

"Oh, good. I love her music. Have you talked to Rayven?" I asked.

"Yeah. Rayven's on her way to meet us for a drink too. She called me after I got off the phone with you, fussing about her day not going so well. You been so busy lately, we felt like we were losing our drinking buddy." Christian finally stopped talking and stared at me for a few seconds.

"Why are you looking at me like that?"

"I'm really digging that new cut on you, Tracey. It frames your face perfectly." Christian continued to stare, just like I'd done when I first cut it. It was a dramatic change from what I was used to. For the past eleven years, I had sworn by weave only.

"Yeah, I let Shuronda talk me into cutting it off. You know she just opened a new salon on Delmar, right? It's called Studio Posh. It's really nice in there. You should go check it out." I could barely get the words out my mouth. I had already downed one glass of Margarita and was eager to start on my second.

"Shuronda from that one salon, 911? Dang, she must be getting paid. I thought she was still in North County at that one shop. Remember when your mother was pissed at us for driving to West Florissant and she was certain we would get shot." Christian roared an obnoxious laugh at the memory. Of course I remembered, Mother bitched for a whole week about it. I, on the other hand, didn't find it that funny.

"Yeah, thanks to your mother she thought Ferguson was the new ghetto. That's funny though, haven't thought about that in years." I smiled at the old memory.

"Don't blame Gertrude's craziness on me. She just doesn't want her precious daughter to get hurt." Christian laughed again, a little louder than she should've.

"Anyway fool, Shuronda left them a couple of months back. Where has your late self been? It was seriously about time for her to leave there anyway. Her clientele was ridiculous and the other girls were getting jealous, in my opinion. That's simply because everyone in St. Louis knows if you need your hair done, Shuronda is the one to go to." I turned my head around to give her a view of the back. Her face said exactly what I already knew, I looked damn good.

"Yeah well, you know Moni, at MJ2 is my girl. I can't have anyone else in these naps, but I really like how Ms. Shuronda did yours." She stopped and stared at me again. It was really weird. "Really brings out how pretty your face is. Girl, I just don't have the patience to wait in a shop for hours. I have things of importance to do."

Christian played in her long, lightly colored hair and stared oddly into space. I knew then, she was definitely intoxicated. Her mind was gone somewhere far. Under normal circumstances she resembled a dumb blonde with the bright, hair that seemed to be bleached and the spacey looks, but this was different. I followed her gaze and immediately saw what had her distracted. It was them…our true enemies.

Megan and Leah, two girls we knew from childhood, had come into the club. Leah spotted us and waved. We waved back, pretending to be genuine, especially with Megan. She'd been caught in Christian's bed with Chuck, on more than one occasion. When they headed towards our table, I knew that trouble would soon follow.

"Wow, Tracey, you really looking good girl. What's your secret to not getting fat like most people we know?" Megan spoke in a smug tone.

She purposely addressed me to ignore Christian. I looked her up and down and noticed she was wearing the same shoes as Christian.

"I've always looked the same Megan. Unlike most, I don't have to try so hard being something that I'm not." I gave her the same attitude she tried to dish out. If I wasn't good at anything else, I could make a person feel low with little effort.

"That's real funny Tracey. I always found you to be rather comical. If your professional hoe job doesn't get you far, being funny sure will. Speaking of funny, nice shoes, Christian. They don't come out until next spring. I guess we both have connections." Megan boldly stared Christian in the eyes. She was daring her to ask how she'd gotten hers.

"My shoes come with a million dollar house, five cars, and

a thirty-five million dollar football contract. What comes with yours besides a wet ass?" Christian shouted over the music. It looked as if she was ready to kill Megan.

"Hmmph, mine comes with similar amenities minus the needs of a Body Magic girdle." Megan rubbed her hand down the sides of her nonexistent waist. We all knew that Christian struggled with her weight and it was a touchy subject for her.

"Come on ladies, we're better than all this. No need to fight over silly things," Leah nervously stammered.

Even though Megan was her best friend, she never condoned her relationship with Chuck. She hated messy situations and spent a great deal of her time diffusing Megan's messy situation.

"What do I look like fighting this tramp over my own damn husband, Leah? Fights are for kids. Snapped, is a real life show that happens every day."

Out of the blue, Christian pulled a razor blade from her Birkin bag. My eyes couldn't believe the scene before me. Where in the hell had she gotten a razor blade? When had she gotten so bold to pull it out and try to harm someone?

"Christian, put that shit away. If anyone is worth your life, it is most definitely not, Megan." I grabbed the blade from her hand and quickly put it in my purse. I too, hated Megan, but I wasn't about to go to jail because of her ass.

"Please, who do you think you're fooling? You know exactly what it is with your husband, don't play yourself. I'm done with his lousy ass anyway. In due time, you will be also." Megan talked as if she wasn't scared just a second earlier. I wanted to give Christian the weapon back, just so she could hurt her.

"Leah, would you please take your friend to the other end of the club? I love you and all, but this trash you hang with, I can't stomach the likes of her." I really liked Leah, but I was willing to cut her off if she didn't get better control of her friend.

"At least I can stand in the mirror and see exactly who I am. I like men and I love money and I'm out here to get it. You chasing it for free, which just makes you a conniving slut!" Megan shouted loudly, drawing more attention than necessary.

"Megan, you want to be one of us so bad, you slut yourself around for money. Keep trying honey, we were born this way," I told her harshly. "You, however, were taught to be." I had enough of her ass and was done with the uninvited visit.

      "Tracey, you can continue to sit around on that high ass horse of yours if you want to. But I have the power to bring you down. Now, shall we play a little game of truth or dare." Megan stared at me pointedly. I looked in her eyes and searched for the bluff behind them. Sadly, I found none. Did she know about me? Megan shot me a disgusting scowl, then turned and walked away.

Chapter 4

I sat with my posture still intact, but my expression hadn't changed. "I hate her tacky ass so much. She's a despicable human being at best." I was pissed that Megan had completely ruined our good night. The plan was to chill and not worry about any problems.

"Girl fuck her! She and anyone else who have ever crossed me, will get what's coming soon." Christian laughed and took another sip of her Martini. I couldn't put my finger on it, but her laugh made me feel uncomfortable as hell. I watched Christian closely. Something was definitely different about her.

"Are you going to let the food get cold, or continue to have a good time?" Christian asked me. Her mood had switched from sour to happy in less than one second.

I looked at the feast on our table and dove into one of the chicken wing baskets. I wished I was at home because I would've eaten those bad boys with my bare hands. Since I wasn't, I picked up my fork and tried to act proper, like a lady was supposed to.

"Tracey, look at you holding that fork the wrong way. I don't know why I bother to teach you anything proper. Do you know how much money I spent on etiquette classes for you? You will never get it. And your hair? Why on earth would any woman want to be bald like a man?" Christian turned up her nose and imitated my mother.

I couldn't help but laugh because she had her down to the nasally annoying shrewd voice and repulsed look. "She's really nuts, Christian. I haven't spoken to her in three days, so I expect some of her hell to blow my way soon."

"Three days? Yeah, when she touches down she's going to make your life miserable," Christian said, taking another gulp of her martini.

"I guess she's still pissed that I'm moving out before getting married. You know in her book living alone, is the ultimate taboo," I commented while continuing to laugh at Christian's attempt to move her body like my mother.

"Technically Tracey, you don't live with her, since you stay in the guest house anyway," Christian stated.

"That's the exact thing I said to her and she waved me off. She claims to have something more important to worry about, other than my silliness, as she not so politely put it."

"Lord Tracey, you know her and my mother are planning the fall charity ball together for the hospital. I don't know why they just don't stop pretending they like each other. They're worse than the women on those Real Housewives shows, catty as hell. I've never heard so much bickering and arguing at one time." Christian talked loudly as she glanced nervously around the club. I hoped she wasn't still looking for Megan.

"Glad I'm not a part of that drama. I'm ready to have me a few drinks and let loose. Damn, work, Mother, and any other drama that could possibly come our way. Here's to us, nothing and no one can come between us." After we clicked our glasses, Christian quickly downed her martini in one gulp.

"Whoa, what's wrong Christian? I've never seen you drink like that and why are you looking nervous like a crack head? What's on your mind?" I asked with a voice full of concern.

"I found lipstick on his shirt. I thought he was still messing with that bitch, Megan. But you heard her, they're done." Christian's voice was barely above a whisper.

"Christian, she's lying. You saw she had on the same shoes. You know that lipstick stain is more than likely hers." I hated that Megan even came over to our table.

"Something is up with him and I'm not sure what. He's getting so reckless with his cheating. He doesn't care with who or where. His phone rings all night long, but he has it locked. Then last week, I found lipstick all over his collar." As Christian's lip quivered, I was so not in the mood for one of her dramatic breakdowns.

I didn't know what to say, so I stayed quiet and listened. It seemed like the right option. I had played the, Chuck is Cheating, game before. Christian liked to vent, but never liked hearing advice.

"I can't remember the last time we made love. The only thing he does is find a way to complain about my weight and how he can't get into me like he used to. That really hurts my feelings, but I try to ignore it."

I bit my bottom lip at the thought.

"I'm a good wife to him, Tracey, and more understanding than any woman would be. I can't even count how many times he's cheated. But I make him pay by running up his damn credit card though." Christian quickly signaled for another drink. I felt bad for her; she was my best friend and didn't deserve what she was going through.

"You're right, you don't have to take that. Chuck is a complete asshole for not wanting a beautiful woman like you. You've lost a lot of weight these past few months, everywhere we go, men try and step to you. Hell, even if you weighed 200 pounds, his black ass is lucky to be with you." I was used to being her voice of confidence. Chuck had turned her self-esteem into nothing.

"Excuse me ladies, do you mind if I sit with you two hookers until my real friends show up?" Without turning around, Christian and I both knew that voice. It belonged to the one and only Ms. Rayven Starr.

"Sure, but this is the blacks only table, so I'm assuming that you are African- American," Christian stammered. We all burst out laughing at the inside joke.

Rayven was born a white girl, but she had some soul sisters trapped inside her. We didn't get along at first because she would always let me know that she was a lot "blacker" than I was. This debate caused plenty of arguments until I finally gave up and accepted the child as one of us.

"Ha, you two are so funny I forgot to laugh. If I wasn't black, how would you explain these hips and ass? Y'all just jealous of me," Rayven said in an exasperated sigh.

As she sat across from us, I couldn't help but admire how beautiful she was. Her tanned skin was just one shade lighter than Christian's high yellow ass. She was 5'8 when she wore six inch stilettos and her body was to die for. She hit the gym six days a week and her arms, abs, and legs showed her dedication. Her long, brown hair draped perfectly over her shoulders. She recently got a bang, which was a major step for her. She hated the idea of cutting any of her hair. I thought it brought out the color of her eyes perfectly.

"Your hips are the product of bacon and your ass is full of silicone. That doesn't equal black sweetie. Now, me on the other hand, all natural baby." I ran my hands down the side of my body and stuck my tongue out at her.

"Bitch boo, your body is wack. Your yellow ass has so much white in you, you're one step from being my sister," Rayven snapped. "And did I interrupt a funeral? Why were you two looking so down when I walked up? This is still a club isn't it?"

"Why are you asking so many questions, Rayven?" I asked pointedly.

"Whatever Tracey. What did I miss? But if it is too damn depressing, don't tell me. Hell, I only want to talk about men and their winkies right now." Rayven reached for the pitcher of margarita when Christian smacked her hand.

"You didn't interrupt anything, Ms. Nasty Girl. I don't know about Tracey, but I, prefer not to talk about the male anatomy tonight. Furthermore, how old are you and why are you saying winky? Say dick. And you just walk your boney ass in and sit down ready to eat and drink without ordering anything. You hate margaritas yet you love them when they're free," Christian snapped at Rayven.

"Damn, who are you, the margarita police? Let a sister get a drink before you bash her! And you know I don't play about chicken wings, so I don't have to pay for them. Hmm, let's see. You're in a foul mood, so am I wrong to assume that you two were discussing Chuck, the diseased bum hole?" Rayven signaled for the barmaid who promptly swooped to the table with a Midori Sour. She was a regular and tipped higher than she should have, so the waitresses always catered to her.

"Rayven, you shouldn't talk about Christian's husband like that! I hate his ass too, but we should be cordial. Don't be rude!" I remained shocked at her statement about Chuck, but we all knew he was the type of person you hated to see coming. Everyone could see that except for Christian. He had a way of working a spell on her. Or maybe she did see it but decided to ignore it.

Either way, I knew that the conversation would only get worse if we didn't change the subject soon. After four drinks my head was already spinning. I felt like I only had another ten minutes before I needed to lay down, especially if I didn't get some water soon. Maybe I was getting old, like that hoodlum with Shanice said. I used to be able to drink pitchers of margaritas and could stand tall.

"It sounds to me, like someone is jealous of me being married. Unlike some, who shall remain nameless, I prefer to sleep with the same man and not several of them. I'm used to single ladies hating on me though. Say what you want Ray, but I'm the one with a ring on it," Christian said as she twisted her hand Beyonce style. We all laughed at her attempt to lighten the mood. Rayven quickly frowned. Something was bothering her and I could tell it was about to come out.

"If you knew better, you wouldn't be yelling that so proudly." Rayven blew her bangs out of her eyes.

"Look, I've been hearing some not so good things about Chuck. You know I know a few of the players and they're all talking about some new chick that has his nose wide open. Apparently he's keeping her on the hush tip, but they say he's more serious about her than any of the others. She's not really new though, it's been about a year."

Christian didn't speak a word. She just stared into space. If the moment wasn't awkward enough, I felt close to passing out. Those margaritas were simply not for the faint of heart. My head was sweating and I needed some cold water ASAP.

"I'm not feeling so well. I have to use the bathroom," I blurted out as I fought to stand up straight. "Watch my food and make sure, none of them pesky insects, don't find their way to my plate. And if you two start fighting before I get back, I plan on kicking some ass myself. Y'all know I'm the toughest, so please don't make me flex in here."

I laughed and stumbled away to the bathroom with a really heavy heart. I hated seeing my friend hurt. She really was a great woman who didn't deserve what Chuck put her through. He and his mistress were both flat out wrong!

"Looks like someone has had too much to drink. Where's all that sophistication you proclaim to have?" Megan stood next to me in the bathroom mirror.

"Something is wrong with me. I don't feel so good." I leaned against the counter looking for support.

I looked in the mirror and could see the sweat beads pouring down my face.

"Just maybe if you were a little nicer to me, I would be able to help you." Megan laughed as she continued to fix her hair.

"I'm serious Megan. I don't feel so good. Just help me sit down." I grabbed her arm and continued to plea for help.

"I'm not helping you do a damn thing. Matter of fact, I'm going to be the one who bust those skeletons out of your closet." I know what you've done! But this time you won't weasel your way out of it!" She pushed my hands off her arm, causing me to tumble to the ground. The coolness of the bathroom floor brought forth some relief and before I thought about how unsanitary it was, I was knocked out.

Chapter 5

"*Wake up, St. Louis! You know they say the early bird gets the worm. Don't keep hitting the snooze button! Wake up! Wake up! Wake up!*" my radio blared next to my king-sized bed.

Jarred from sleep, I tried to open both eyes. My God, my head was killing me. Staci Static and Mz. Janee weren't making it any better. I swear they were the rowdiest radio morning show personalities I'd ever heard. They kept me laughing though, especially when they did their segment, Put 'Em On Blast. I was always amazed at what people called in and said. Hearing about the less fortunate always kept me entertained. Once again, I hit the snooze button shutting off their show.

This was the reason that I never like to go out on a weekday. Christian could sleep her drunkenness off in her bed. Me, on the other hand, I'd have to peel myself out of bed and go into the office. Pieces of last night randomly shot through my head. I was so glad that Christian and Rayven helped me out of the bathroom before anyone saw me passed out on the floor. That was beyond embarrassing. I guess I'd drank more than I thought.

I had just dogged Shanice out just yesterday about acting like a ghetto smut and there I was acting worse than her. I'd even dug a little into her background as soon as she left the office only to find out that she grew up in downtown St. Louis in the Cochran Projects. At least she'd graduated at the top of her class, even though that wasn't really hard to do considering the public high school she went to. She also had an associate degree in business administration. I also found out that her father had been gunned down in front of her back in '95, leaving her mother to raise two kids on her own.

I guess everyone wasn't as privileged as I was, and that was too damn bad in my book. Even if I had stayed with my real mother, I was sure I would've still been in the same position I was in now. You had to work hard for things and never become a product of your environment, like my father and I did. He too stayed in the hood, but he was now a surgeon. Shanice, at this point, should thank me for helping her take a step out of the ghetto. I didn't care if she'd only been with me for a day. That was actually an honor for someone like her.

I rolled over to look at the clock realizing it read 8:30 a.m. Shit! I had a meeting at 9:30 with this chick who did promotional work. Suite Ballentine, or some crap like that, was the name of her company. Saying she was anal about punctuation was an understatement. Her assistant e-mailed me a million times about the itinerary of our meeting. But I loved to support young black movers and shakers like myself, so I chose her firm. They hadn't been around for long and I wanted to be the one who introduced them to the world.

"Damn, boo, yo place is the business for real," Mr. Bound for jail said as he walked in my room naked from the waist down.

My heart stopped pumping. Literally. "What in the hell are you doing in my house? And why do you not have on pants?" I screamed, but as I sat up I immediately saw that I was naked and he must've been "doing" me.

Oh My God!! Suddenly, it all came back to me in a flash. Jesus take the wheel, drive the car, be a fence, and all those other things I hear church women say. I was on the brink of a Holy Ghost faint and I couldn't even remember this guy's name. Maybe I drank more than I thought, or maybe he followed me home and raped me. That surely sounded more believable than me voluntarily sleeping with him.

"Yo, you know good and damn well what I'm doing here. You called Shanice and got my number last night. You hit me up all drunk and stuff, talking 'bout what you wanted me to do to you."

"Sir, I highly doubt that." I rolled my eyes at the thought of talking dirty to him.

"You better believe it baby. I ain't never turning down no chance to bag no classy lady like you. Shit, you know what I'm saying. You got it Lil Ma, this world is all yours." He had the nerve to stand there and rub himself.

He was looking somewhat sexy, despite all of the ugliness

coming out of his mouth and his despicable act of masturbation.

"Excuse me, uh. This is embarrassing; I don't even know your name. Clearly, I was drunk as hell and you took advantage of that. I wouldn't even let you park my car, let alone sleep with me."

I tried to cover myself up so that he couldn't see my body, while trying my hardest to remember talking to Shanice the night before at the same time. Why would Shanice give me his number when I was clearly out of my mind?

"Look here boo, you can drop that sheet, cuz I done seen every inch of that body. You look great for a cougar, by the way." He peeped under the cover again and let out a long whistle. "Tez, my name is Cortez. Obviously you don't know a damn thing about yourself because I parked something much better and bigger than a car last night."

"I'm seriously having some trouble remembering what took place. Can you fill me in?" My brain was in overload trying to think of the moment he and I spent together. The hangover was making any thinking impossible.

"Dig this. You and I made mad music last night. I was banging yo back out and you was feeling it. So, now that you sober, you wanna try and diss. If this was the streets, I would smack the shit out yo mouth and then make you suck something with them swollen lips."

"Who in the hell do you think you're talking to? I'm not the normal ghetto hoochies you're used to." He'd pissed me off by disrespecting me. I could do a lot of things with my lips, but it sure as hell wouldn't be him.

"Ok, since you some kind of lady, you get a pass. Stuck up and all, I'm cool with you Lil Ma, yeah I fucks wit you big time." Before I could respond, his cell phone rang.

He turned his back to me and never said a word, he just listened. I was sure it was one of his thousands of baby mommas he probably had, trying to figure out where he was at. That was the perfect time to get him out of my house. I hopped out of the bed, naked as a jaybird, since he did make a point by saying he'd seen what I was working with before.

"Uh Tez, right? You need to leave. I have a meeting that I need to be at this morning. Besides, this should've never hap-pened. I apologize if I came onto you, but I wasn't in my right frame of mind."

"Can't you see I'm on the phone," he mouthed like he was speaking sign language.

I was trying to be nice, but I was three seconds away from calling my security at the community gate. Why in the hell did they let him in anyway, did I give him the security code, too?

"Yeah….yeah…yeah…I got you," he said to the person on the phone.

Seconds later, he hung up his phone and stared at me. Not in a malicious kind of way, more like a deep, meaningful stare.

"You gotta go," I said firmly.

"That's ok Lil Ma. Like I said, we cool. The way I threw it at you last night, I'm sure you'll call me back. But please, check that uppity attitude at the door. It's not attractive at all." He was still laughing as I threw him his pants off of the floor. It was driving me insane.

"Get out now! Say what you want, Tez, or whatever your name is. We may have done something nasty, but if you don't leave my house within the next five minutes, I will call my father back here as well as the Chesterfield Police! And I'm sure you have warrants!"

"Whateva, Miss Snobbie."

"Play with me if you want! I'll have you arrested quicker than you can blink!"

I threw out my tough girl attitude because I didn't know what the hell happened for real. All I could remember was all those damn margaritas and Christian bringing me to my parent's house. Thank God they rarely come back here to the guest house. If they saw this thug, they would have me committed to the nut house.

"You know what Lil Ma, Shanice was right. You're a complete bitch! It's really sad too, 'cause you one beautiful woman. But you the type that like to look down on people, just because you in a higher position. Yet you call me late at night, ready for whatever. You just like the rest of these hoes, so don't flatter yourself." Tez looked at me as if I was dog shit on his shoes.

"Tracey, what's going on? Is everything Ok:" The banging on the door startled us both. That voice had me shook.

I gasped for air.

"Tracey, you in there?"

The banging continued.

It was Anthony! He'd never just popped up at my home without prior notice.

"Tez, you have to go now. That's my fiancé at the door." I pleaded with him desperately.

"Fiancé? Where's the ring?"

"I don't wear one, damn it! Now go!"

"Where in the hell you think I'm going?" Tez looked at me incredulously.

"Get in the bathroom...now! Just let me talk to him and then you can leave." My heart raced a mile a minute. I picked up his remaining clothing and pushed them towards him.

"You proving my point about how much class yo ass got. You didn't say shit about no damn fiancé last night."

"Look, I don't have time to explain this to you. Please, just go in the bathroom."

"Like I said earlier, you need to get yo'self together. I ain't with no chicken head shit." Tez grabbed his clothes and walked towards the bathroom, taking baby steps which pissed me off.

Did he just try and check me? Damn! He was sexy as hell. Uneducated, ghetto and borderline obnoxious, but sexy nevertheless. What in the hell had I gotten myself into?

BAM BAM BAM BAM!

Anthony's furious knocks had come harder than the last time. I quickly slipped on a robe and my engagement ring that I rarely wore, and opened the door, letting the morning October chill hit me in the face.

What in the hell are you doing in here? And who were you talking to? I thought I heard voices?" Anthony angrily asked.

"I was on the phone hollering at that dumb ass new assistant of mine. Sorry I made you wait." I gave him a slight smile, as I tried to pacify the situation.

"Do I look like I believe that?" Anthony asked barging his way inside.

My adrenaline pumped. Did he know I had someone in the house? Who could've told him, I wondered as my face became flushed. "What are you doing here?" I asked as I pulled the belt to my robe tighter.

I hadn't expected him to just barge in. This was new for

Anthony to be so forceful. My eyes quickly swept the room for any traces of Tez.

"Oh, so I have to have a reason to see you now?"

"Of course not. It's just not like you to pop up."

I tried to smooth things over. I didn't want him to think that I was acting suspicious. Hopefully he couldn't tell that I was nervous as hell. I had done a lot of things in the past, but I had never been caught up. This was a new experience for me.

"Maybe I should've called first, you look like shit," he said while turning up his nose.

"I don't really feel that good. I went out last night," I stammered over my words.

"I can tell. You're really letting yourself go, with all that drinking and partying that you do."

"Anthony, I'm not trying to be rude but, what do you want this early?" I purposely ignored his rude comment because my nerves were already on edge.

"I came by to give you a warning."

"A warning? You're not my father," I blasted.

Suddenly he moved forward landing on my four-thousand dollar couch which was positioned just five feet away from the closet that Tez now occupied. *Oh GOD! I was Busted*! I prayed that Tez wouldn't move or cause anything to fall down inside the closet. The whole situation had me flustered. I knew it was just a matter of time before I was caught. I impatiently looked at the clock on the living room wall as Anthony seemed to be in deep thought as he rambled about me and my lifestyle. Then, all of a sudden, Tez poked his head out the door causing me to nearly die.

"Tracey, what are you staring at? Have you heard a single word that I said?"

"What? Oh, I'm sorry Anthony, baby. I didn't hear you."

"Oh, so now I'm baby. You've never called me that, ever. Anyway, I said that Christian called and said that you had a little accident at the club last night. Why must you continue to embarrass me like this?"

"I told you that I'm not feeling that well. I need something to make me feel better."

I was trying to think of ways to quickly get Anthony out of the house. He seemed rather comfortable on the couch and it didn't look like he would be leaving anytime soon, so I figured I'd give him something that always made him run away. *Good head.* Seductively, I sat down beside him and placed my hand on his thigh.

"Well, you were feeling well enough to go out last night. Maybe you should've been at home in the bed," he said.

"I hate being in that big bed all by myself. I need some company," I coyly replied as my fingers made their way to his zipper.

Before he could put up a protest I was on my knees and had his pants down to the middle of his thighs. I thought he'd flee from me as he normally did. But when he didn't I knew I'd have to put it on him strongly. Without hesitation, I placed him inside of my mouth. Anthony didn't put up a fight as the sensation shot through his body like a speeding rocket. As long as we'd been together he never liked for me to service him with my mouth. So why was he allowing it now? His moans and groans rang loudly in the room, giving me motivation to continue. It only took about two more minutes before he jumped up with a hard-on.

"Tracey, what in the hell is wrong with you? On your knees like a two dollar whore. I don't even know who you are anymore," Anthony screamed at me as he pushed me down to the floor.

"What the fuck? We're engaged Anthony, it's what normal people do," I said while trying to get up. He pushed me back down and balled up his fist as if he was going to hit me.

"No wife of mine will walk around acting cheap. You just remember that," he said as he stormed out the door.

I had never seen him so angry, but at least felt good that my plan of getting him to leave had worked. Tez opened the bathroom door wide, startling me. "He's gone, so go," I told him, sort of upset that Tez had seen me give oral sex to Anthony.

"Aye, if ole boy don't want it. I'll take it any day. You had that fool hollin like a lil bitch," Tez said as he stood in the hallway laughing.

"Just get your stuff and get the hell out before I have you thrown out!" I yelled at him and charged towards my room. If he had any sense, he would be long gone before I got back out.

Chapter 6

Just three hours had passed since my drama at my house with Tez and Anthony. But now, I had bigger fish to fry. I paced the floor letting him have it like he was officially my man.

"You're such a hoe," I told him bluntly. "I'm not sure how I ever fell for someone like you, but this has got to end."

I listened to him tell one lie after another. The worst part of it all was that I couldn't tell a sole about him. I'd blasted him as soon as he answered my call. I wanted to know who the chick was that everyone had seen him with. There was someone new and I wanted to know who it was. Was she of royalty like me? Or some video bitch with a big ass? Probably implants, I sneered.

Suddenly, my line beeped. I didn't even tell my soon-to-be ex lover that I had to go. I just clicked over knowing he would still remain on the line blurting out lies about his infidelities.

"Tracey, I'm pulling up outside your little office. You know how I hate to wait so please be down when I get there. You have five minutes, so be ready."

That voice made the hairs on the back of my neck stand up. It always sounded like a threat, never a warm invitation. I stared at the receiver for a minute, not surprised that the person had hung up. I was in total disbelief that I had to deal with this, when I was still sorta hung over. Five minutes? I couldn't be ready in five minutes. There were so many things I'd rather be doing than dealing with this. Quickly, I returned to the other line and told my secret lover I had to go.

"Shanice get in here now! Hurry up!" I screamed like a lunatic because the madwoman who ran my damn life would be arriving in five minutes.

My mother, the very woman who could turn my sugar into shit, was on her way for a surprise visit. I hated when she just popped up like I didn't have a damn business to run. She didn't respect it at all. She felt that a woman's place was at home, raising a family, looking pretty and spending her husband's money. Not being independent herself, she firmly denounced anything that had to do with that movement.

"Shanice, come on. What's taking you so long? I don't want my mother to come up here and see you. I can't deal with having to explain who you are." Obviously, she didn't realize how crucial it was for me to be ready and downstairs so that Mother wouldn't come up.

The last thing I wanted was for my mother to have to meet Shanice. She would rip the poor girl to shreds with one look. Lord, what was I going to do? I needed to hit my suit with the iron, since Mother didn't condone any wrinkles. And touching up my makeup was a must. Oh My God, the list could go on and on about what this woman would complain about.

"Yeah, what's good Boss?" Shanice finally appeared at the door. "You look hella crazy." I wanted to shake the little ghetto bunny smart. She was so damn stupid.

"Shanice, how many times do I have to tell you, to watch what you say? Being ignorant is not a cute trait. My mother is on her way. I need you to plug in my steamer, so I can knock the wrinkles out of this suit, and get me my Mac makeup bag. Make haste about it because I only have about three minutes left." I didn't give Shanice time to talk, as I stripped down to my underwear in the middle of my office floor. She stood there looking at me like I was the one who was crazy.

"I'm sorry Boss, you gone really need that makeup bag, cuz you got hickeys all ova yo body," Shanice laughingly said. I looked at my body in the floor length mirror, and found no humor in the hideous marks on my body.

"Somebody got knocked down last night fo sho. It was Tez, wasn't it? I knew when you called me last night, it was sure to go down," she ignorantly laughed.

"Speaking of that, why in the hell would you give me his number?" I was still pissed that I had to hide Tez in my closet and allow him to see me servicing Anthony. That was such an embarrassment for someone like me. That scene could've easily turned into a really big disaster.

"You were drunk as hell and I don't know for sure, but I

heard Tez got that good stuff. I saw it once in a pool, but he's like my brother, so you know, nothing ever happened. Lord knows I don't need any more cold blooded niggas, messing up my life." Shanice started laughing again at her rambling and my obvious embarrassment.

I got dressed so fast this morning I didn't even notice any marks all over my neck and chest. That low class Tez, or whatever his name was, had obviously put this childish crap all over me. If my mother's plans were to go shopping, which I'm sure they were, she would surely notice it.

"Tracey, what in the hell are you doing?" The voice of hell asked in a disgusted manner.

It had only been four minutes since the call and she'd made her little boney way upstairs just to piss me off. She must've been downstairs the whole time and was just playing a game to make me sweat.

"Mother, what are you doing up here? I thought you said for me to come down. I was on my way down now," I stuttered and stammered over all my words. She really discombobulated my whole thought process.

Everything about her look said, she didn't play. Her gray tweed Chanel dress was heavily starched and her black peep toe Louboutins were shined to perfection. Her hair was neat in a tight bun and drastically pulled her eyes towards her ears. She scared the hell out of me, even when she wasn't trying.

"Why are you in your office in your undergarments? Who in the hell wants to see that flab?"

"Ummmm. Shanice is getting a few wrinkles out of my suit, Mother. I just took it off for a few minutes."

"What are you, a size eighteen now? I don't know why in the world you would cut your hair like that." She looked me up and down with pure disgust.

"Please, Mother. I had a rough night and I can't take all the screaming and the hollering today."

"You should try to get some sleep because those bags under your eyes are awful. And the next time you and Anthony have sex, you may want to advise him to refrain from putting whore marks all over your body. I honestly thought he had a little more class than that." Mother finished her verbal assault with her nose turned up. She totally ignored that I had a rough night. She stood waiting on me to answer all of her questions.

"Mother, I'm still a size six, same size I've been for years now. And if you came to the guest house more often, you would've seen my hair by now, it's been this way for a whole damn week. I swear you're impossible to deal with." I tried to mumble the last part under my breath as low as possible. When she turned back towards me briskly, I knew that she'd in fact heard me.

My mother walked close in my personal space, but I wasn't about to back down. I was hung over and sick of her constant nagging. Jesus would have to come down from Heaven, before I apologized. I stared back at her with a defiant glare.

"May I ask, just who in the hell do you think you are speaking to that way?" My mother spoke her words angrily, and I could smell the mints that she thought masked her morning cup of whiskey.

"Mother, I wasn't trying to disrespect you. It's just that I really had a long night." I mentally noticed that I'd begun to whine like a child. Whenever she and I talked, I found myself pouting.

"I brought you in this world and you best believe I will take you out. Two minutes flat and I could erase your whole life." I'd heard those cliché sayings so many times in my life. It was like she really believed that she gave me life or something.

"I know, Mother. Trust me, I know all about your capabilities."

"As I was saying, you've been looking rather bloated lately, has Anthony impregnated you with a bastard? If so, you can start planning the wedding now. No grandchild of mine will come into this world in sin and disgrace." My mother was always relentless with her attacks on me. It had become a natural occurrence early on in life.

However, I wasn't feeling it at all today. I was tricked into sleeping with a possible crack slinger, who for some reason I kept thinking about. He sucked hideous marks all over my body. And now I had to listen to her talk shit to me. Before I knew what came over me I lunged at my mother and wrapped my fingers around her fragile throat.

"You're such a bitch!" I spoke the words just as harsh as she had spoken to me seconds earlier.

"Is your mission in life to ruin all of my years on earth?

CHRIS RENEE 47

Maybe you need to see how it feels to be critiqued." I watched as
she cringed, choked and changed a few different colors. "How
about for once you stop acting so damn frigid and sleep in the
same room as your husband? Give the man some ass for goodness sake!"

"Tr-a-a-a-cey- I thought I heard her attempting to say. But I
squeezed tighter and kept preaching. "Stop drinking and smoking
your life away, and please, sit down at the table and eat a pork
chop. You're what, a size negative four now?"

My mother grabbed my hands, and tried to remove them
from her fragile, little throat. Her eyes begged for forgiveness, but
that just made me choke harder. I laughed a murderous, deep
belly laugh at how ridiculous she looked. The bigger her eyes got,
the harder I screamed. Nothing had ever felt so good. I'd wanted
to choke her since kindergarten. I laughed harder as Shanice
rushed toward me and tried to pull my arms from her neck.

"Tracey! Tracey! What's wrong with you? And why are you
standing there laughing? Maybe you should see my shrink, too."

"Yes, I agree," Mother chimed in. She'd snapped me from
my blissful daydream of choking her. I blinked several times to
gather my thoughts and quickly checked my emotions.

"Get dressed and let's go. I'm sure that suit wasn't that
flattering on your shape anyway. I wanted to tell you that last
month when you bought it. We can stop in Nordstrom and find
you something more suitable. Cicely, my personal shopper, called
and told me that they have some new things coming in today."

Once again my self-esteem dropped two more notches.
"Mother I'm really tired," I announced as Shanice handed me my
suit.

"Let's go, Tracey. And I'm sure you don't even have a
gown for the charity ball. You most definitely won't be wearing
your hair like that, so make an appointment for a sew in," she ordered. She once again focused in on how short my hair was.

"I love my hair like this. I think it makes my face look a lot
brighter."

"Trust me, it's a lot of things but bright isn't one of them.
You also need shoes and those bags under your eyes are
screaming for a facial…maybe even botox. I already know Christian and that wretched mother of hers are going to try and up-
stage us. So I really need to make sure that you're dressed

appropriately."

"Mario has already picked me out several dresses Mother. I don't need any help in that department."

There was no way in hell that I was going to wear something that she wanted me to.

"You wouldn't want to disappoint your father anymore than you already have, now would you? I'm sure the dress that Mario has is just wonderful, but it just won't do for this event," she ranted then ran down the list of things I hadn't done or needed to do.

What part of, I didn't want to go to the store with her, did this woman not understand? I thought to myself. I felt like shit and she made me feel worse. Being around her wouldn't do me any good. I was desperately thinking of some excuse to get out of her surprise little outing.

"I can't afford to be any later Tracey, so if you would please make haste, we could be on our way. You know, you really need to work on being on your A-game at all times. What if I would have been Anthony on my way with a surprise for you?"

"We don't surprise each other, Mother. So I'm guessing I'm good in that department." I shrugged my shoulders. I seriously didn't care what she was talking about.

"Maybe that's why you aren't married yet. What kind of woman doesn't live to be surprised with fabulous gifts by her man? Never mind that question, your level of couth has never been high." Mother straightened the bun on her head and looked at me sternly.

"Mother, do you mind if I skip this little unannounced appointment? I asked slipping my camisole and skirt back on. "I have some really important things that I need to take care of. I'm not sure they can wait either. Besides, I don't feel like pretending as if we enjoy each other's company."

"Is it too much to ask for a daughter to spend time with her mother?" Her voice cracked as if I hurt her steel feelings. "You only get one mother Tracey. You would think that before I die, we could become closer. Not to mention, that it's your place to attend these kinds of events. How else will anyone know how important you are?"

My mother had some unnamed disease since I was about thirteen, one she could never name. Just out of the blue one day, she saw the coming glory of the Lord. Since then, she'd been using that as her weapon of mass destruction against my father and I, whenever we didn't want to do something that she did. He and I both knew she was as healthy as a race horse.

"Mother, of course I want to spend time with you, but I'm really busy. If you would've called first, I would've told you that over the phone. There is this big meeting coming up and it could really bring in a lot of money for me." I mustered up a smile, when I really wanted to run to the bathroom and puke.

"I don't understand why you keep this little business open. You could achieve so much more by marrying a wealthy man to take care of you." Mother stated that so matter of fact, I almost believed her. She looked around the office as if the government had just condemned the place.

"Mother," I said, with more pleading in my voice. At that point I decided to put my jacket on, and slipped back on my shoes.

"I'm walking towards the elevator Tracey. You should be as well. Don't make me wait long. You do know how I hate waiting, right?" She strutted towards the door, leaving behind her scent of Chanel.

I grabbed my purse and ran my hand over my suit just to make sure I looked perfect. It was never a choice with Mother. If you just did what she said then no one would get nagged to death.

"Yes, Mother, I hear you loud and clear. The whole St. Louis can hear you." I mumbled the last part under my breath.

Shanice heard me and she gave me a slight hi-five as I took a few steps towards the elevators. I hoped like hell I could make it through the day without having a nervous breakdown.

"Hey, Boss, while you was in there with yo mamma you got this package." She nervously handed me the Tiffany box, as we both saw Mother walking back toward us.

We locked eyes as we thought about the last package that I'd received just the day before.

"Well, what are you waiting for? Go ahead and open the thing. I told you that Anthony was good enough for a surprise or two." Mother snatched the package out of my hand and eagerly opened the box.

I couldn't see its content but I could tell from her face that she wasn't pleased.

"What's going on with your life, child? This is dreadful. Are you dealing with college drop-outs or something? I'll talk with your father about getting you some security. You're really going to need it." She threw the box on Shanice's desk.

It tumbled over and Shanice screamed loudly. I stood in total shock as the dead mouse with the noose around his neck stared at me bug eyed. Whatever was going on had really started to scare me.

"That's just Rayven playing a silly prank, Mother. There's no need to get all dramatic." I pretended to not be bothered by it. But really, I wanted to know, who wanted to see me dead, and possibly with a noose around my neck?

"Who in the hell do you think you're fooling? You have no clue who sent this trash, do you?"

"Mother, I said drop it. I don't feel like talking about it," I snapped.

"You know just as well as I do, that any number of people could've sent you that. You're the most hated woman in St. Louis," she continued becoming more amused with each word she spoke. "You're like the black version of Kim Kardashian just with no sisters and certainly no friends.

I frowned. "I wouldn't go that far, I have plenty of friends."

She threw her head back in a fit of laughter, wiping away the tiny teardrops that escaped her eyes.

"Friends? Do I have to remind you of how you embarrassed me when you got caught sleeping with the Mayor's married son?"

"No you don't, Mother," I responded while balling my fist tightly.

"Or how about when you acquired this little magazine of yours by stealing the company from your own cousin? What is now called Totally Chic should be Totally Stolen!"

Again, more laughter from her.

"Are these reminders even necessary?" I asked through gritted teeth.

"Certainly they are! You can't get to the level that you are without pissing more than a few people off, silly child."

"You would know, wouldn't you, Mother?"

"I paid my cost to be the main bitch. Unlike you, there isn't a living soul who would be brave enough to even think of crossing me.

I had to keep my cool, even though I wanted to kill her on the spot. If she had guessed for one second that I was really shaken, she would never let up.

"Let's go, Mother." I walked ahead of her as she stared at me oddly.

I tried to remain confident, one false move from me and she would know that I was worried as hell.

Chapter 7 ————————————

    The afternoon with Mother was a complete couple hours of hell. She talked endlessly about all the silly little things that she'd accomplished in her life. Things I'd heard countless times. Then she had me call around investigating the package that was sent to my office. I even tried to contact UPS to find out if they had a return address, which they didn't. Everything seemed to be going wrong in my life, especially the part about hanging out with Mother. The most surprising thing was that she didn't drill me about Shanice. She made one sly comment asking me where I'd found her. I pretended to not hear her, just so she could go on with her next conversation. Of course that meant to talk about me again. She then took a million and one shots at my appearance. It was impossible for the two of us to have a civilized shopping experience together.

    The best part of our outing was the end when she dropped me off at the Mercedes service department to pick up my truck. Driving a nice car had always put a smile on my face in the past. I'd switched between the latest Porsche to a BMW to my newest baby all in six months. This time I vowed to keep the white, GL Benz truck. I got in, gripped the wheel and sighed wondering what my next move would be.

    I called Anthony to let him know that I was on my way to see him when I got his voice mail, so I sent him a text. I needed some sexual healing after the dreadful day that I had. I had covered the spots that the Tez guy left on my body. I couldn't remember anything I had possibly gotten myself into with him. I thought hooking up with Anthony would do me some real good. It wouldn't be the best sex ever, but it would be familiar.

    I really wanted to call another friend of mine, who always found the cure to itch my scratch. He had some addictive love and I had to wean myself off it. He was also very obsessive and I didn't want to get caught up in his drama. He was far too dangerous for me to be around. He was one of three secrets that I would take to my grave. No one knew about him, not even Christian. Yet, as bad as I wanted to dial his number, I knew Anthony was my safest bet.

We'd been seeing each other for the past eight months and engaged for the last two. Courtesy of our mothers, we were set up at one of the who's who picnics. We didn't grow up together like Christian and I, but his family had attended several events throughout the years.

His mom and dad were both lawyers and both grew up in South County St. Louis. His family was pressuring him for kids and a wife, and my mother was pressuring me for kids and a husband. Put us together and it was one big forced relationship.

I'd grown to love him though, and actually missed his company from time to time. Fireworks never shot off in the bedroom, but he served a purpose, and we had some fun together at times. Hopefully, he would be just as happy to see me and could help me take my mind off that mess that happened with me and Tez.

I'd tried to reach Tez on his cell as soon as I got out of mother's car. I would've left him a message, but listening to a three minute song from a rapper, telling some girl to bend over so he can see it, was something that I was neither use to nor did I care to hear. That song fit him perfectly, just low class and disgusting.

I still couldn't believe Shanice gave me his number when she knew I was drunk. I couldn't wait to get back into the office and let her know that his name was now forbidden in my office. Ugh! How she went on and on about the anatomy of Tez angered me as I drove crazily, turning one corner after another. Please! He was all right, I mean really he was packing, but I couldn't remember if he could throw a hip or two. Besides, a wet ass couldn't pay any bills. He was broke as hell. I didn't even know why I bothered calling him. Other than, I wanted to curse him for putting those marks all over me. Every time I saw them, I got pissed all over again. If I knew where he lived, I would've gone over there and slapped the hell out of him.

Lucky for him, I'd just pulled up to Anthony's house. I sat in his driveway and waited for him to arrive. I hoped he checked my message and would be coming home soon. I could've easily used the spare key he gave me, but I liked to give Anthony respect by not imposing. More so because I didn't want him freely using mine.

My cell began ringing loudly just as I pulled my engagement ring from the glove compartment. It scared the hell out of me. More than likely it would be Christian, calling to see how my day went. I answered the phone without taking a look at the number and slipped my ring on.

"What's good Lil Ma? Just saw that you called. I'm not really surprised thou. You calling for round two already?" That voice was enough to make my knees buckle. Something about his arrogance was a turn on, and a complete turn off. How was that even possible?

"I think not, you ghetto asshole. I called you earlier to tell you that I don't appreciate the hickeys that you put on me. I run my own damn business and going to meetings with marks all over my neck and chest isn't cute at all. I know that you aren't use to a real woman, but that is not something that I want or need in my life."

I kept reminding myself to stay strong. Don't let him know that he could get to me. He was probably like a stray cat, feed him once and I would never get rid of him.

"Chest and neck?" he chuckled. "Girl you need to go in the bathroom and get a mirror and look at the ones I put down below, on your pussy. You must don't check yourself on the regular," he said with a laugh.

"You really should find better words to use when you are speaking to a lady. While that may turn your little hoodrats on, it is appalling to me. How you ever had sex with a woman before is beyond me." As quick as he turned me on, I was now in off mode. His choice of words killed any sparks that were brewing.

"Why? You got a pussy don't you? What's there to be ashamed of, it's just a word. Do me a favor and slide your fingers between it. I know it's probably swollen from last night, so go slow. Move yo hand over to the right of yo clit, and you'll find the first mark. That's my trademark, it's called the Tezzery." He moaned in the phone and I couldn't stop myself as I slightly smiled.

"The Tezzery? How cheesy of you?" I rolled my eyes and

put as much sarcasm as possible in my voice. "First of all, again, watch how you speak to me. I don't have to be verbally abused by you, and furthermore, I'm not in high school. So you and I will not be having phone sex. You do nothing for me sweetie. You're broke and uneducated, the two things my mother and I despise the most."

"You don't know the first thing about me woman. Good thing I ain't trying to get busy with yo momma then, right? You kept mentioning her last night. I'm really not into the threesome thing, but if you want me to smash yo mom, just say the word." He chuckled again, and I could see that it was all a game to him.

"Boy, my mother wouldn't even walk down the same street with the likes of you. Lose my number please, and make sure you never stop by to visit Shanice again." I was sick of his smart ass mouth. I wanted to end the call before I hurt his feelings.

"Check this though, Ms. Bougie. I'm downtown at the Radisson in room 314. I'll be here all night. Be here by nine and make sure you wear something sexy. I prefer nothing, but if you too prissy, figure out something that'll satisfy me." He hung up without saying anything else.

There was no way in hell I was going down to some funky little hotel to have sex with a gutter rat again. A cheap ass hotel at that. Just who in the hell did he think I was? There was no way in hell I was going down there naked or fully clothed, to have sex with him. He wasn't even my type and so beneath me. But the nastier he talked to me, the more turned on I had become. Most men liked to cater to me and took care of my every whine and groan. But not him, he was a complete asshole, who didn't mind telling me about myself. Regardless, I wasn't about to go and meet him today, tomorrow, or never.

I looked at Anthony's house again and tried to make the decision of whether I wanted to go in or not when a set of blinding lights blared in my rearview mirror. I couldn't see all the way, but I was certain that it was Anthony's Escalade. I started to get out when the truck flew past the driveway.

There was a woman sitting in the passenger seat. Her face was covered with black shades and a black hat tilted to the side. I blew the horn to get their attention so he could stop, but I knew that he already saw me in his driveway. Whoever he had in the car with him didn't belong. And he obviously didn't want me to see. I picked up my phone to call the son of a bitch, but it was already ringing. Somehow my fingers had dialed a different number.

"I'm on my way right now, just give me a few minutes." Angrily I ended the call and threw my ring back in its spot. Two could play Anthony's little game. I knew the best way to get over a man was to get under one.

Chapter 8

Within five minutes of when I first saw him, I allowed him to explore my body as he pleased. To say he was shocked when I showed up would be a lie. He knew I would come. He anticipated my need for him. I banged on the door hard as hell. I wanted to hurry inside his room before anyone saw me.

"Tez, it's me Tracey are you in there?" I couldn't believe I was standing in the hallway, semi naked and he had the nerve to not be there.

What kind of game was he trying to play with me? I couldn't help but wonder. Good thing I didn't know anyone who would come to the Radisson. Trying to explain why I was standing outside a hotel room dressed like a hooker, would be too embarrassing.

"Tez, if I have to knock one more damn time, I'm leaving! You bastard! Play your games with someone else!" I was pissed that he had the nerve to try and play me. I turned to walk away, when the door miraculously opened.

He stood on the other side looking like a reincarnated Greek God. I saw Tez's body the other day, but didn't get a chance to admire it. Either he worked out a lot or had just gotten out of jail.

Six feet even, his body was so toned and fit. I couldn't find an ounce of fat anywhere. If I had to guesstimate I would say he weighed about two hundred and fifteen pounds. His chocolate skin was illustrated with several tattoos including: The twenty third Psalms down his right arm; a huge burning gun and knife on his stomach with the words "NO WEAPONS FORMED AGAINST ME" scribbled in block letters; a R-I-P Big Tez on his side; and across his shoulders and back, he had a huge cross. He must've been in the shower because his body was dripping with water beads.

"Tracey, close yo mouth, and then close the door. You acting like you ain't neva seen a man naked or something. Make yourself comfortable, I'm almost done in the shower."

He stared at my breast as they spilled out of the "hoochie number" I had on, and walked back towards the bathroom. I could have just bit his little chocolate behind, it looked so smooth and sweet. Instantly, I became super horny. I wasted no time discarding the little clothes I had on and ran towards the bathroom like a track star. Somehow we made it into the shower ass naked. There was no conversation at all as we groped, moaned and groaned. We were locked in a passionate kiss as the water beat down on us. Tez forcefully pushed me against the white, vinyl, and the coolness from the wall made my nipples tingle.

"Do you mind if I play with yo monkey?" he asked while he licked inside my ear. I tried not to grimace, but again his word choice irked me.

"Can we not talk while we're doing this? I'm not a ghetto linguist and words like monkey turn me off." I wanted to not be annoyed and just get what I had come for, the sex.

"What's wrong, Ms. Bougie? You don't like hearing monkey? You said pussy was too vulgar, so it's now a monkey. I don't give a damn what you call it. I just wanna know if you want me to play with it or not."

"Yes, I do want you to play with my vagina. That's the proper term for the word, I hope you know. Just shut up and put your fingers in me now." I was so wet and hot. I rotated my hips, so that Tez' fingers could easily enter me.

"Down girl. We gone do this my way. I won't be inserting nothing, not until you beg me to put my fingers in yo monkey." He kissed me harder, and with more purpose than the first time. My whole body was flushed with excitement and I wasn't sure if I could wait another second.

"Stop playing Tez! Why are you torturing me? Can I get what I came for please?"

"What you come for, Ms. Bougie? You came so I could kiss your lips?" Softly he laid his lips upon mine.

"Ohhhhhhhhhhhh…." I moaned

"Or what about yo neck?"

I thought I would melt as his tongue traced figure eights

upon my collar bone right along with the water beating on my back.

"Oh, I know what you want kissed. You want me to kiss this monkey don't you?" He kneeled in front of me, and barely grazed his tongue back and forth between my thighs.

I grabbed his head and tried to push it deeper, but he wouldn't let me. I was frustrated, with his little game of tease.

"I wanna hear you say the word. Now, let me know I can play in your monkey."

He was such a cocky bastard. Why in the hell did I have to say all of that nonsense just for some sex? "Please Tez, I can't take it, just do what you are going to do already." I dug my nails in his back. I wanted him to feel the pain I was in.

"I know what I'm gone do, but I want you to tell me what I'm gone do it to. You have to use my words and not yours. Besides, I know you can get freaky. I saw you remember?" I knew he was speaking of what he saw me do to Anthony. He stuck his tongue out farther and flicked it back and forth like a snake. I was on the verge of a black out. I knew that, playing his game would be the only way for me to get what I wanted.

"Please play with this monkey or who gives a damn what you call it, just do it." I felt utterly ridiculous saying the word. I almost burst into a fit of laughter, it sounded so stupid. I made a mental note to mention that to Rayven, only she could get a kick out of something so stupid. But by any means necessary was my state of mind because I wanted him more than anything.

Hearing those words was as if he found the golden ticket to Wonka Land. He didn't hold anything back, as he plunged head first between my thighs. His first lick drove me insane. I didn't want to act like I'd never gotten my clit lick so inhaled to keep from moaning. I could tell right off the back Tez was a master at performing orally. He probed here and there with his fingers and tongue causing me to go bananas.

"Damn, boy." I finally let some words escape from my lips. "It feels sooooo good."

It was as if he was down there painting a picture, the way he took long, strokes, eating me whole. I used my right hand to hold onto the wall since Tez was licking me faster and harder.

"Shit! Oh Shit!...Don't...make...me...me...me..."

Tez had me going so crazy I couldn't get out the fact that I didn't want to cum. He kept licking and plunging his tongue deeper until my legs started to buckle. I could hear my ears pop as my eyes shut tight. Quickly, I started humping his face with one leg raised in the air hoping like hell this would never end.

"I'm cumming Tez, I'm cumming! Please don't stop. Don't you dare stop!" I screamed so loud, I was afraid someone would call the front desk.

Tez continued making music with his mouth, as I yanked his head around. I heard about an out of body experience before, but that was the first time I ever felt it. I crumbled on top of his head and slowly slid down the wall.

"Damn, boy!"

He picked my exhausted body up and laid me on the bathroom floor. After running out into the bedroom then jetting back inside, he made sure his condom was on tight, then dove into me.

Where in the hell had he been all my life? I thought, as he moved and grooved to every curve of my body. This man was the missing piece of the jigsaw puzzle to my life. He wrapped my legs around his neck and gave me the slowest, nastiest grind possible.

My words became inaudible, and it was possible I spoke a foreign language. We spent the whole night laughing and talking. He really wasn't that bad when he actually spoke clear English. Even with that new found fondness of him, I still had to ask myself, *what in the hell was wrong with me?* It was fun, no doubt, but what about when I had to go back into the real world. The world where, sex wasn't the only thing we had in common. Where could we go from this moment?

******

By the time the next morning rolled around I was still asking myself, what were we doing? I kept asking that same question over and over in my head as the morning sunlight blared through the window. I mean, I didn't even know Tez, like that, but here I lay, doing a full eagle spread naked on the floor of his hotel room, ready for his morning treat.

Oh God, if Mother could see me now with my pussy pulsating waiting for Tez to tear into me… She would surely die from a heart attack. The thought alone was enough to put a smile on my face, but Tez actually entering me made me cheese even harder. Thoughts of my mother drove me to throw my ass back at

Tez even harder than he was giving it to me. In my mind I was paying my mother back with every stroke I gave.

"What you tryna do, get a nigga hooked or something?" Tez moved so seductively. "Who knew lil Ms. Bougie was a down low freak?" He rolled his tongue across my lips.

"Not my fault you can't keep up," I moaned in between my thrusting. Damn, he felt good. "I thought you thugs knew how to work it. I guess that's just an exaggerated myth, huh?" I didn't want to admit it to Tez, but he seemed hell bent on digging for oil between my walls. Stamina was his friend, and I appreciated their companionship.

"Auh…auh..auh," I cooed as he hit my spot.

At that moment I saw Tez's eyeballs shift to the back of his head.

"Damn, I ca- ca- ca- can't hold it, I can't pullllllllllllll out. It fells soooooo good, Tracey. Please don't be mad!" Tez groaned as he pulled what little bit of hair I had left. He kissed me one last time and rolled over completely out of breath.

I almost forgot what had really just happened. I was so deep in thought.

"I'm at a loss for words. I'm sorry boo, I shoulda pulled out. But I'm telling you, Ms. Bougie, you straight got my mind gone."

"It's ok, I'm on the pill anyway. But next time, mind gone or not you will not slip up again. You cool and all that, but I don't even know your medical history." I didn't even know why I told him that lie.

It was nowhere near okay for him to be depositing himself inside of me. Hell, I was the one with everything to lose. I had over $600,000 in the bank and a hefty trust fund that he could possibly benefit from if we had a child together. And I was too damn old to be whipped. My mind raced. And what about Anthony? Even though the bastard had some chick in his car, I at least owed him enough respect to tell him the truth. I couldn't go on pretending any longer. I wasn't happy with him at all. And he certainly didn't satisfy me in bed.

I had no desire whatsoever, to continue playing around. Being with Tez made me realize there was so much more to experience in life. My mind had just been made up, on what I wanted to do with my personal life. But I knew better than to let good dick cloud my judgment. That was for ghetto girls.

"You know Tracey, I hate to hear people say cliché shit, but I really could lay with you in my arms forever and a day. I'm surprised though, but you ain't that bad, once you stop acting all snobbish and shit." Tez pulled me closer to him and began to kiss softly, up and down my neck.

I could lay with him forever too, but time on the outside kept ticking. Mother's charity ball was less than ten hours away, and the rest of my day would be spent preparing for it.

"Me too baby. Unfortunately, I have an event that I have to attend tonight. I won't have much time to do anything other than, get ready for that." I rubbed my lips across his goatee. I loved how the soft hairs tickled my face.

"You should take me with you, Tracey. We'd have fun. You said everyone in that world is stuffy as hell anyway. At least I can keep you company." Tez winked at me and began to play with my cheeks. It wasn't long before his hands cupped my breast. If he worked himself up again, this would make the fifth time we had sex. I wanted to focus solely on that, but him asking to come with me had shocked the hell out of me.

Keep me company? No way in hell was he going to step foot anywhere near that ball. Everyone would laugh if he showed up with me. I wouldn't even know how to introduce him and my mother would probably die from shock.

"As fun as that sounds, you can't come. All the seats have already been filled anyway." I wanted to change the conversation, because it had made me nervous.

"But if it's yo family's lil thing, I know you can get me a spot in there too, right?" Tez persistently asked.

I didn't say anything because I didn't want to hurt his feelings. I was going to try my best to keep him and my real world as far away from each other as possible.

"Aww I get it, yo silence speaks volumes, Tracey. I'm good enough to dig yo back out, but you can't be seen with me?"

"I didn't say that Tez, you did."

"You embarrassed by me, or some shit like that." He roughly grabbed my face and I thought he was going to flip out on me.

"Of course not. I just need some time to tell my parents about us first. Hell, I don't even know what to call us. What would everyone think if I just showed up with someone new? I do have a fiancé. They wouldn't understand this, I barely do."

This was only our second time together. Even though I was feeling the way he touched me, I was not about to take it to a more serious level. I thought this was just about sex. What was wrong with modern men? They were getting sex confused, like women used to.

"Understand what, Tracey? The fact that you a grown ass woman scared of yo peoples, is some funny shit to me. I can't understand bullshit." His nostrils flared up like the devil.

"No, that's not what I'm saying. I just need to let them know, I'm seeing someone new. They still think that Anthony and I are together, so imagine their surprise if I showed up with someone different. I never said I was embarrassed of you." My mind scrambled fast as hell. I tried to figure out a better lie to keep him at bay.

"Yeah, ok, Tracey. God forbid, if they cut off your credit cards or some other Beverly Hills 90210 shit like that. I thought you were a grown ass woman. Maybe you should call me when you get that together." Tez pushed my body away from him and got up like he was running from a fire.

He was pissed. Why was he making it so complicated? He and I were really nothing more than two people having great sex. If I took everyone that I had sex with to every event, Mother would disown me. What was the big rush to go around those people at the Charity Ball anyway?

"Tez," I called out.

I got no response.

"Tez," I called again.

I had too much on my mind to play mommy to some little ass boy. Suddenly, my cell phone rang. I moved with the speed of lightning to retrieve it from my purse. As soon as I saw that it said UNKNOWN, I started not to answer, but crazily, I did.

I quickly realized someone wanted to play games. One second after another they just breathed into the phone never saying one word.

"Hello," I repeated loudly.

Still nothing.

Chapter 9

    The History Museum was lit from top to bottom with beautiful white Christmas lights. White lilies adorned the stair casing leading into the main corridor. The long black carpet that lined the floor was plush, but not thick enough for one to trip and fall. I could hear the St. Louis Symphony serenading the crowd with a slew of boring songs. Each table in the hallway held glass trees, with the seating arrangements of each guest. Knowing my mother, she had probably seated all her enemies in the back, away from everyone and everything, just to make them feel unimportant.

    My mother and Christian's mom, Mrs. Santana went all out with decorating. Each went above and beyond the necessary preparations, just for bragging rights. On the outside, people couldn't even tell that they had a love/hate relationship with one another. They were both the queens of fake, and easily put on their happy smiles when they were being watched. I felt slightly out of place in my over the top Badgley Mischka ball gown. My mother had insisted on me wearing this taffeta monstrosity. The color was black, which was always a favorite color of mine, but the puffy bottom made me look like a blackened cloud. Not to mention, the fabric itched my ass like hell. Something told me that I would spend most of the night digging wedgies out of forbidden places.

    The horrendous dress was nowhere near my first choice of what to wear. I had my heart set on a simple Herve Leger backless gown, which hugged my body in the right places. Mother, however, thought it looked tawdry and expanded my hips. It was no sense in arguing with her about silly things, so I took the quiet way out and wore her choice.

    I watched all the other stuffy black tuxedos, and extra pressed designer ball gowns parade around me. I could see some folks felt just like me. They attended by force; more than likely, by their parents, who were just as equally snobby as my mother. Most of us rebelled against the whole socialite scene by the time we hit twenty-one. Then there were others like myself, Christian, and Anthony, who didn't want to disappoint our families. So, we forced smiles on our faces, just to save the peace.

I was more than amused to see the Petersons, an older married couple of forty-five years, getting freaky on the dance floor. I wasn't sure if Mr. Peterson had taken Viagara or what. He'd begun to dry hump his wife as if they were the only two around. The Petersons always showed out on the dance floor. When we were kids, we would seek them out at every event, just for a good laugh. I looked at the other faces to see their reactions, and many were horrified at the spectacle. Not I though, I actually found myself wanting exactly what the Petersons had, real love.

Suddenly, I felt someone invade my space. "Finally, I get to lay eyes on my fiancé. I almost didn't recognize you." Anthony stood close behind me and kissed my neck.

"I guess not. You've been busy lately," I said with sarcasm in my voice.

"You have too, Tracey. It's the life we chose."

"I think you've been choosing something more than work lately." I paused to hit him with a smirk. "I think you're practicing more than law."

Anthony seemed to be in deep thought. His black Gucci tuxedo was tailored specifically to fit his 5'8 frame. His line was fresh, as if his barber hit it the second before he walked in the gala. I leaned into his chest and allowed his Dolce&Gabana cologne to hypnotize my sense of smell even though I knew he was full of shit. I started to question him about the person in his car, but quickly decided to leave it alone for now.

Once upon a time, Anthony was all I needed. Well, that may be exaggerating a bit. He was just a friend that I never thought about romantically. I hadn't been faithful to him never a day in my life. Nevertheless, he was all I needed for this pretend socialite world.

"Awwwwe baby don't be like that. I've been really busy this month," he finally stated. After this big case coming up, I'll be able to relax more."

"Sounds good, some relaxation will do us good." As I

spoke the words to Anthony, I realized, I was truly talking to the wrong man. I didn't want to relax with him, not even a little bit.

That damn Gertrude was staring at us from across the room, signaling her approval of Anthony and me. I never understood her devotion to our relationship. She was always encouraging me to pressure him for marriage. I lied and told her that he wasn't ready just yet, but it was really me.

"So, you've been working really late, huh? Cranking the midnight oil every day has to be tiring. I can see bags under your eyes." He stared disapprovingly at me. I could almost see my mother, staring through his eyes. He sounded just like her.

"Yeah it's tiring. I've just been so stressed lately. But I don't get how my eyes, make you look bad though. I'd recently gotten a facial and hadn't seen any bags. However, I sure could use some sort of relief. I'm hoping that you can give me some." I licked my lips, to ensure Anthony of what kind of release I was looking for. Even though I had just left Tez's arms, I still felt it was my duty to please my fiancé. I snuggled a little closer to him so he could feel what he was missing.

"Must you act like an indecent whore in front of all these people? My parents and boss are over there for goodness sake! Besides, you haven't been home in two days. Don't think I don't realize it!" His tone had changed completely.

"Anthony, don't let me start on you!"

"Oh, it gets worse Tracey. I know that you haven't been wearing your ring!"

Quickly, he lifted my hand. *Thank God I had it on*.

"Have your fun now because once I marry you, your days of being a whore are over, Tracey." He glanced around trying to see who was looking at us.

He was so damn uptight, and at that moment I wished I had brought Tez with me. I was sick of Anthony always trying to criticize me. More often than not, he reminded me more and more of my mother. My instincts told me to give him a piece of my mind, but I knew *she* would have my head on a platter. So, being nasty nice was in order, for this moment only.

"You know Anthony, taking the stick out your ass every now and then wouldn't hurt. You don't have to step on my esteem, just to build yours up. Everyone here, including your parents, knows that you are a grown man with needs. Maybe if you took your balls into your own hands, you would understand that. As for what I do with my body, that's none of your damn concern. And so since we're throwing stones, I guess I should let you know that I did see you and the bitch in your car!"

"Quiet down Tracey. You don't know what that was about," he warned.

I continued to smile as people passed us by. Anthony had known from the jump that I slept with other men. He said he would be okay with that, until we got married. Why bring it up now? Besides, I never said it was okay for him to sleep around.

"Well, maybe if you weren't so boring neither of us would have to go elsewhere for sex."

"It's not like you have your own set of balls, Tracey. You're nothing more than, your mother's puppet. How dare you attack my manhood, when you still stay at home with, Mommy and Daddy?"

Anthony shocked me, speaking to me in the manner he was using. He'd never said such hurtful words to me before. I had told him I would move in with him soon, but that wasn't good enough for him. "You self righteous bastard I…" attempted to shout.

Anthony kept a straight face and wouldn't even look at me as he spoke. "You may want to turn that frown of yours into a pretty little smile. There are too many important people here for you to put on the ghetto welfare act. My boss and his wife are on their way over as we speak. Try not to fuck this up for me. You know I need to make partner at my firm and I want to run for office soon."

My mouth simply opened wide. Anthony's Jekyl-Hyde syndrome went into overtime, as he cheesed and laughed as his boss walked closer to us. I'd had enough of this bull already, and some fresh air was in order. I could still feel Anthony giving me the side eye, so I hurriedly walked away. I stopped the *Eventful Eats* waitress as she walked by, and grabbed two glasses of champagne and a plate of stuffed crab shells. The way the night was going I knew that only getting drunk and eating until I burst, would save me from killing myself.

I'd purposely starved for the past week, so that I could fit into my dress and not have any alterations. I'd rather not eat, than have Mother go on and on, about my fluctuating weight again. I wolfed two of the shells down without even chewing much. I found a nice quiet spot in the corner and watched my parents chat with the Mayor and his wife. If I didn't know any better, I could've sworn that Mother was flirting with the man, right in front of his wife and my dad. She laughed at whatever was being said and coyly rubbed her hand up his arm. My mother had a way of seducing whatever man was in her path. I was willing to bet, she was boning the mayor.

. "Hey, Tracey! You're wearing that dress honey child! Your body is to die for, bitch! Have you been working out? Doesn't she look nice, Christian?" my gay boyfriend, as I so wonderfully called him, Kensington said.

He and Christian must've arrived almost simultaneously. They both walked up to me, looking as if they wanted to be anywhere else besides the Gala.

Kensington eye-balled me as if he was straight. He was wearing the hell out of a black Gucci tux, but had opted out of wearing the bow tie and left the top three buttons undone. His hairless chest had been smothered in baby oil. That must've been a move to piss off his parents. Their noses were so high in the sky, they sniffed clouds daily. They didn't approve of his alternative lifestyle and had all but wrote him out of their will. He just wouldn't leave though.

"Yeah, she looks good, but what else is new? Tracey always looks good, and always has to outdo everyone whenever she gets a chance. But I know that dress was not her choice, it's not showing enough cleavage. It doesn't look sluttish, like the rest of her clothes. I'm sure Mother chose the perfect look for her perfect little daughter," Christian said with despicable sarcasm as she briefly looked me over. She quickly turned her head and continued to scan the crowd.

I could tell by her body language, she wasn't in a good mood. I silently questioned Kensington and he nodded his head 'yes'.

"Christian, you look beautiful too doll face," I warmly told her. "I don't know why, all the snide remarks, but you really do look good. Have you lost weight? These women in here should be scared." I looked Christian up and down, because she really did look that beautiful.

She had on a soft butterscotch Yves Saint Laurent Grecian gown, and her hair was pinned on the side with a white lily. Even her makeup was flawless. My friend was truly a gorgeous woman.

"What do you mean, did I lose weight? What? I don't look good when I'm fat? Besides, you just saw me the other night. Save your condescending ass remarks for someone who really gives a damn about your opinion Tracey."

"Christian, what's wrong with you? I just said that you look cu…"

Christian cut me off, and moved close to my face.

"I look cute for a fat girl? Wow! And I thought my weight didn't matter at all to my real friends. Look, I'm over this damn place and all you phony ass people. I need some air. Do me a favor and leave me the fuck alone!"

Christian stormed off, leaving me and Kensington staring after her. We both were confused as hell. How could a compliment set her off in the wrong way?

"Did I say something wrong Kenny? I mean, I can't understand how she got so mad at me. You just said that I lost weight and I didn't get all pissed off. I should go find her and apologize, because I really didn't mean anything by that." I was worried about her and hated arguing for no reason.

"Child please! It has nothing to do with you, and everything to do with that no good ass husband of hers. Look at him, over there whispering sweet nothings into that tramp's ear. If he's gonna cheat, it should be with me," he hissed between his teeth. "As fine as that man is, I would even re-do his dreads for free; tasting his neck along the way."

"You're so nasty Kenny."

"So I've been told," he said fanning himself. "But he's the biggest dog walking the face of the earth." Kensington nodded towards the patio. Sure enough, Christian had found and confronted Chuck. He had the nerve to be smiling unashamedly in Megan's face. Suddenly, Megan stood off to the side and laughed as Christian screamed at Chuck.

"Oh my God! This is going to get ugly real quick if someone doesn't stop it." I'd never seen Christian this mad before and it kind of made me nervous. "Why would Chuck try and pull a stunt like this knowing she came with him tonight?" I spoke to Kensington, but really the question was rhetorical.

Of course, he knew she was there. He drove the car that she arrived in. Her mother was co-hosting the event. The point was, he just didn't give a damn.

"Tracey that man can't help it honey. Of all the hoes in St. Louis, he sleeps with Megan. That's a damn shame, I hear she has herpes. Now that may be a rumor, but it's my job to keep folks informed of the possibilities." He ate another stuffed shell as his eyes darted across the room.

"Herpes?" A lump formed in my throat. I got worried. But if he has them then so does Christian." I couldn't fathom the idea of my friend having a disease that she could never get rid of.

"Do you think he really gives a damn who he gives that mess too? I also heard he was in the strip club last night and blew ten grand in an hour. He's one sorry piece of shit if you ask me." Kenny flipped his hands in dramatic fashion as he talked. He was truly a diva.

"Nobody asked you, Kensington, with your crazy self. I wouldn't be surprised if Megan did have an STD, she's nasty as hell. How in the heck do you know what goes on in those strip clubs? You don't like women." I playfully slapped his arm.

"I may not get down with the fish, but you will be amazed how straight men talk, while creeping on the down low. I keep my ears to the street child, and therefore I stay well informed." Kensington remained nonchalant about the situation, and helped himself to some more of the shells on my plate.

"You're insane. And obviously hungry."

"These stuffed crab shells are to die for honey; they almost taste better than sex. Who is the catering company, Tracey?" Kensington barely looked at me as his eyes were glued to a slender young man across the room.

"You're silly as hell. Nothing is better than sex, but the catering company is *Eventful Eats*. You should look her up if you host a party. This is Mother's third time using her, so she really must be good. Enough about food, let's go and do our friendly duty, and break up this little debacle before something bad happens." I sat the plate on the table, ready to go save my friend.

"Fighting is so not cute. If I do nothing else, I keep it cute. I can't risk messing up this beautiful face. I just got my nose done last year boo and I don't need Chuck breaking it."

"Yeah, you're right about that. He never liked you much

anyway." I thought about our options and decided that hanging low was best. "Besides, there goes Mrs. Santana getting up from the table ready to do some damage control." I figured she was pissed that they'd caused a major scene.

Kenny saw her strutting toward us. "Oh shit, here she comes. You know when the old bitches get mad, none of us have peace." Kensington nodded to our right.

Mrs. Santana kept her eye on Chuck and Christian's movements but chose to stop right in front of Kensington and I as she watched her daughter and son-in-law chew each other's heads off. She didn't say anything she simply gave me this strange look, the same one she gave me at least once a month. This time there was a slight smirk behind it. I never understood Mrs. Santana nor how she felt about me. But I was certain she hated me just as she did my mother. Within seconds, she'd stormed off and joined the argument.

"I'm sick of your shit, Chuck!" Christian screamed at him.

"What did I do now? I'm just sitting her talking to a friend," he replied condescendingly.

Megan stood next to him laughing at the growing scene. She loved all the attention that she was receiving. She secretly hoped the scene would make the gossip section of the paper. I on the other hand wanted to secretly murder Chuck.

"Friend my ass. You think you and this bitch will keep disrespecting me like this!" Christian continued to holler.

"I don't know what got you all gassed up, but I suggest you calm down before I embarrass your ass." Chuck looked around at all the faces, eager to be in someone's business.

"Yeah, Christian, you need to chill. You got yourself looking real stupid right now," Megan chimed in.

I wanted to interrupt but I knew inserting myself in the mix would make things worse. I saw her mother bud in and grab her arm attempting to pull her away.

"I'm talking to my husband, unless you want me to make this situation about you, I suggest you leave," Christian said angrily.

"Girl boo, you don't scare…" Megan started to reply.

"She doesn't have to go anywhere. You don't own shit. We're just standing here talking. You just go back to doing whatever the hell you high society people do," Chuck interrupted as he continued to laugh.

"That's enough, Chuck!" Mrs. Santana roared.

Chuck laughed even harder. "No disrespect Mrs. Sophia, but I'm grown."

"I'll have you ruined in this town, Chuck."

"I bet you wouldn't think this shit was funny if I cheated on you," Christian interrupted.

Chuck laughed even harder at her mentioning cheating on him.

"Who would want your fat ass, besides me?" he replied.

Megan laughed so hard her champagne flew out her nose and mouth.

Christian stared at him with wide teary eyes. She couldn't believe that he was really standing in front of Megan talking down to her. And I couldn't believe what I was hearing. My fist got tighter and tighter listening to every word coupled with Megan's God awful grin.

Christian's mother stepped in between them. She knew better than anyone the situation was about to get worse. Christian was totally oblivious to the audience that had formed as she continued to scream and holler obscenities at Chuck.

Just when I thought the scene couldn't get any worse, Christian threw her glass and hit Chuck in the head. Blood spurted out the side of his head and onto his tux. My mother smiled big as the scene grew bigger and people started pointing and talking. It didn't matter that Christian had obviously snapped, she was just happy that the Santanas had been embarrassed by the fight.

Everyone who was anyone in their lives watched with delight and witnessed the whole thing. It wouldn't have surprised me, if my mother had invited Megan on purpose. Why Mother included her, I could not understand. She was one evil bitch. She always got her way, regardless of who she had to hurt in the process.

"Tracey, who is that nice piece of meat looking at us?" I followed Kensington's gaze and realized the man that he had gawked at was my new stylist, Mario.

"That's Mario. He's an up and coming stylist. Before you ask, hell no I can't hook you up. I really like his style and you will not mess with my clothes honey. Besides, I need to go and check on Christian. You should, too."

"No, you go ahead and play hero, I have other things on my mind." Kensington walked away towards Mario. I tried to smile, but Christian's sobs had washed away any happiness.

I watched as Christian's parents walked her out of the museum. My heart really hurt for her. I knew that her mother would be all in her ear all the way home. Christian seemed to be at a breaking point, and no one was safe whenever someone was at their lowest like that. Meanwhile Chuck's sorry ass wiped his head with a napkin and tried to walk out with his head held high, trying to save some dignity. But it was pointless; we all had been a witness to his cheating and disrespectful ways. The bloody napkin was an indication that Christian had gotten tired of his infidelity. The crowd quickly dispersed as the excitement ended. Everyone had gone back to their boring idle chatter as if nothing had happened. I noticed a girl crouching down on the patio, trying to make herself unseen. I couldn't be certain but she looked just like Shanice. What in the hell was she doing here and who invited her? I started to make my way towards her when Mother ambushed me.

"Did you see that scene that your friend just caused? I swear those Santanas have no couth whatsoever," she said while laughing.

"Mother, I don't have time for this right now. I'll be right back."

"Don't dismiss me like I'm not even standing in front of you."

"It's not that Mother. I just see someone that I know. I'll be right back," I said through clenched teeth.

I turned around and walked towards the area where I'd noticed Shanice, but she was gone. Maybe I was just tripping. I looked around to see if anyone had noticed the uninvited guest, but they all were focused on the performance that had begun on the stage. I did have more than a few glasses of wine. But I could've sworn she was just standing over there.

Damn, my life had gotten crazy!

Chapter 10

"Shanice. Shanice. Shanice! Get in here now!"

I swear dealing with her, was like working with a child. I'd been waiting for her to get to work so that I could run back out to the bank. Mondays were never my favorite and for some reason they made me extra bitchy. Besides, Shanice was four hours late! I had been dying to ask her if she had the nerve to crash my mother's charity ball on Saturday night. I started to call her at home but I didn't want to seem like I was nuts if it wasn't her.

"Shanice! Do you not hear me calling you?" I screamed louder this time.

Her attention span was about as long as her skirts. The makeover did nothing for her lost soul. She was back in her hoochie wear and tear. I thought that she would take the money from petty cash that I told her was available, and buy a few more outfits. Wishful thinking on my part was my guess.

"What's good Boss, I was just 'bout to go into the kitchen and watch General Hospital. That Sonny Corinthos, is one fine ass white man!" Shanice was smiling, like she and I were friends and it was cool to watch television at work.

"Where were you Saturday night?" I grilled.

"What? What do you mean, where was I? I was at home with my kids, not like its yo business or nothing," she stated defensively.

She was a semi-pretty girl, who would look a lot better if she cleaned up her act. A personal trainer and a dietician wouldn't have hurt her either. Although she wasn't fat, she was a lot thicker than she probably should've been; short, and my guess…a size 10. I was certain she ate bullshit on a regular; probably pork bacon, fat back meat, and fried chicken with lard.

"I thought I saw you somewhere, that's all. I knew I was

tripping, no way in hell would you have been able to get into the same party that I attended anyway."

"Ugh, ok. But what you want Boss?"

"Shanice, I'm really trying to give you a chance, but you're not cutting it. In fact, I'm gonna have to let you go if the issues aren't fixed immediately." I gave her one of my famous, I'm trying to be patient with you looks.

"Damn, what I do now? I did everything you asked me and ain't messed up in hellas." She had a confused look on her face.

"Maybe if you weren't so focused on watching fictional TV, you could do your job. You dress like a whore, you talk like a gutter rat, and you forgot to send the final draft of the December issue to the printer?"

"I sent it to the printer like you asked, Boss. I'on know what you tryna pull!" She herself was just seconds from going off on me. I could tell by the way her nose continued to flare out.

"I have deadlines, Shanice. If I don't produce my product then I don't get paid. This has caused a complete set back. Do you not realize, this is a company that does not thrive on stupidity?" If looks could kill, her mother would have been in a black dress singing hymns.

That was exactly why I didn't want to hire her ass in the first place. I tried to be nice and now I had to work extra hard, fixing her problems, which trickled back to being a major problem for me.

"Wait, what did I do Boss? You don't even listen to me! I haven't done anything wrong, what's wrong with you and why you taking it out on me?"

"Shanice!" I interrupted.

"But I swear I did my job. I did nothing wrong!" Shanice rolled her neck and eyes and I wondered, if it was a mistake to confront her.

I didn't want to have a fight with her and no one was around to save me. I saw enough, Jerry Springer, to know that ghetto girls fought dirty. "You haven't done anything right either Shanice! What in the hell am I paying you for? Not to watch soap operas all damn day, I can tell you that much. I don't need to babysit someone all day, that's why I don't have kids."

"Well, if you recognize that you don't have kids, what in the hell makes you think it's okay to talk to me like this?" She balled her fist at her side as she spoke.

"Before I left last week, I told you that the final copy needed to be sent off by Friday. It's like I have to hire a stupid coach, in order to get you to understand me." I may have been scared, but I would not back down. I put too much work into my magazine to have her ruin it for me. "And if you would stop having babies maybe you could think a little better!"

"I love my kids!"

"But do you know who their fathers are?" I asked with a serious expression.

"Aww nawl, hold up. First of all who in the hell do you think you talking to? You calling me a hoe? Boss, you slept with Tez after meeting him one time."

"Shanice, you're skating on real thin ice, all in my damn personal business."

"Thin ice, my ass. You ain't about to keep talking crazy to me," she yelled.

"First honey, a lady should never raise her voice like a man. You really need to calm down."

"A lady? You were whored up in a hotel room with a man you barely know. And believe me there's something you don't know about Tez. He ain't what you think."

I grabbed my chest hoping she would tell me more. "Shanice, I'm sorry." I was hoping to lighten the mood and earn myself some brownie points with her. I needed to know what she knew about Tez. Then I stopped to think, maybe that was her comeback since she knew I was feeling Tez. It was all a trick; Hood Trickery 101.

Crazily, my thoughts flooded with images of Tez right in front of Shanice. Even though he pretended to be pissed about not going to the charity ball, his true feelings showed yesterday. He'd called constantly until I finally answered telling me that we had to hook up soon. He even said that he had a nice surprise coming my way soon. That boy had a weakness for me, and I knew it.

By now Shanice had become teary-eyed and didn't realize I was in my own little world. "Boss, I tried to reach you, but the phone kept going to voicemail. For your information, I personally delivered the final copy to the printers Saturday morning and it will print on time. So now you should feel hellas stupid." Shanice rolled her eyes again as she spoke. I thought her five dollar, fake eyelashes would fly off. I stared at her like the circus freak she was to me.

"I hardly ever feel stupid, Shanice." I made sure I took all anger from my voice and got down to business. "Whether you completed the task or not, don't you ever in your life speak to me that way again. I'm the boss! Keep it up and you will find yourself back in the welfare line." I really did feel kind of stupid, but she would never know.

"You are the worse kind of woman, Ms. Tracey. Why? Because you don't even know who the hell you are for real. Naturally you assume because we're from different backgrounds that you're better than me."

Shanice's bottom lip quivered and I actually felt bad that she was about to drop tears. I hadn't intended to hurt her feelings. Well maybe I did, but I didn't think she would break down and cry for real. I never broke down and cried when Mother would go in on me.

"Well, let me tell you something, Boss, you're not. You're weak and spineless. Yo momma dogs you out, and you too scared to let her know you're grown. I have tried to work my hardest here, even though you constantly turn your nose up at me. I don't have to take this! I quit!"

She stormed her ghetto behind out of my office and I felt good for all of ten seconds. I should've felt great. Finally rid of her and all the other unnecessary drama she brought with her. I did owe her an apology since she'd completed the task. I was use to receiving a confirmation email, but I guess there wasn't one since she personally delivered it. Actually, I felt like crap, she didn't deserve for me to take out my frustrations on her. She called herself telling me a thing or two and for some reason I admired her for that. Shanice had something that I didn't. Courage! I picked up the phone, pressed the intercom button, and called her back into my office. When she walked back in, I crossed my arms and began.

"Shanice, I didn't mean it like that, I'm just frustrated as hell. It has nothing to do with you and I hope you can accept my apology." She remained silent but I knew she wanted to stay. Welfare recipients needed money, right? She had calmed down drastically but I didn't want to entertain her dramatics at all. I still needed to get to the bank. I apologized again, so she could either stay or go. I was going to try and pacify her a little more but someone had entered the front office causing Shanice to run out front.

"I'm coming!" she shouted.

That was my sign that she still wanted her job.

"You have a delivery at the front desk, Boss," Shanice said through the intercom just seconds later.

Hurriedly, I entered the reception area and was met by a beautiful bouquet of lilies.

"So, you're staying, Shanice?" I was all smiles.

"At the end of the day, I got bills to pay. Just treat me with respect, Boss. Here's your card that came with the flowers," she said while throwing it on top of her desk.

There was no need for me to look at the card. I knew that an arrangement that beautiful and expensive had only come from one person. I guess he still didn't get the message that I didn't want anything else to do with him.

"Hmm, I guess hoochies come rich or poor. Mighty funny how those flowers came from a dude name Charles, when you sleeping with Tez and Anthony," Shanice mumbled under her breath.

I tried to pretend as if I didn't hear her as I made my way toward the elevator. I didn't owe her ass any explanations at all. "Shanice, I'm going to the bank. I'll be back."

I thought I saw her roll her eyes as I stepped onto the elevator. The moment the doors closed, I thought about my life. Things seemed to be spiraling out of control with all of my men, especially Anthony. He hadn't called and I hadn't either. I needed spice in my life, I told myself stepping off the elevator. I took the rare chance of thinking about my other men as I strutted to my car. Some thoughts made me laugh, others made me cry, and some thoughts I'd take to my grave. Then suddenly things brightened for me. I stepped toward my truck with a smile on my face.

True to his word, there was an invite on my windshield. The envelope was deep, dark purple with fancy silver writing. I opened it and the invite slipped out.

YOU ARE CORDIALLY INVITED TO TURN ALL YOUR SEXUAL FANTASIES INTO REALITY. ANONYMITY IS A MUST SO YOUR SECRET IS SAFE BETWEEN THESE WALLS. FEEL

*FREE TO BRING THE "TOYS" OF YOUR CHOICE. SEXY AND
COMFORTABLE ATTIRE IS RECOMMENDED!*
*15433 BELLEFONTAINE ROAD, THE FESTIVITIES
START AT 10:30PM*
October 31st

My heart fluttered. This was the surprise Tez was talking
about. How sexy? He certainly knew how to turn me on, even if
he was sending me an invite for an event that was a little over two
weeks away. Instantly, I got excited and scared all at the same
time. I was terrified of attending a sexual party, and wished that
either Christian or Rayven could go with me. I preferred Rayven,
but ever since she started some insane private investigator side
job she hadn't been in town much. Her parents had pressured her
into following in her father's footsteps by working for the District
Attorney years ago so I guess she'd decided to rebel. Maybe
that's why I'd decided to go through with going to an orgy, just because Gertrude would despise it. It was not something no one in
my circle would even consider. I couldn't believe that I, Tracey
Robbins had considered it. Granted I was freaky, but this was on
another level. I couldn't wait! Damn, cocaine, lust was a hell of a
drug.

Chapter 11

I'd spent nearly three weeks with Tez and seemed to be having the time of my life. Tonight was a big night for me and I couldn't wait until things got moving. The fact that I'd shaved the kitty completely bald still had me shocked as I strutted from the bathroom headed to grab my wig. I needed to see myself in a mirror from top to bottom. I couldn't believe that Tez was able to get me to open up like no other man I'd ever known. The thought of me going through with a sex party had me ready to down another glass of Riesling. I kept checking the clock making sure that I left my house on time prepared to meet Tez, ready to screw his brains out. He and I had been spending countless evenings together doing what we both loved.

Sex.

More Sex.

Lots of sex.

And good sex.

For weeks now, I'd wanted to invite him to my house, but I couldn't run the risk of my mother seeing him. She would surely flip out and scare him away and I couldn't allow that to happen. I was beginning to think that we had a chance at being together. Maybe even a boyfriend- girlfriend situation. The fact still remained that Tez came from nothing. Besides meeting in hotel rooms to have sex, we had gone out on a couple of dates here and there. Not my normal top of the line restaurants, but I was really liking some of the low-budget places he took me to like Ruby Tuesday's and Houlihans'. He even took me to one of his 'homeboys' birthday party at the Tap Room. I was nervous as hell when I saw a security guard using a hand wand to search us for weapons. His roughneck looking friends with face tattoos didn't make it any better. They were dressed so inappropriately. However, I must admit that they made me feel welcomed and I had a ball.

It was crazy how I grew up in St. Louis, but I had never been to a lot of places in the city. My parents forbade me to travel out of the safer areas of West County, when I was growing up. With Tez, it was like I was seeing the city for the first time. When we were together, I could just be Tracey and not some manufactured version of myself.

When I stepped in front of the full length floor mirror, I gasped. My all-black leather jumpsuit with the nipples and the crotch area cut out had me spellbound. I almost didn't believe it was me. I looked damn good. My mask covered my eyes only. I had my stylist Mario hand sew purple Swarovski crystals around the edges. He knew I loved anything that was Swarovski. The pink ostrich feathers that he also attached, matched the color of my whip perfectly. I wanted to put a bit of a twist to it, so I decided on a hot pink wig that was shorter than my own hair.

I was going as Catwoman, not really original, but it was sexy as hell and as comfortable as one could possibly get under the circumstances. Damn, I nervous. Who wouldn't be? Well actually, I knew some people who wouldn't be, but damn-it, I was.

I wanted to stop and call Christian telling her what I was about to do. But she'd been acting extra crazy since the charity ball so our conversations had been very short. Besides, I hadn't given her any information on Tez just yet. Plus, I knew people loved to judge things they didn't do. Anything out of the ordinary and they started to label you with all these fancy –isms. Hell, I had already judged myself severely enough. I still didn't know how I let Tez talk me into it. Well, yes I did.

I thought back to my original conversation with him when I told him I was afraid and that I didn't really want to go.

"When you with me ain't nothing to be scared of," he told me one night after making, long, nasty, love.

"I know Tez, but if Mother ever got wind of something like that, I would be finished." I felt nervous as I even thought about it.

"Tracey baby, damn! Can we have just one day without you talking about yo damn Mama? Damn, I feel like she's always involved with us. You'll love the party," he added. "Stop worrying."

Maybe he was right. I did need to grow up, and not worry so much about Mother. And yes, I did need the party.

"What if I can give you all your fantasies in one night and no one will have to know who you are?" I remembered his muscular arms being folded behind his head. And the sexy look on his face made me want to do any and everything he asked. It was crazy how connected I felt to him that night. I wanted to tell him that I loved him, but I wasn't really sure if that was the emotion that I felt. I was wise enough to know, lust will make you do some crazy things. And that's exactly why I grabbed my purse and headed out the door.

Ten minutes later I found myself driving twenty kilometers below the speed limit. I was shook, wanting to turn around. Who were the people who would be at this place? And what would happen if I knew someone who was in attendance? Tez assured me that my identity would be a secret because it was a masquerade ball, but I was beginning to worry again.

In all honesty it was the perfect season to let loose. Halloween! The only time for freaks to live out their fantasies and become whatever their hearts desire if only for one night. I was no exception to the rule; I knew that what happened in the next few hours would change me as a person. I kept telling myself that I was ready to put on my grown woman amour and go through it. No more boring Anthony.

However, my nerves were racing like Flo Jo in the '84 Olympics. I figured that a joint and a shot of Grey Goose would be able to calm them down. I prayed they had drinks at the event. Everything about the moment had to be just right. Suddenly, my cell rang.

"Hey, you still coming right?" Tez eagerly asked as soon as I said hello.

"Yes. I told you that I would and I'm a woman of my word," I said as I pushed my foot down a little harder on the pedal. The fact that he was waiting for me made me excited to do this with him.

"Good, I just told my patnas that you was coming to twerk something."

"Patnas? I've never even heard you mention you had friends."

"I can't be telling no woman all my business. What kinda dude do you think I am?"

He seemed slightly annoyed with me. "Damn, don't snap

at me. If your friends are going to be around, why can't one of mine come?"

"This shit is a very private affair, so telling anyone else is not optional. I was told that I can bring someone, and I really want you to fulfill your fantasy with me."

"I know baby, I want this for us. I'm just nervous. A friend coming would have made it easier for me, especially my girl Rayven." I sucked my lips. "I'm on the street now," I ended with a whine.

"Ok, cool," he responded and then quickly ended the call.

I pulled in the driveway of the address that was on the invitation, and my heart began to race. It was as if I could hear my blood as it calculated the precise time for each pump. My stomach was in knots and I wasn't convinced that it was just the alcohol.

"What the hell are you doing?" my inner voice kept asking me over and over.

"Would you shut the hell up?" I screamed out loud, completely forgetting that I was the only one in the truck. I just kept driving slowly. Then my phone vibrated, putting a cease to the constant chatter in my brain. It was him again! Too nervous to answer I let the call roll to voicemail. Soon after the call ended, a text came through.

"What's wrong Ma? You good?"

I watched the words on my screen so closely that they all began to blend together. Am I good? Not exactly, it wasn't like I signed myself up for stankness every day. I looked around at my surroundings. All I could see was the large home in front of me reminding me of a big house on the hill with about fifteen steps that had to be climbed to make it to the front door. On each side of me the area was completely filled with woods. At that point, I thought about backing up all the way down the long driveway. Then that all changed. The taps on the window began. I rolled the window down and mentally told my nerves to take a hike.

"You straight?" Tez asked, while putting his head inside the window to give me a kiss.

Instantly, his smell molested my nose. I found myself inhaling and exhaling his essence over and over. His lips were slightly parted and seemed as if they begged my tongue to trace their outline.

"Yeah luv I'm good. I was just putting on some lip gloss." Once the words slipped out, I realized that my lips were already at the point of being considered juicy. Any more gloss, it would've ran down the sides of my chin.

"If you scared baby we don't have to do this," he whispered softly in my ear.

Obviously he knew I was lying and past the point of being scared. But he had already opened my door, which let me know he wanted to do this with me.

"I promise you won't be forced to do anything, we could just watch," he said gently.

He grabbed my hand and pulled me close to him as he closed my door. Before I could change my mind or resist, he held me in a tight embrace. His hands groped everything as he begun to kiss me. I could tell from the way he sucked my lip, he was sending a nonverbal message of his desire. I thought he was going to suck my face off with the intensity he put into it. My stomach was queasy and I could feel my lower muscles as they jumped rapidly.

I had to have him right there! I didn't care about the people in the house, or the people that drove down the street for that matter. All I knew was this man filled me with an insatiable desire, and I needed to feel him immediately. My fingers couldn't move fast enough below his waist as they unbuckled his pants.

His eyes showed surprise, but the shock didn't labor his kissing and touching. I wasn't sure how we got on the other side of the truck, away from the traffic, closer to the trees, but we were there. He roughly spread my cheeks apart as he kissed the back of my neck.

The heat from the engine burnt my nipples as he rubbed his head up and down my clit. With one hand on my hip he secured his plunge into me. Tez grabbed my hair with the other and pulled my head back so that my ear was close to his mouth.

"You got it so wet for daddy. Tell me what you want me to do with it?"

Tez knew I hated dirty talk, but insisted on doing it. Between the pain from the heat on my nipples and the pleasure from him teasing me, my words were stuck in my throat. Besides, who had time to concentrate on words?

"So, you not gone tell me what you want? That means I

can get it how I want to right?"

"Oh God, Tez!"

I wanna play with it, Tracey! I'm a take my time in this shit, you know I don't like to rush." He shot off all kinds of words and phrases.

Next thing I knew, he'd entered me. Tez' stroke was so good I thought I would pass out. He wasn't a humongous man in stature, but his stamina made up for all that. I knew that ten more deep thrust and my g-spot would be purring a sexy song. I tried to slow his pace, to prolong the action but he had declared in all-out war on my insides. He ripped my mask from my face, and with the string he tied my hands behind me. His hands were now inter-twined with mine and he started to grind.

"Ooh shit that feels soooooooo good, soooooooo good," I repeated over and over. I could even hear myself as I growled a time or two.

His stroke had completely taken all of the proper out of me. It was time that I really showed him what I could do to a man. There was no use in trying to stop the inevitable, so I threw it back at him real hard.

"Ooh that's my girl, give it to me. Let's cum together baby. You want me to cum?" Tez grunted forcefully.

"Yes! Oh God, yes I want you to cum." Those were always the right words to say to him. They always gave him a new found flow of energy and he dug deeper.

"Tell me where you want me to cum, Ms. Bougie!" Tez grunted and moaned louder than me. I knew exactly what he wanted to hear.

"In me Tez, I want you to give it all to me." I screamed so loud, I was sure the neighbors heard, but at that moment I didn't give a damn.

Our legs shook simultaneously as the truck rocked side to side, almost in a violent manner. My ears popped and slob had escaped the corners of my mouth. He was lying on my back with his sweat dripping all over me. Heavy, breathless kisses were planted on my neck and upper back. It was eerily quiet as we both tried to catch our breaths. I wondered, what he thought of me. Had I done too much, by allowing him to have me out in the open like that?

It seemed as if time was frozen, as our breathing turned to

normal levels. Then the claps and the cheers started from the various cars parked around us. Several couples had pulled up, but never made it to the front door because they were watching us. I looked around and noticed that some of them had even started to have sex on top of their own cars. The loud moans and groans sounded like a sex musical. Three women even had the nerve to pull out some toys and began sexin' each other on the front steps of the mini-mansion.

"Aye, I need to holla at my boys, then we can go inside for some experimenting," Tez said to me.

"Don't just leave me over here by myself. I don't even know these people," I nervously replied.

"You'll be fine. Quit being so damn scary," he said while walking a few feet away to a group of men standing off to the side.

Even though most of the people were off talking and into their own thing, I was still embarrassed at what I had done. But it wasn't like I knew any of them personally so why should I even give a damn, I asked myself.

"Wow, what a performance. I'm sure your mother would be so proud," a voice said from behind me. I turned around and stood face to face with Megan. She had on a dress that was so short, all of her ass was hanging out. "Are you following me now, stalker?" I asked.

"Please don't flatter yourself. I'm here to make money, as usual. Looks like you are here just to get fucked," she replied snidely.

"Get the hell out of my face, Megan. Money is only a concern to broke ass people like you."

"Damn, what you heard, I'm nowhere near broke. Matter of fact, I see my money walking up anyway," she said as she started to walk away from me.

Good riddance, I thought as she switched her plump ass in her six inch heels. Every man, including Tez, was mesmerized at the sight. She stopped in her tracks and turned back around to me.

"Oh, by the way, don't worry I'll keep this lil secret of yours locked away with the other stuff I know," she uttered.

Quickly she turned around and continued on with her prance. I silently contemplated chasing her down and kicking her in the back. I had to figure out a way to get rid of her before she blabbed whatever she thought she knew.

If running into Megan wasn't enough as soon as Tez and I got inside the house the open sex in every hallway, doorway, and stairwell had me feeling dizzy. It was like nothing I'd ever seen before. One guy had his pants down near the stairwell, showcasing the biggest penis I'd ever seen in life. The woman he groped appeared to be older and for some reason kept staring at me. Her face was hidden from the mask she wore so I didn't know if I knew her or not. Instantly I got nervous and nudged Tez along.

Out of the blue, the woman stepped to me, lifted her mask, and begged me not to tell I'd seen her there. Little did she know, I wouldn't have known her identity if she'd kept the mask on.

"I'm serious Tracey. I'll be ruined if anyone were to ever find out I was here."

That was enough for me. "Let's go Tez," I told him firmly.

"Thirty minutes, baby. Just give us thirty minutes. I wanna do something to you that's never been done before."

He grinned devilishly. And of course I walked away with him headed to some secret room.

Chapter 12

The next morning my phone rang uncontrollably. I opened my eyes and looked at the digital clock on the side of the bed. I'd taken the day off, and had planned on sleeping all day. However, someone felt the need to call and harass me. I reached for the cell phone and saw that it was Kensington.

"Sweetie, someone better be dead," I blasted. "Why in the hell are you calling me when you know I'm off today?" I hated talking on the phone early in the morning. Besides, my voice sounded like my breath was kicking.

"Oh my God! You little stank whore! I had no clue you had it in you, Tracey. I mean, I know how you got down back in high school, sleeping with all those different dudes, but this day and age I thought you were on the prudish side." Kensington fired off tons of other words at me while I became even more annoyed.

He had always been a rambler. Born under the sign, Sagittarius, he did this talking thing for a living. I didn't want to play games with him today though. I was in need of serious rest.

"Kensington, what in the hell are you talking about?" I rolled my eyes toward the ceiling. It was too early for a drama queen production.

"It's Thursday morning you damn hoochie. You know what that means? The *St. Louis American* came out today; guess who's all in the Partyline section?" He played coy, obviously he knew something that I should.

"Who? My mother? What else is new? She always makes the paper. I think Delores Shante is fascinated with her bitchiness or something." I wasn't interested in this conversation. I wanted to sleep more than anything.

"Holy shit! I didn't even think about your mother. Lord Tracey, what in the world have you done? I have to be there when she attempts to kill you." He cackled in my ear.

"Kensington, you're scaring me, what are you talking about?" Now he had my interest piqued. I sat straight up in the bed. What had I done to make my mother murderous?

"I'm not too certain where you are on this picture, but girl-friend I need to borrow that outfit. Were you Catwoman for Hal-loween? And that wig, Miss thang, is the business," Kensington rambled, but I didn't hear anything after Catwoman.

My spit was now lodged in my throat and I couldn't speak. Surely my heart ran a thousand miles a second. How in the world did he know about the Catwoman costume?

"Girlfriend, you are in the paper bent over the hood of your truck with a nice looking fella behind you. From the look on your face, ole boy is putting in some serious work." I heard Kensington shuffle the paper around as he spoke.

"I'm in what? There is no way possible that I'm in the paper. Oh my God! Mother is going to kill me!" I was in disbelief as Kensington told me the details of what he saw in the picture.

"Tracey, what happened? Where were you? And who in the hell is that fine ass man working you over?" Kensington shot off a series of questions as I tried to gather my thoughts.
I didn't see any cameras there last night. I was so busy being a slut I didn't even look around for cameras. Who could've possibly taken a picture? I thought Tez said that was a private affair any damn way. I trusted him! That bastard!

"And what about..."

I cut him off as I slouched down under the covers, pulling the sheet up to my nose. "Kenny, please slow down with the questions. I have the worse hang- over ever. I have to concen-trate on what I'm going to tell my mother. Oh Lord, I've never been so terrified in all my life. How did the picture get to the St. Louis American?" I was scared shitless. I was in the one paper that every black person in St. Louis read, other than the Evening Whirl.

"Well, I can't help you Ms. Thang, not unless I know what's going on? Who is this man? And more importantly, why didn't you invite me?" Kensington was so nosey and wanted every detail.

"His name is Tez, and I met him sometime last month. He's a little rough around the edges, so that's why you haven't met or heard anything about him. I'm so embarrassed; I don't know what the hell to do." I still didn't understand how someone took that picture. That could possibly ruin my whole damn life.

"Ok, so what he's rough around the edges. I meet rough guys every day. It's no big deal, trust me." Kensington was down playing the moment, but he and I both knew Gertrudes' wrath. She was nowhere near as easy as his parents.

"Mother would never approve of him, Kensington," I told him throwing all the covers off the bed. "He swears like a sailor, wears saggy jeans, and I'm not even sure he's finished high school. But I do know that he's exciting, spontaneous, and what I've been missing."

"So what about Anthony?"

"Uhhhh, I'm working on that. But now's not the time to worry about him. I'm just thinking about Tez. He said that damn party was private, I should have known better." I paused to hit myself in the forehead as I swung my legs off the edge of the bed. The anxiety had taken a toll on me.

"Oooooohhhhhhh, so Ms. Goody Goody is getting worked over by a thug. I love the drama in all that Tracey! Enough with the secrets honey. Tell me all about last night. How is it that you got bent over the hood of a car?"

I imagined Kensington sitting on the edge of his seat, ready for my soap opera. "I'll tell you, but you better not speak a word to another soul. I know how loose those lips of yours can be at times. I went to an orgy party," I blurted out in shame.

"A damn orgy party! My word, this man has changed you into a different person and I'm jealous. I love orgies!"

Kensington screamed so loud in my ear, I had to remove the receiver before I went deaf. I thought about the events of last night and how they had already come back to haunt me. I put my trust in Tez, and somehow that backfired.

"Okay Kensington, don't judge me. It's not like your trife self can anyway, but you know what I mean. I really didn't know it was an orgy until I got there. Here's how it went down." I took a deep breath and began to play back the events of the previous night. I'd started off with the explosive sex that Tez and I had then moved to the kinky things that we did with complete strangers once we got inside. As I told him step by step, he would fall out with all types of screams and cries; mostly from jealousy. Before long Kensington said he'd just had an orgasm off my stories so I decided to tone things down.

"For me, Kensington, that was enough excitement to last me for the rest of the year. I came, I saw and conquered. Well maybe not conquered, but I was definitely satisfied. There was no doubt in my mind. With Tez, was surely where I wanted to be. I just had to convince my parents that he was all I would ever need." I paused and smiled at how good I felt when Tez was between my legs.

The question remained in the back of my mind; would I be willing and ready to give up my parent's world and live in my own? A few months back, I probably would've said no. As it stood my own world wasn't looking so bad.

"Where can I find me a Tez at? He sounds like one hell of a screw, Tracey." Kensington shook me from my thoughts. He had found amusement in one of my greatest failures.

"I wonder how long it will take Anthony to flip out when he sees the paper though. You know how he is about being embarrassed in public."

Leave it to Kensington to really bring up another issue. "Shit! I forgot all about Anthony seeing the paper. He would be devastated when he saw the picture."

"The hell with Anthony," Kensington announced. You need to turn on the radio. They talking about the party last night, girl! You're ruined Tracey!"

Quickly, I leaned over the side of the bed and pressed the button for the radio to come on. Bile rose from my gut as I heard the words *orgy of the year*. Sure enough they were about to clown me:

Rumor has it that St. Louis' most loved to be hated socialite was feeling a lil freaky last nightttttt," Staci Static roared over the airways. She was caught red handed at an orgy party! No need to make sure you heard me correctly people, because yes I did say an orgy party!

Apparently it was a masquerade ball because everyone was hidden behind masks except for Ms. Tracey Robbins. From what I could see in the picture, it was tied around her hands while she was having sex with some man, who wasn't her fiancé by the way! If this ain't a soap opera in the making, I don't know what is. I'm dying to know who else was at that party, hiding behind those masks. Y'all know Tracey don't hang with the unknowns, so I just bet all the local celebs were in that spot too. Rich folks be on that kinky stuff!

Tracey, if you out there listening, girl someone is out to get you! They sent us these pictures anonymously and said there was plenty more where that came from. What have you done girl? Karma is a bitch and it looks like she's coming for you! We hope you can out run her in those Louboutins.

Something in the milk ain't clean y'all! We'll keep following this story until we get down to the bottom of it. Got something to say? Hit ya girl, Mz. Janee up and let's talk…

As that snippet ended so did my life. What was I to do now? The entire St. Louis population would now judge me.

Chapter 13 ——————————

I hung up with Kensington after hearing Staci Static and Mz. Janee on the morning radio show. I immediately rushed to pull out my ipad and looked online. On every local blog, there was that same picture of me and Tez bent over my the hood of my Benz. I was mortified knowing there was no way to erase what happened. I turned off my ipad and immediately rushed to call Tez, feeling a little dizzy in the process. He would certainly get a piece of my mind for not protecting me. It rang and rang until the voice mail picked up. I didn't even consider leaving a message. We needed to have a real conversation. I hung up and called again. After getting the same results, I opted for a long, hot shower. I needed to clear my mind and call both Mother and Anthony. I figured they'd want answers by now.

As I stepped inside the shower, I thought about how Anthony had blown my cell up earlier. I could only now assume, he too saw the pictures. I didn't want to be mean to him, but I really needed to find a way to break off our little situation. He and I weren't seeing to eye to eye on much lately anyway, and stringing him along seemed unfair. If he hadn't already seen the paper, he would surely flip once he did. Men in power like him, hated to be made a fool of, especially because of his political aspirations. But facts were facts. The whole time we'd been together I cheated on him, probably because his sex game rivaled that of a seventy-two year old man. No spice, no excitement, and heavily laced with routine. That was the nicest way to describe our sex life. Even with all his flaws, I still thought he deserved the truth, and that was what I would give him.

I even considered telling him about Tez, describing the way he made love to me, describing the way he made me feel as a woman. Then I laughed. Anthony would find some snobby way to make me feel like an idiot. At that moment, I closed my eyes and allowed the hot water to cascade down my body. I'd really gotten myself into some shit, but facing Mother would be my first priority once I got dressed.

******

Nearly thirty minutes later I'd thrown on some juicy sweats and a Victoria Secrets Pink t-shirt. I knew I'd become depressed anytime I allowed myself to rush from my house with non-matching attire and my hair slightly out of place. I was nervous as hell as I walked up to the driveway of my parents' home, with no coat, wind blowing in my face. Even the dizzy spell from earlier was back, but I was on a mission. A free-Tracey mission. For some reason, the house looked bigger and seemed more intimidating than it normally did. We had always been a small family of three, plus my nanny and the maid, so I never understood why the house had to be so big.

My father's Jag was not in its normal spot, which meant he was on the course playing golf, or out of town on one of his many business trips. I wanted to talk to him and Mother at the same time. That way he would be able to play mediator like he normally did. Unfortunately for me, Anthony and my father were very close which meant he may not have wanted to hear my story anyway. And even though my father never pressured me, I knew he wanted me to have an upstanding man who came from a prestigious family. Anthony was that guy in his eyes. And when the dust settled, Anthony was everything that Tez was not, well except for sexy and good in bed. Of course I couldn't tell my parents that.

I stopped in front of the door just before grabbing the knob wondering if turning around was the better idea. I hadn't been this afraid since I flunked every class freshman year at Berkeley. Mother bitched for three months straight as she worked her magic and got my failing grades switched to passing ones. I smiled thinking about how she could've possibly made that move to help me or my self-esteem. Then I frowned knowing that she probably did it to save the family name. "No Robbins family member received anything less than grades of honor status," she once told me.

As I entered the foyer of the great house, I searched the table where the newspapers normally sat. I saw the St. Louis Post-Dispatch, but the St. Louis American was nowhere to be found. I sighed with relief. Hopefully, something was going right in my life and Mother hadn't looked at it. I prayed that the odds were in my favor, but I wouldn't know until I faced the devil herself. Then it hit me, talking to her later was a better idea. Going to see Anthony first made more sense.

I turned to walk back out the house, when I heard noise coming from the great room. Mother would kill someone if they left the television on while no one watched it. She may have been a bitch to her daughter, but to the world, she was the Green Earth Queen. Preserving St. Louis's Energy, was one of her charitable organizations. I opened the door to the great room and almost passed out.

"What the hell?" I screamed at the scene before my eyes.

A man stood there with his stiffly pressed khaki pants and underwear around his ankles. His head rolled back as he moaned and groaned at the oral pleasure he was receiving. The sound was all too familiar to me.

"Tracey," he said, pulling himself out of her mouth and struggled to pull his pants up.

It couldn't be! No way, was I seeing what I thought I was. I blinked a couple of times, because I had to be in a state of delusion.

"Hello, Tracey dear," Mother said.

She didn't even try to pull herself together and wipe the slob and semen from her mouth. She sat on the couch and smirked like the cold-hearted bitch that she was. I became nauseous and my whole body underwent an outer body experience.

"Oh my God! Anthony, what are you doing with her?" I knew the answer, but the question just flew out of my mouth. Anthony and my mother were engaged in sexual relations and I wanted to puke.

"I can explain. It- it-it isn't what you-you-you- think," Anthony stuttered.

He fell over his pants leg, still desperately trying to pull them up. He was mumbling an inaudible explanation. Mother, the queen of all evil, sat her shrewd ass in one spot, with a look of disgust on her face.

"Tracey, have I not taught you how to be a lady and knock before you enter a room?" Mother asked.

She had the nerve to question my womanhood, even

though I just caught her in the midst of sucking off my fiancé. "Seriously Mother, are you crazy? Do you want to be me that bad, that you fucking with my boyfriend in my father's own got damn house? Oh my God what kind of monster are you?"

"You better watch who you're talking to, young lady. I don't give a damn what I did, you will keep yourself in check."

Mother put the smirk back on her lips and I wanted to slap her face. The tears immediately poured out of my eyes causing my vision to blur. The unrelenting smirk on her face felt like a knife wedged in my back, which caused me to cry even harder.

"Yes, you want to be me," I sobbed, barely able to get the words out.

"Be you? My God child, why would anyone, and especially me, want to be you? I'm trying to help your relationship you foolish child. Anthony didn't want to play your games of hide and seek anymore. It seems he was looking for you last night and he was worried sick that something happened to you."

"Stop lying Mother!"

"No, seriously, he flew over here this morning to make sure you were okay. Imagine our surprise, when we opened the paper and there was his fiancé and my daughter being treated like a common whore!" Mother stopped talking and placed her hand over her heart. "I almost fell out my chair as I saw my daughter, bent over the Mercedes truck that I bought her, like a prostitute.

"That's right, Tracey, what was I supposed to think?" Anthony added.

I shot him a deathly look as mother continued.

"My family's reputation means everything to me, and I will not let you or anyone else ruin it. Do you understand, child?"

My glare remained on her lips.

"Don't you see that if I had not been here to convince Anthony that you are worth waiting for, the wedding would be called off? He's willing to forgive the fact that you are a no good slut, and will still marry you. It'll take much more for me to forgive you though," Mother stated so simply that I stopped crying and just looked at her.

All the years of her belittling me and treating me like trash, I finally had enough. For some reason unknown, she hated me. I wanted nothing further to do with her or him. Cheating was one thing, but to sleep with my mother, in my father's house, was downright unforgiveable.

"I will never forgive you for this Mother, I swear not ever! And you Anthony…you can save your forced marriage because I don't want it! I stood by you when I should've been off doing my own thing. You can't even fuck for goodness sake. And why in the hell would you go there with my mother?" I was livid as spit flew from my mouth and landed on his face.

"Tracey, I swear it's not what you think? I was pissed damn-it! You have completely embarrassed me, but I was willing to hear your mother out like she said. You and I can still get married and you can keep your little boy on the side. If I want my career to take off, I need a wife," Anthony pleaded.

"A wife? You both are fucking crazy. How dare you think for one second that I would want you, after what you've done? I would give you your ring back if it were on my finger, but because I never wear it anyway, I'll donate it to charity," I told him with vengeance. "I'm done with you Anthony!" I wiped any remaining tears from my face and walked out my parent's home. I didn't even look back as I heard Anthony calling my name.

"Tracey, please!"

There was really nothing left to say. There would be no way for him to right this wrong. He knew how I felt about the way my mother treated me. He knew about all the tears I had cried, and the therapy I was seeking because of it.

I hopped back in my truck and cried really hard. I was completely devastated over the fact that Mother would stoop so low. How could she claim to love me, but do everything in her power to ruin me? I felt nauseas again and knew that in any moment, I would throw up an empty stomach. I'd been feeling this way even before seeing Anthony and my mother, but this was different, it was painful. I drove off like a mad-woman with no destination in my mind. I picked up my phone and called Christian but it rolled to voicemail again. Tez also didn't answer and I didn't want to call Rayven because she was out of town working on some case she'd taken pro-bono. Strangely, I always found myself alone in my darkest hours.

I stopped at the liquor store, picked up two bottles of my favorite wine, Reisling then drove to my office. That was the one place that always made me happy. My business symbolized that I could prove my mother wrong when it came to survival; since she'd always told me I would fail.

Suddenly my cell rang. Speak of the devil, I muttered. "What is it Mother?" I answered with spite in my voice.

"First off Tracey, get over it!"

I couldn't believe this woman!

"Shit happens, so I think you're being unreasonable. I've already called the St. Louis American and demanded that they retract their story. I told them that picture was from your college days. Just let me handle everything. Believe me, I know what's best for you."

"Mother, there's nothing you can do to make any of this right." It was too late for that. She and Anthony had done what they thought was right. And the picture was out there for the world to see. My main concern was , who took the picture and why?

As my mother rambled on, I decided to hang up. There was nothing she could say that I wanted to hear. Hating Gertrude Robbins wasn't a strong enough word. How in the hell does my enemy know what's best for me? How in the hell can my enemy, be the one person who is supposed to be the one who loves and protects me? I picked my cell back up praying for the strength to call my dad letting him know just how horrible of a person his wife was. I didn't want to cause him unnecessary pain though, and a betrayal like that would be devastating to him, so I hung up.

Truthfully, I wasn't sure Mother and Anthony had anything to do with the way I currently felt. Yes they hurt me deeply but it was Tez that had me stressed. Here I was willing to lay it all on the line for him, but I didn't even know that much about him. I needed him bad and he was nowhere to be found. I called his cell ten more times, and not once did he answer. It was now turned off and going straight to voicemail. Calling it seemed pointless.

Still my fingers pushed the numbers, like they were the key to my salvation. I started humming the melody to the rap song that played on the outgoing message. I had called so many times; the song had grown on me.

"Tez, its Tracey. I'm not sure what's going on, but call me. Somehow this picture of us made the paper and Mother and I had a fight because of it. I just really need you right now. Please call me. I haven't been feeling too well, throwing up and feeling dizzy. I think I'm pregnant Tez, so I just need some support.

Chapter 14

I pulled out of the garage from my gynecologist's office crying like a crazy woman. Even though it was day two of my misery marathon my tears hadn't slowed. I had an important meeting in less than two hours, yet I couldn't stop crying. So many mixed emotions flooded my system as I picked up my cell phone and tried Tez again. I needed to tell him the news from the doctor.

As soon as his message ended, I began my shouting session. "Tez, I didn't think that I would have to keep calling your ass like this! I know good and damn well you see that I'm calling you. It's been over a week since we've seen each other, you no-good motherfucka. If you call yourself trying to play me, you can think the fuck again. I do the playing! You got one more chance to call me, or else!"

I slammed the phone down so hard that I scared myself as I swerved just missing an old woman crossing the street. I smiled and mouthed my apologies hoping that little incident wouldn't make the papers. I thought about what else I should've said to Tez when my cell rung. I knew that last message scared his ass.

"Oh, so it takes an irate message for you to call me back?" I yelled into the phone.

"Umm, Tracey, are you okay? This is Christian and what irate message did you leave me?"

"Girl, I thought you were someone else. Never mind what I said."

"Are you sure you're alright, you sound mad as hell?"

The nerve of her. I hadn't heard from Christian since the night of the gala. She too knew I'd been calling her like crazy and the lack of returned calls had me not wanting to talk to her much.

"So, what's up Christian. I'm not feeling so good right

now."

"Sorry to hear that Trae, I was just checking on you."

Who did she think she was fooling? Just like everyone else in St. Louis, I was certain she'd seen the picture of me and Tez in that uncompromising situation. I just didn't know why it had taken her so long to call.

"I'm holding on, Christian. But get to the point. We've been friends forever so let's not drag this out."

"You're right. Girllllll, I saw the paper. Wow, Tracey girl! What in the world are you involved in?" Christian sounded like my mother. I knew she wouldn't understand the Tez situation.

"I'm not involved in anything, Christian. I met a guy that I really like, and we hooked up. Some bastard took pictures and sent it in to the paper. That's it." I sighed then waited for a response from her. When I didn't get a sign of positivity or negativity, I continued. "Anyway, what's up with you? Last time I saw you, you were in a Waiting to Exhale moment, blasting off on me first, and then Chuck later. I've called you several times since then."

"Girl you silly as hell, I wasn't waiting to exhale. That night was a complete misunderstanding."

I couldn't believe how Christian's mood swings were changing back and forth. She now seemed so sweet and at ease like nothing in the world bothered her.

"Chuck was only getting Megan's phone number because she has a jewelry line called Bella Brown. He was going to buy me something special." Christian sounded convincing, almost like she rehearsed that bullshit of an excuse. Now I was certain an alien had taken over Christian's body. No way in hell would she go for that line of bull that Chuck told her.

"Ohhhhh, is that so?"

"Yep. It was all one big misunderstanding."

I took a twenty second pause. "Christian, you sure you're okay?"

"Oh, I'm feeling great! But anyway, I saw you and Anthony in the corner booed up at the gala. I can't wait to pick out my maid of honor dress. It'll be the first time, the maid of honor looks better than the bride."

A lump formed in my throat. She'd now changed her disposition again. "Christian, I think we both need a vacation. Maybe we can go somewhere together for some rest and relaxation. I've got so much to tell you, especially about Anthony. So much has changed."

"Maybe. I'll have to check my schedule," she told me bluntly. "But speaking of Anthony, how did he take the pictures being in the paper?" Christian paused then hit me with a crazy laugh. She knew Anthony was anal as hell, and would see nothing humorous about the situation.

"Girl please, Anthony will never get to boo anywhere near this again. Girl, if you knew what that bastard has been up to, you would die from shock. I may have been foul for getting caught in the paper, but he's living a life, that I don't understand."

"Oh, no Trae, so it's true?"

I immediately became confused. Was she talking about Mother? How'd she know? "What are you talking about Christian?"

"I'm talking about Anthony's secret. That's what you meant right? I got wind of a little bit of it."

I got quiet. Does it have anything to do with my mother?"

"Uhhhh, no Tracey. Maybe I should just keep this to myself until I find out more information. I don't want to spread rumors. Do you have time to meet up later and talk about it? Chuck has an away game this week so I have free time. I miss spending time with you, Trae." Christian whined in the phone.

She now had me worried. What other secrets could Anthony possibly have? Hell, I didn't have time to worry about Anthony's ass. "I miss you, too, girl. I have a meeting in a little while, but afterwards I'm free all night. I've got to see you." I breathed heavily hoping the real Christian would surface so I could spill everything to her. "I'm caught in this heavy situation with this guy and I really need some sisterly advice. He has me confused." I felt tears trying to force their way down my cheeks. I was an emotional wreck.

"Who is this new guy anyway? And how long has it been going on, because you sound way too serious?" Christian's tone had once again become judgmental.

"I don't have a lot of time to really talk now, but I met him through Shanice."

"The hood rat from your office?"

"Yes. They're play brother and sisters." I felt like an idiot using those words. "I admit, I was skeptical at first, but girl he can

106

CHRIS RENEE

stroke it like none before him. It's only been a month, but it feels like forever!" I smiled and rubbed my stomach.

"Whoa, whoa, slow down, girl. This is too quick."

I had just come from the doctor's who'd confirmed an early detection of pregnancy. But Christian was making it difficult for me to want to share the news. "I love him Christian," I blurted.

"Wow, just like that and you're in love? That sounds pretty stupid. You met him through Shanice, the girl that works for you?"

I hated the fact that she was still harping on the fact of how I met him. "Christian, you would love him."

"Ahh, no. He would never fit into our circle. You need to think rationally and not with that hot box of yours, Tracey." Christian spoke with disdain in her voice. "You're always fucking the wrong men."

That comment hurt. She had always been there to help me through each heart break and now this. "I don't need a lecture, Christian. For once, I just want to do what makes me feel good. And Tez does that. He loves me; I just know that he does." I tried to convince myself that he was in love with me, like I was with him. That was also exactly why I wanted to talk to Rayven, and not Christian. Rayven would love the element of him coming from nothing, but a master at the art of long stroke. She would think it was so Romeo and Juliet like.

"You already have someone in our circle who loves you. Anthony would give his last breath to you, but you don't realize that. If you don't open your eyes, you may miss what could possibly be the best thing to happen to you," Christian pleaded with me.

"Anthony does not love me. He proved that by sleeping with my mother."

I heard Christian's loud gasp clear through the phone. That revelation had shocked her just like I knew it would.

"So yeah, like I said, Anthony and I are a thing of the past. It's really no big deal, I was over him anyway. Hello?"

I could hear her as she softly whimpered through the phone.

"Are you crying, Christian?" Since she called me, her mood had switched seven times exactly. "Maybe you need to see a doctor. Mental health maybe," I suggested. "You've been through a lot."

"No. I'm just shocked."

"Are you sure you're alright? You're really acting strange?" I had started to question the stability of her sanity.

"Yeah, I'm okay. I think I should stop by now Trae. This is all too much."

"News flash girl, I'm not staying at my parent's estate anymore. I'm at the Four Seasons. Been there for the last five days."

"Oh God! I've missed so much. When are you going back to your place?"

"I may not," I said matter of factly.

Christian began sniffling and sobbing again. "Christian, I'm going to call Dr. Griff. He's a psychiatrist who works for my father. I know him very well."

"No, don't do that." She snapped out of her misery quickly. "I'm okay. It's just that you and I both deserve to be happy and in love. The thought that we may never get that is unbearable. Between your mother and Chuck, we've had enough pain to last a lifetime. I just want us to both have joy."

I was starting to feel like I had my good friend back. Her words were so sincere. "We'll get it sweetie, don't you worry. Love is in our destiny! I have to get ready for this meeting, but let's have dinner later tonight." I glanced at the clock and saw that it was after two p.m., I was close to being late.

"You're missing the point, Tracey. The love that you're waiting for, will not always wait for you. You need to open your eyes before it's gone. You should be planning to have kids right now," she preached. "But good luck on the meeting and I'll see you later."

I stopped her just before she ended the call. "Christian, thanks for being there for me. I would feel bad letting you hang up after that comment. "I gotta tell you this." I paused as chills sped up my spine. "I'm pregnant, girllll! I'm pregnant!" I repeated with joy.

Christian abruptly ended the call, leading me to believe that a nervous breakdown was on her horizon. She didn't even let me say bye or tell me congratulations. The thought of the baby, our baby, made me think of Tez.

I know I said I wouldn't call again, but I needed to hear his voice. I dialed the memorized numbers and waited patiently as it rang. On the third ring, a recording came on, saying the number was not in service. I stared at the phone in disbelief. Why would his phone be cut off? I just called his ass ten minutes ago and it was working. What in the hell was going on?

Chapter 15

"This bitch has really lost her mind. She's gone too far!" I screamed as I hit the steering wheel when I slammed on brakes in front of my office building. What a way to ruin my news of being pregnant. I shook my head in disbelief at all my expensive things laid out on the sidewalk. Mother knew that Mario had just ordered me the spring collection of Dior and Versace. I figured between jealousy and being caught with Anthony those were reasons why she'd tossed my things out onto the pavement. She was pissed at me because she'd gotten caught? Insane!

My mother was on a whole new level of crazy. If I had one wish it would be to kick her ass. I had been staying at the Four Seasons so I would not have to run into her. I'd gone home last night when I knew she would be gone only to find out that the locks were changed. I tried to get one of the maids to open the door for me so that I could get my belongings when I was informed that Mother already had them delivered to my office. I thought she was just lying to piss me off because I knew I hadn't received anything. Pulling up to work and watching these bum ass people going through my stuff almost sent me over the edge. I threw my truck in park and angrily jumped out bulldozing my way toward my stuff. I snatched my new Kate Spade satchel out of the hands of one of the pesky homeless chicks who always hung around outside the office building.

"Do you know how much this cost?"

"Ask me do I care," the woman taunted as if she'd done nothing wrong.

"Get the hell away from my shit," I yelled at her.

My nostrils flared as she opened her coat and laughed hysterically at the Armani dress of mine she had stashed as well as my Neil Lane diamond studs. I tried to grab her again when she quickly spun around and ran towards the Metro Link station.

Quickly, I'd decided to let the woman make a run for it while I skimmed over my things trying to mentally memorize all the items I had stored in my closet. I cursed under my breath once I saw my jewelry box was open and no longer containing the pink Rolex watch my father had given me for my eighteenth birthday. As if I hadn't had enough bull to deal with, my eyes darted toward the construction workers who were playing catch with my Victoria Secrets underwear. The bitter one made sure that I saw him throw a pile of my lace panties in the mud.

"I guess you pissed off the wrong person huh?" he asked me with an attitude.

"This shit doesn't mean anything to me, sweetie. I can get a new wardrobe worth your whole year's salary in less than thirty minutes," I replied harshly.

"Well, ain't it nice to be rich? Too bad you don't have a place to live. Bitch, you not about shit. Obviously your man thinks the same, that's why all your shit is out here on the ground."

I felt the tears almost spill over the brim of my eyes. I wouldn't let him see me crying though and I didn't bother correcting him on who'd thrown my things out. I didn't even give a damn about any of it. I counted it all a lost as I knew that I would never wear the shit again since their crummy hands had touched it. By the time I walked into my building I felt lower than ever before. I totally ignored everyone who spoke to me. I was like a walking zombie, void of all feelings. Life goes on, I kept telling myself. I didn't have time to worry about foolishness. My main concern was my business. My mission was to continue pressing forward, regardless of what people were saying about me. As I strutted, I attempted to pump myself up with confidence.

"Jealous people will talk Tracey, it just comes with the territory." My mother would say that to me every day. I didn't know her reasoning for it then, but it all made sense now. People were jealous of me because I would never have to waste a manicure on washing dishes, or wiping ass for a living. The little incident in the paper gave them fuel to talk about me, but it only caused my fire to burn brighter. I had even made it to one of the national blogs. The rule was always, any talk was good talk. The cliché sounded good, but the truth was that three accounts had been lost because of all the bad publicity thus far. I had to get Totally Chic hot again.

I stepped onto the elevator thinking about mother's guidelines for cleaning up mess. It was clear that whenever things hit the fan, she would clear it up immediately. I had decided to adopt that same cut throat attitude with both my haters and my men. It had been two weeks since I last saw Tez. He hadn't called, nor texted me back. If he only wanted a sex buddy, he should have told me. I could handle just sleeping with him without all the attachments. That's actually, all I was doing in the first place. Then I got to know the real him. And it felt good to know I was capable of receiving real genuine love. I knew having his baby would cause Mother to write me out of the will, especially if she knew that I was having a child by a street thug. But what was I to do? The word *abortion* entered my mind. I didn't know what I was thinking even getting attached to the idea of Tez and I being a family. I paused then clutched my stomach as I stepped off the elevator. The realization hit me…No baby showers with Tiffany's stainless steel pacifiers or rattles. Not one penny of a trust fund would be set up similar to the one Mother had set up for me. She would definitely convince my father to stop funding my business. That thought depressed the hell out of me.

"Hey, Boss," Shanice said to me with a smile.

Her facial expression changed when she looked at me closely. I had become ill, maybe from the pregnancy, but more than likely from depression. "Shanice, we've got a busy day ahead of us. Hold all calls unless Rayven calls."

"Everything okay, Boss? You don't look so good," she asked awkwardly.

She hadn't said anything about my clothes being outside but I knew that she had been through them as well. I could see the pile underneath her desk but decided she needed them more than I did. "I'm fine Shanice. Just bring me something to settle my damn stomach before my meeting," I yelled, changing my mood swiftly.

"Gotcha Boss," she said as I hurried into my office and shut the door. My reasons weren't justified for treating Shanice that way.

She really had improved her work ethics. She even managed to set up a new meeting with that Suite Ballentine chick who had a client who was opening a night club in downtown St. Louis,

Eric Stevens of Stevens Enterprises. We would run his ad in our magazine for six months and the deal would bring some serious money into my life. So serious, I could finally allow Mother to cut the purse strings and leave my life alone. First thing on my agenda was to find myself a new, permanent home. The amount of drama that surrounded me just couldn't be healthy for any life. If there was a God like people said, then I was sure he wouldn't just let people suffer like this. My blood pressure was through the roof and I needed some immediate relief.

"Just relax Tracey," I kept chanting to myself.

Shanice burst through the door. "I ain't really know what you wanted so I just made you some toast," she said handing me the burnt toast and a Sprite.

"Thanks, Shanice. As you would say, my bad for snapping at you earlier."

"It's cool. I've known you long enough to know when you just acting like a bitch. I mean, not feeling well," she quickly corrected herself.

I raised my eyebrow at her before speaking.

"I guess I deserved that. I'm just nervous about this meeting," I explained.

"Speaking of that. They just arrived. You want me to send'em in?" she asked.

I wasn't sure if I was just tripping but her voice had a mischievous ring to it.

"That will be fine but give me a few minutes. I want to seem really busy," I replied.

Shanice walked back into the reception area and I started rummaging through papers on my desk. I laid out the layout for next month's magazine, pleased with what I came up with. I felt a slight migraine creeping on me. My hormones were raging and my stress level was at its max. I was not about to let my health ruin my chances of making this money. I knew the deal was mine. With any luck he wouldn't be a complete asshole and the meeting would run smoothly and quickly.

"That's what I like to see, my baby momma smiling and glowing. You are just as beautiful as ever," Tez said while standing in the doorway.

I sat frozen in my chair as I looked at his handsome face. I wanted to be mad as hell and super dramatic by slapping him.

But he looked damn good. I'm talking, sweep everything off my desk and make love on sight good. I continued to stare at him, trying to dissect every single detail about this man.

"Tez! What are you doing here? I've been calling you like crazy! You bastard! I left you message after message, with no response from you."

"I had to dip out of town for a lil minute. Me and a few dudes had some business to attend to," he responded.

"What do you mean, some business? Are you a drug dealer? You told me that you weren't into anything illegal but I've never once heard you mention a job." I asked him the questions that had been on my mind since I met him.

"I do all kinds of shit. I dabble here and there in whatever will make me money," he said while making himself comfortable in the chair.

I looked at him skeptically but decided to drop the question since it was obvious he wouldn't explain fully. "Yeah, okay but why is your phone off and why in the hell are you dressed like that?"

He really shocked the hell out me. He just showed up like nothing had ever happened. However, it was his attire that completely confused me. I was used to seeing him in that tall, t-shirt thingy. Today, he was dressed in a very nice gray pinstriped suit, with a lavender collar shirt underneath. I wanted to immediately jump his bones. Where were his baggy saggy pants and monogrammed shirt? No doo rag or baseball cap either. Who was this stranger?

"Well, I came to deliver my baby mamma some flowers. If I can remember correctly, lilies are your flower of choice," he said while extending his arm with the flowers.

"I never told you I like lilies. Who told you that? And what are you doing here?" I asked again, still perplexed.

"I have a very important business meeting to discuss with a Ms. Tracey Robbins." He flipped his phone open and showed me the scheduled appointment.

"Uh no, we don't have any business. You just up and disappeared, Tez so I really can't talk about this right now. It's obvious you got my messages, but I seriously have to run."

"Damn, you talking to me like you don't even know a nigga."

"I have an important meeting with an Eric Stevens right now and you will not mess it up. This deal could seriously bring in a lot of money for me."

I wanted to wrap the conversation up. There was no way I wanted my new client to see me involved in baby daddy drama. He chuckled and it irritated the hell out of me, that he found my situation so damn amusing. I looked at him as if he was nuts, and he laughed harder.

"How you gone have a baby by me and not know my name? You damn rich people are insane," Tez said while moving to my side of the desk.

"Seriously Tez, what in the hell are you talking about?"

"Allow me to formally introduce myself. Hi, I'm Eric Cortez Stevens. CEO and owner of Stevens Enterprise, it is my club that you will be featuring in your magazine. Pleasure to meet you madam." He grabbed my hand and placed his lips to it.

"What? I don't understand, Tez." I snatched my hand away from his lips, and stood trying to wrap my mind around what I was just told.

Tez was not a thug, but really a business man? He was on his feet and not just some nickel and dime hustler, like I thought he was. I had been dodging his love because I thought he had nothing to offer me. Somewhere Cupid was laughing his ass off at me. I didn't even know how to process what was happening.

"Close your mouth girl. We don't want you getting lock jaw unnecessarily, now do we?" He smiled widely.

"Seriously Tez, what are you doing here? I don't have time for games, so if that is what you looking for, I suggest you find a ball of some sorts." The nerve of him pissed me the hell off. Who was he to try and play me like a nobody?

"I already told you, boo. I'm the one you meeting. What, you shocked I'm not some bum ass street thug like you thought?"

"Actually, I'm very shocked. You made it seem like you had nothing really going other than running with a rough crowd."

"Nawl baby girl, I never confirmed that, I just didn't tell you right from wrong. A man like me can't be with any woman just because I have money. I need to really know, if you down with me. I'm still kind of on the fence about your little snobby ass, but I find you an interesting task to conquer, Ms. Bougie." Tez pulled a wad of cash from his pockets. I guess that was an effort to impress me.

"An interesting task to conquer? Is that all I am to you, Mr. Tez. I love money like the next girl, but plastic is even sexier. You have any credit cards on you, Mr. Big Shot." I walked towards him wanting to get in his personal space.

"I got everything you need right here," he said while grabbing his crotch. "You know I'm Mr. Exclusive."

"Speaking of your exclusivity, I thought you said we were at a private damn party that night," I said while slapping him upside the head.

"We were. I saw our picture in the paper. I don't know who could've done that bullshit. I was giving it to you good though," he laughed.

"It's not funny. That ruined my whole life. I've had clients to pull out on commitments to the magazine, people talking about me behind my back and on the radio, of course. I mean it's crazy. Things have been going bad ever since."

"Girl, you are dramatic as hell. What could possibly be so bad?" he asked.

"Well, I'm currently homeless, pregnant, not speaking to my mother, and I can't get my so called boyfriend to call me," I purred at him. Instantly I sat on his lap placing my nose right under his. He talked a good game, but I knew that his ass weakened around me. Typical man in my book, he lost all sense of control when he smelled a woman in heat.

"None of that stuff that happened to you matters now. Daddy's home," he told me lovingly.

It felt so good to be in his arms again.

"I got some things to talk to you about after our meeting. I missed you though girl, I needed to clear my head. Lord knows, I couldn't wait to get back to you." Tez slid his tongue across my lips and squeezed me tightly.

I closed my eyes and waited for his hands to roam as they pleased. Tez, gently pushed me away from him, stood up and walked out the door towards the conference room. I could hear him as he gave orders to Shanice as they moved down the hallway.

I couldn't believe he worked me up and then left me hanging like that. I couldn't wait until the meeting was over. I wasn't even sure, how I would sit through the whole thing.

Whenever he was near me, I wanted to rip our clothes off and engage in slutty activities. But first, I would grill him about why he lied about who he was. I wasn't doing bad for myself, so he had to know I didn't want his money.

Shanice had to know that he was not the person I thought he was. Yet, she never said a thing to me about it. I had spent countless moments telling her about why I couldn't live my life with him. I made a mental note to get with her when he left, so I could get as much info about him as I possibly could. Then it hit me...the words she spoke weeks ago, saying Tez wasn't what I thought. I wondered what else I didn't know.

Chapter 16

Apparently, Shanice's words meant nothing to me I'd fallen in love with this dude. We'd spent every day together for the past two weeks, only separating when I had to work. Each day he had surprised me with something new; one day with a limo picking me up, transporting me all day,and another day with a masseuse showing up at my office, just to name a few. I never knew he had it in him, and even though I liked not having to ask a man to do anything for me, I could really get use to the princess treatment he'd been giving me.

"What you over there smiling at?" Tez asked me as we pulled up to *Mike Shannon's Steakhouse.*

"Nothing really. I just can't believe how happy I've been lately. It just seems so unreal." I rubbed his thigh lovingly. I found myself wanting to touch him every single second of the day.

"This is nothing, Ms. Bougie. I plan on giving the world to you and my baby. I got some big money coming through real soon." He pulled my face close to his and placed a kiss on my lips.

"Tez, I know you said you're not in the streets anymore, but I don't want you to do something stupid to make a lot of money fast." I chewed my bottom lip nervously at the thought of him and me not being able to raise our child together. "I like the legal Tez, the businessman."

"All you have to do is sit back and look pretty. You leave the financial burdens to me. Trust me when I say, lack of money will never be a problem for us, not after this deal." Again he tried to reassure me.

Something in his eyes told me that however he made this money would not be a good thing for us. In fact, I felt a cold shiver wash over my soul. "I just want us to be happy. We won't need illegal money once I tell my father about the baby." I tried to ease the mood by bringing the baby back up. Nothing seemed to make Tez happier than talking about his unborn child.

"Speaking of which, let's go feed my lil boo. I know she has to be starving since you barely eat." He gave me a slightly evil glance as he got out the car to open my door. It was crazy how he'd already claimed our little one to be a girl.

Tez had been trying to stuff me with food ever since he found out about the pregnancy. I didn't want to gain a lot of unnecessary weight, so this baby would have to make do with what little food I put in my body. Becoming a beach whale was something I wasn't going to become.

"Thank you luv. And for the record, I do eat. I just don't want to pack on a lot of pounds. Nothing is worst than those big bloated pregnant women," I commented as we walked toward the restaurant.

"You be on the wrong shit sometimes. Don't make me hurt you about my seed," Tez said as he opened the big, glass double doors for me.

The restaurant was beautiful but the smell of beef instantly made my stomach turn cartwheels. I looked around for the bathroom and locked eyes with Megan. This bitch always seemed to appear when I didn't want her to. She was sitting near the front bar, at a circular table with Chuck. They were fucking holding hands! I thought she had sense enough to leave him alone after Christian clicked out on them at the gala. I spun around fast looking for a quick exit. I didn't feel like being bothered with her and I certainly did not want to see Chuck.

"Aye, Tracey, look. There go running back, Chuck Jones. Let's go congratulate him on a good season. That dude killing shit this year," Tez said as he dragged me by the arm toward their table.

"Tez, no, I don't think that's a good idea. It looks like they're having an intimate dinner," I said pretending not to know them personally.

I could think of a million reasons why I didn't want to go over there. I prayed I wouldn't have to use any of them. Once I realized Tez didn't have any intentions on releasing my grip, I dug my hands into his palm, drawing blood. I hoped that pain would be enough to stop him in his tracks.

"Girl, what in the hell is wrong with you? I almost lost my manners and slapped the shit out of you." Tez's voice was loud causing the other patrons to nosily look our way.

"Tracey, is there a problem? You cool?" a male voice asked.

Without turning around I knew that it was Chuck at my side. I could smell his signature scent of Versace cologne. The scent I knew so well.

"Yeah, I'm fine. I almost tripped and my fingernails dug into my date's hand." I quickly came up with a lie. I was completely embarrassed by the loud altercation.

"Wait a minute, y'all know each other?" Tez asked.

"Yeah we do and who in the hell are you?" Chuck sized Tez up, causing Tez's good mood to do a complete swing in the opposite direction. He knew something wasn't right.

"Aye, play boy. I respect yo hustle on the gridiron but you need to take some of that bass out yo fucking voice," Tez said while moving closer to Chuck.

He stood toe to toe with Chuck and I was frightened that this could turn ghetto. With Chuck being a football player I knew that news of this would spread. I looked around at the other customers and watched as they all looked on in horror. The hostess looked slightly nervous. Her expression told us that she was seconds from calling the police. I knew that Chuck and his football star status would be going home and Tez would wind up in jail.

"Seriously guys, it's not that serious," I interjected.

"I'm not the one with the problem but if any nigga wanna get dealt with, that could be handled too." Tez's voice became deep and harsh. He wasn't about to back down.

"Really Tez, this is my best friend's Christian's husband, Chuck. So, let's keep things cordial. He was just looking out for me."

"She's in good hands, bruh," Tez said followed by a nod of the head. "Worry about your wife over there."

"Oh, that's not his wife." I smirked. "He's having dinner with trash." I nodded at Megan and rolled my eyes.

"The name calling is real cute, Tracey, but I'm not in the mood." Megan stood up like she was ready to rumble. "However, I'm entertained at how you being a whore is finally coming to light. You sleeping in the gutter now?" She laughed looking at Tez.

"At least he isn't married you cum dispenser. Get your own man, bitch," I angrily yelled at her.

"Get my own man? Whose man are you currently fucking, Tracey? Besides your best friend's hus…"

I cut her off. Megan knew too much and this game was beginning to get dangerous. "Shut up Megan!" I turned to get a quick look at Tez who had his jaw hung low and seemed to be in deep thought. Then I glanced back at Chuck who'd taken two steps toward Megan.

"I got this," Chuck announced like he was in charge of the situation. "Sit your ass down, Megan and shut up! That's all on Tracey if she wants to be a slut. Just keep that shit away from my wife," Chuck spat as he cut Megan off.

I was appalled. How dare he speak of me that way? "You're sitting here with St. Louis' professional groupie and you tell me to keep my slutty ways away from your wife. Your ass is nuts. Fuck you and fuck, Megan."

"Wait, what did she say? Yo ass sleeping with who?" Tez asked in disbelief. He hadn't gotten over Megan's comment. "I'm hoping I didn't hear her correctly."

"It's not what you think Tez. We can talk in the car. I don't feel so well. Can we go baby?" I turned towards Tez begging him to leave, but he wouldn't even give me the respect of answering me. He looked at me with disgust and snatched away from my arm.

"Wow, this is really some shit," he commented while probing Chuck's facial expressions. He really wanted a straight answer from him.

"Tez, Megan, doesn't know when to shut the hell up. I don't have a clue of what she's talking about. She's drunk and envious, pleaseeeee, let's just leave," I begged.

The look in his eyes told me that he wasn't convinced by my little performance. He quickly stormed away and I followed like a lost puppy.

"You're worthless, Tracey Robbins! You're a fucking whore! But don't worry. I'm going to let everyone know that you're fucking your best friend's husband!" Megan shouted behind me.

Tez stopped in his tracks and turned to look at me.

"Damn, I woulda never ever thought yo ass was living foul like this. Is this shit true," Tez asked? "It must be," he added, looking deeply into my eyes.

    I couldn't bring myself to answer. I was so ashamed that not only had Megan told Tez, but she also told almost all of St. Louis. He hurriedly pressed through the big, double doors and left the restaurant. I continued to hold my head low with shame. I didn't want to make eye contact with anyone but Delores Shante, the gossip writer from the St. Louis American, who made it her business to clear her throat so I could see her. My eyes begged for a little mercy. Once this new little piece of gossip made the paper I would have no where else to go but to the projects with Shanice.

Chapter 17 ──────────────

Tez ran almost every light just to drop me off back at my hotel room as quickly as possible. He was so angry about the run in with Chuck and Megan that he wouldn't say a single word to me. He didn't even make sure I made it up to my room safely as he burnt rubber flying out the parking lot. I sulked from the elevator all the way to my room wondering why everything in my life had turned to shit. I'd heard of Karma, but damn, I deserved a break. I opened the door, kicked off my shoes and quickly rushed over to the mini bar near the living room area of my suite. I needed a small shot of tequila to calm my nerves

Minutes later the knock on the door startled me but I quickly smiled at the thought of Tez coming back to check on me. "Yes, I knew I had that nigga hooked," I chanted to myself. I ran to the bathroom and picked up the bottle of mouthwash. I took back two cups full and quickly washed my face. If Tez knew that I had a drink while pregnant he would really flip out on me.

The banging on the door continued as I took my dress off and stood in my underwear ready for some good make-up sex. I didn't want to take the chance on Tez questioning me some more so I figured seducing him would keep the topic of Chuck off his mind.

I slid my feet back into my Giuseppe sling backs and briefly paused at the mirror on my way to the door. I looked ready for anything and I hoped Tez felt the same way when he saw me. Eagerly I yanked open the door with a slight grin on my face only to be disappointed.

"You? What the hell are you doing here?" I asked demandingly.

"What was all that slick shit you were talking tonight?" Megan asked as she barged inside my room. She looked me up and down with pure disgust on her face.

"Bitch, you followed me? What kind of deranged shit is that?"

"Never mind me following you. That was easy. But you need to put on some clothes so we can talk."

"I don't have shit to say to you. I already couldn't stand your ass but after what you did tonight, I could never waste my breath on you," I said while yanking the thick, white robe off the couch and pulling it tightly around my body.

I was pissed that it hadn't been Tez who knocked on the door. And the whole idea of random people being able to knock on my door wasn't sitting well with me. I was going to have to look into getting my own place soon.

"You're such a whore," Megan blurted out for no reason.

"Get the hell out Megan."

"No, we have some business to discuss and I suggest that we do it now," Megan replied as she made herself at home sitting comfortably in the chair to my right.

She opened her purse and pulled out a white envelope. I looked at her stupidly, wondering when she would begin this little conversation. After just staring at each other for seconds, possibly even minutes, I decided to take the bait. "Alright, Megan! What is it? What's in the envelope?" I asked sarcastically. I couldn't imagine her having anything worth knowing. She was only trying to aggravate me as usual.

"Well, since you asked," she began as she sat up in the chair with a wicked grin on her face. "This right here could possibly change your life."

She paused again awaiting my response or reaction but I just stood confidently waiting for the unwarranted visit to come to an end. Megan exhaled slowly and opened the envelope. There were pictures of me and Chuck making love in Christian's bedroom.

I didn't speak a word but I looked at the pictures so hard my vision went blurry. Where had she gotten those from? Did she actually take them or had someone else? And what did she plan to do with them? All those questions and so many more ran swiftly through my mind.

"Where did you get those Megan?" I quietly asked again.

"That doesn't matter. All that matters is I have proof and I'm going to make sure that everyone knows about it too, especially Christian," she smugly remarked.

"Megan, don't do this, please, I'm begging you to just leave this alone. That was a big mistake. You'll hurt a lot of people if you go through with this."

"I don't give a damn about any of the people involved. I'm done with Chuck. He just proved what a jack ass he is when he was about to fight over you, like I wasn't even sitting there. I'd be a damn fool to just let you win."

"There is nothing for me to win, Megan. I don't want Chuck, sorry to be the one to inform you. I'm asking that you not tell anyone about this. Especially Christian."

"Give me one good reason."

"I can write you a check, name your price. We both know that you need the money," I said while walking towards my purse. I didn't want to pay Megan but I didn't want Christian to find out either. Megan needed the money since she was now financially poor, so I knew that a check would keep her quiet.

"I don't want your fucking money, Tracey. You think I need anything from someone like you? I rather see you fall than take a dime from you," she spewed at me.

I turned around with the check in my hand when I saw her eyes light up briefly. Money was like a drug for someone who didn't have any. "Look, everyone knows about your family going broke. It's okay, shit happens," I told her sounding like my mother. "Like I said, name your price," I repeated as I shrugged my shoulders.

"I want all of it."

Megan's eyes spewed revenge. I figured this would get harder as the minutes went on. "What? Girl your ass is nuts for real. There's no way in hell that I'm going to give you all of my money. You may as well go ahead and tell whoever, I don't give a damn," I said in disbelief.

Megan began to talk extra slow accentuating each word with spite. "You either give me every last cent or I swear I'm going to tell anyone who will listen!" she yelled as she waved the pictures in my face again.

"Get the hell out! It's not that important to me. No way in hell will I ever switch places with your broke ass," I screamed back at her.

She ran towards me with her fists balled, shocking the hell

out of me. The first blow actually surprised me. I felt myself becoming woozy as she continued to hit me, each time below the
eye. I threw my hand up to stop her from hitting my face, hoping
for no bruises or scars.

"Megan, what in the hell is wrong with you? Are you
crazy?" I attempted to step back but the luggage cart which I
never wanted to return was behind me.

"I'm sick of your shit, Tracey! You don't deserve to live this
life," she hollered with each blow.

One of her fist landed wildly in the center of my stomach. I
almost doubled over in pain when I felt the cramp that immediately followed. I threw my hand up and connected with the side of
her face. I flung her back and she fell against the coffee table.

I paused momentarily I tried to get my breathing pattern
together. My stomach hurt like hell and all I could think about was
my child and Tez. "You crazy bitch, I'm pregnant! You punched me
in my damn stomach!" I yelled at Megan.

She was lying on the floor not saying anything. She was
perfectly still but her eyes were open giving me the chance to
whip her good for all the pain she'd caused both me and Christian. I kept panting hoping my heart rate would slow when I began
to worry.

"Megan, get the hell up and get out of here before I call
the police on you. If something is wrong with my baby, you can
bet I'm going to have your ass arrested."

I moved towards her and kicked her in the ass as pay
back for the hit to my stomach. But I noticed the red fluid pouring
from her head. I slightly panicked confirming the bad feeling that I
had.

"Megan, this shit is not funny! Get up." I shook her leg in
an attempt to wake her from what I thought was unconscious-
ness. She still didn't move. Her body appeared to be lifeless. I
kept telling myself not to panic. Not to cry. I didn't need any extra
problems in my life. Quickly, I sat on the floor beside her and
checked for her pulse, there was none.

At this point I knew it was time to really freak out. I sup-
pressed the sob that was trying to escape my throat. Megan was
fucking dead! I hadn't meant to kill her; I was just trying to protect
myself from being hurt. I sat beside her not knowing what to do. I
leaned over the table and picked up my phone from the floor. I

quickly called Tez's number. Of course he knew what to do, people like him dealt with death every day. After the phone rang several times it rolled over to voicemail.

"Fuck!" I yelled in frustration.

I was going to have to get rid of Megan myself. There was no way in hell I would let anyone find her in my room. I wanted to call the police but after the argument that she and I had earlier, everyone would think I did it on purpose. I got off the floor and ran into my bedroom. I threw on a pair of Tez's old sweats that he left behind. I didn't want anyone to notice me so I threw on the hot pink wig from the Halloween party that was in one of the boxes on the luggage cart. I placed an old tattered Howard University hat on that belonged to my father and pulled it down low over my eyes.

Swiftly, I attempted to roll Megan into the comforter from the bed that I'd laid on the floor. Yet as soon as I tried to lift her body, I knew I hadn't thought things out clearly. Her body weight seemed to double. Truly, I needed help. Normally her 105 pound body would be easy to carry, but as dead weight she was heavy as hell. I could barely lift the lower part of her body without using every ounce of my strength. Out of the blue, I thought about the cart. Within minutes, I'd managed to remove all seven boxes and the hanging luggage pieces from the bell hop cart. With all the strength I could muster, I lifted the upper part of Megan's body first. Then perspiring like crazy I struggled to lift her bottom half to finally swing her body snugly onto the cart. Quickly, I threw two long, hanging Gucci luggage bags on top to camouflage what I was really carrying just in case someone saw me. As my heart thumped, I pushed with all my might to get the cart down the back hallway which led to the garage.

By the time I got to my truck, I was sweating like a pig. My breathing had intensified and I could've sworn a heart attack was near. I repeated the same strenuous job as before when tugging and putting Megan's body into the car. I kept turning around hoping no one would come out the doors behind me. Finally, she was in securely and I took off like a race car driver. I sped through the streets of downtown praying that I wouldn't get stopped by the police. I just needed somewhere to drop her body off. With all of the homeless people down here I knew that it would be awhile before anyone found her. I pulled over on the side of the Riverfront and

128 *Wealthy & Wicked*

thought that the Mississippi River would actually be my best bet.

My heart felt the weight of what I had done as I watched the bag slowly float towards the bottom of the river. I was really happy that it was her and not me though. Megan was a disgusting person who would wind up just like her parents, broke and in jail. I turned back towards my car when the police light glared in my face.

"Everything ok ma'am?" The white officer asked.

My heart started to beat rapidly and I felt my palms sweat. How long had he been standing there and why hadn't I heard him pull up?

"Yes, everything is fine. I couldn't sleep and I just came out here for some fresh air," I nervously replied.

"This is a dangerous area for a young woman to get some fresh air in," he said as he shined his flashlight on my truck and then back at me. "Someone like you doesn't belong down here. You should go ahead so that I make sure nothing will happen to you."

"Thank you officer, I'm leaving right now," I said, looking back at the river. The bag with Megan's body had completely disappeared. I breathed a sigh of relief as I waved at the officer and got back into my truck.

This day was a weird one that would go down as one I hoped I would forget. I hated having to dispose of Megan the way I did, but I couldn't risk anyone ever finding out about it either. I would put this in the basket with all of the other million of secrets that I planned on keeping.

Chapter 18

I hadn't slept a wink all night. It had been exactly eight hours since I'd dumped Megan's body and I couldn't remember blinking or sleeping. Six a.m. rolled around and I couldn't believe someone was at my door. I hopped up wondering if it was the police. My mind scrambled. I was so nauseated and unfocused I kept pacing the floor before deciding to finally answer the repeated knocking. One possibility was that Tez had come to his senses.

"Who is it?" I asked with my ear pressed against the door.

"Tracey, open the door."

"Kensington?" I questioned. No one else had his high pitch tone.

"Yes, it's me."

"What the hell are you here so early in the morning for?" I asked opening the door.

"I gotta tell you something honey and I know how dramatic you can be, so I want you to calm the hell down already," Kensington said as I rolled my eyes and he waltzed inside.

I wasn't really in the mood for any more drama. Between last night and the last few weeks I'd been completely drained of any signs of peacefulness. "Why is it that every time someone interrupts my peace early in the morning, it is you with a new dose of some bullshit," I said as I closed the door behind us.

Kensington paced the floor back and forth in his cobalt blue Prada heels. I shook my head as I noticed that he was dressed like a woman from head to toe. I had just purchased the same Miss Me jeans that he was currently switching his frail tail in. His lace black shirt hung open to show the string of pearls that he had draped around his neck.

"Honey, I just don't have a clue how I get myself into these situations. All I'm trying to do is live my life and enjoy myself while doing it. I need some coffee or something, Tracey. Call downstairs and get us some breakfast."

"Kenny, it is six thirty in the morning and I just had the craziest night ever. The last thing I want to do is eat some damn breakfast. "

"I just came from the new club on the East side. I need something to soak up all this damn liquor inside of me. Why you always being so damn difficult?" Kensington sulked.

"Your hands work just fine. You go ahead and order breakfast while I at least brush my teeth. You got me all out of character, standing here talking to you with my breath smelling like yesterday," I replied.

I grabbed my toothbrush as I walked into the bathroom. Kensington immediately got on the phone and called room service. I shook my head as I heard him order enough food to feed most of the homeless people in Downtown. Under normal circumstances I would've told him to leave but my nerves were tore up from guilt. At least the companionship would keep me from cracking. I kept seeing Megan's face which was driving me bananas.

"Kenny, make sure you get me some orange juice and I want it fresh with no pulp!" I yelled into the other room.

When he didn't respond I stuck my head out and saw him standing on the balcony, arguing with someone on his cell phone. *Damn, he moved fast as hell*, I thought. He looked up at me equally guilty and quickly ended his call.

"You ok, boo?" I asked as soon as he walked back in the glass door.

He had a worried look on his face. Whatever he had on his mind he needed to get off his chest before he exploded.

"Yeah, I'm good. That was just some fool who has turned into a damn stalker."

"That's your fault. I told you that everyone can't handle good sex. Especially not men," I replied.

I made myself comfortable on the bed and he crawled right next to me. He still had a weird look on his face. He was really going through something and I felt bad for him as I pulled him into a tight embrace. Little did he know, I needed love too…after what I'd done, I still couldn't believe I was a murderer.

"I don't know how I get myself into these situations, Tracey. If my parents would just stop acting so damn uptight, I wouldn't have to spread myself so thin with all these different men."

"Ok, so you have yourself a new sugar daddy, is that what seems to be bothering you?"

"Uhhhh…" he stammered.

"I personally can't stand having to kiss our parents asses for some money. That's why I hold on tight to my savings. Is he the one stalking you?" I asked patiently.

"Yes, girl and you don't even know the half of it. I just feel so bad. I know better than this. What in the hell is wrong with me? You have to promise you won't get mad at me."

"Why would I get mad at you? I don't care who you sucking or who is sucking you. Not unless it'is Tez. Wait a minute. It's not him is it?" I said while pushing Kensington away from me.

I thought back to how Mother and Anthony had betrayed me and the last thing I wanted was to be in that situation again. I still wasn't able to talk to neither one of them. Anthony had finally stopped calling me after he saw that it was pointless.

"Girl boo, why you getting all stank already? I said sugar daddy, and your boo thang is broke, so you know I'm not talking about him," Kensington replied.

I threw a pillow at him, knocking him right upside his head. Tez was still a sensitive subject for me and to hear someone speak on his money status kind of irked me.

"I'm about to put you clean out of this room if you go there again. I love that boo thang that you're talking about."

"Yeah yeah yeah, love is all good but it ain't paying a single one of my bills. You have your own money so him being broke isn't a problem for you. I'm the broke one in my situations," he said while laughing.

I laughed with him as the banging on the door broke our laughter. Since it was still considered early, room service was quick with their service and food was delivered quickly. I adjusted the belt on my robe and got out the bed. The impatient server banged again as I approached the door. My nerves were still going through shock so I wanted to make sure it wasn't the police.

"Look, don't bang on my door like your ass is crazy," I yelled while opening the door. I was about to say more to the assumed immigrant but it wasn't room service at all. "What in the hell are you doing here and why do you look like shit?" I asked, completely thrown off guard.

"I knew your ass would be here," he screamed into the room.

I could smell the liquor as it danced off his breath. He was completely drunk and wreaked of the smell of urine. His tie hung loosely around his neck and I could spot tiny speckles of slob stained on his shirt.

"You have taken desperate to a whole new level. Are you following me now? And you stink like hell." I turned up my nose and tried to hold down the bile that was racing up my throat. Kensington stood behind me with his mouth wide open. He was just as surprised as I was to see our unwanted visitor. Strangely the two of them kept making strong eye contact.

"Tracey, I need to tell you something now..."Kensington started but was immediately cut off.

"Yeah, he needs to tell you that me and him. We go to-gether now," Anthony said while laughing and sliding down the side of the door landing on the floor.

He was so drunk he could barely stand up. I looked at the both of them with wide eyes. I could not believe what I was hear-ing.

"You what?" I asked them both in disbelief.

"It's not what you think Tracey, I swear. You and Anthony were finished when he came to the club one night. I thought it was strange that he was in there but he asked for me specifically. You know I have to make my money so I didn't turn down his offer," Kensington rattled off.

I just held my chest. "You have to make your money?" I hoped my guess at what he was about to tell me wasn't true. "He's fucking my mother for crying out loud," I yelled.

"What?" Kensington asked.

"Yeah, Gertrude and I are in love." Anthony stuttered proudly while he remained stretched out on the carpet. "And I'm not just sleeping with her. You're just a jealous bitch, that's all, Tracey. Mad because I didn't want your slut ass," Anthony mum-bled.

I kicked him in the ass swiftly with my foot. He was a dis-gusting human being but I would have never thought he was liv-ing on the down low. "So, let me guess, it was Kensington who was in your truck that night, huh?"

Anthony laughed loudly. "You fool, that was your mother."

My head began to thump. "This is all too much. Kensington, you need to get your shit and get out. It's too early in the morning for this. Take your sugar daddy with you."

"Tracey, please don't be mad at me. Let me just explain the rest of the story."

"No, Kenny, I can't handle this type of betrayal right now. I need you both to leave right now." Luckily, my desire to make things work with Anthony was at a zero. I just wondered why I'd never seen any sign of him being gay. I guess that was why he always fought off my head jobs.

"Typical Tracey. When she can't have it her way, she runs. Where are you going now, to the slums, with your little thug?" Anthony asked while trying to remove his body from the floor.

I kicked him in the ass again just so that he could fall back over. When he got up again I decided to give up the thought of kicking him again. I was done with him. And if Kensington really wanted him, he and mother could fight over him together.

"Everyone out!" I shouted while turning back to Kensington who was making his way to the door.

"I swear I didn't mean to hurt you. You know I love you," he replied as he assisted Anthony by the arm.

"I'm not hurt. Really, it's more of a shock. I don't give a damn about Anthony any more. I just don't want to deal with this." I didn't even want to know what they'd done, how they did it, or when it all began. I just needed to clear my head. "Do you boo, make your money the best way you can," I told Kensington.

I closed the door behind the two of them wondering how the world could be so cruel...so wicked. I sat on my bed trying to wrap my brain around what I just heard. Anthony and Kensington are creeping around? The thought caused my stomach to churn and I quickly ran to the bathroom and emptied what little contents I had in my belly. Mother would be so devastated when she found out that Anthony was gay. I looked in the mirror and smiled at the thought. I wasn't going to be the one who told her either. It was pure poetic justice for how she treated me. Payback was a bitch.

Chapter 19

Six hours later and I still hadn't eaten breakfast or lunch, nor been able to think clearly. Once again, Tez wasn't answering my calls, but this time all because of that bitch Megan. I sat in my office doodling all over my twenty-two hundred dollar mahogany desk like a Kindergartener. The artistic hearts read Tracey and Tez forever. I meant it-dearly. Suddenly, my door flew open and the unannounced visitor just barged in like he owned the place.

"Tracey, I know you saw that I've been calling you. I know you're confused about your feelings for me, but you and I are in love, damn it," Chuck screamed as soon as he walked into my office looking like he'd just come from the gym.

"Chuck, I don't know why you don't get what I'm saying to you, you and I can't continue this." I ran to the door and quickly closed it. The last thing I wanted was for Shanice to hear him.

"Tracey, what started out as a mistake has turned into the best year of my life. I know it's been yours too, Tracey."

"Chuck, why are you here? Shouldn't you run off and chase Megan?"

"You know I don't want Megan. She's just something to do," he countered.

He stood in front of me with his brown eyes blazed with anger. Had this been a different day, I might've thought his dark brown skin and long, black dreds were sexy. Today, they made him look like the devil.

"If you don't stop this bullshit, Chuck, you're going to get us caught. I can't risk Christian finding out about us. Besides, like I told you last week, it's over!"

"I think she already knows," he said with a solemn tone. "If you would've been answering your damn phone, you would've known that," he said angrily.

My heart began beating like crazy. I prayed that he was wrong. "Chuck, you know why I won't answer for you. Why can't you just leave it alone, Chuck? Why are you going so hard against my wishes?" Tension filled my voice.

"Because I love you, way more than I love her. I can't continue to play like I'm happy with her."

"Bullshit, Chuck! You love everybody. You were just with Megan last night. And I'm not about to be involved in this unnecessary drama. Our relationship was a mistake, I wish I could take it back, but I can't," I said with tears in my eyes.

"Is that a fact? You loved it when we went to Vegas together. You loved it when I bought you nice things, and you loved it the countless times I made you scream!" Chuck nearly growled at me before spitting out his next set of words. "You must be stuck on that lil punk ass, fake thug you was with last night."

"His name is, Tez, and he's not a thug. He's my new man. I'm not saying this because I owe you an explanation, but more out of obligation to him."

"I should've beat his ass. I had no clue that you were now flaunting that shit out in public. I've been watching you ever since someone sent me pictures of you entering his hotel room." Chuck slammed his hand down on my desk, scaring the hell out of me.

"What do you mean, someone sent you pictures of us? What was on them?" I was now confused on what in the hell was going on. Everyone seemed to have professional pictures of me. Immediately, I began to sweat. What if someone had taken pictures of me dumping Megan's body?

"Are you listening to me, Tracey? It don't even matter what was on them. I can't prove it, but I think Christian sent them," he said.

"No way, she doesn't even know about me and Tez for real. What kind of twisted ass games are you playing? Did you have someone follow me?" I angrily asked.

"I just told you that I didn't."

This shit had gotten way too complicated. Chuck seemed confident that Christian had sent him the pics. He then pulled out a photographer developed version of the pic that appeared in the newspaper. "Where'd you get this, Chuck!" I was certain my face had turned blue.

"I believe Christian sent it to me."

"Are you telling me the truth!" I shouted.

"Why would I lie, Tracey. I want us to be together."

"Get the hell out of my office before I call security, Chuck." I sat down in my oversized black chair and turned toward the window. I was done talking to him. I hated that I had ever got involved with a married man. I would not let him sit here and ruin my life.

"Why you fighting this so tough?" I could tell he would get too close to me based on the seductive look on his face. "You know damn well you want me. You can't resist me and you know it," he leaned over and whispered softly in my ear.

I froze with my chest heaving up and down. "Chuck, please. I swear I can't go on with this." *He smelled so damn good.*

When he inhaled deeply in the crevice of my neck, I felt my knees buckle. Thank God I remained in my seat. But I was so afraid of the way he made me feel, I hopped up and tried to move away from his reach. Out of the blue, Chuck grabbed my ass and pulled me closer to him.

"You don't have to do anything you don't want to do, but I know you want to do this," he said while licking in my ear.

He spun me around and stared deeply in my eyes. I felt the first tear drop and he quickly wiped them away.

"You don't have to cry. There's nothing to be ashamed of. We are two adults who have an undeniable passion for each other. Love is love."

"But at the end of the day, you are Christian's husband," I reasoned with him further.

"I'm yours right now and that is all that matters."

He held my face and shoved his tongue down my throat. I couldn't resist him as he ran his hands up my thighs, lifting my skirt. He pushed everything off my desk onto the floor and roughly threw me on top of it, face down, ass in the air.

"I'm about to punish your ass for making me wait so long," Chuck moaned sexily.

My head spun as thousands of thoughts entered my head. Was I doing the right thing for Christian's sake? Chuck didn't want her so it didn't matter whether it was me or some other woman. Right now I needed love too. I needed to cum hoping to release some of the stress that had built up within the last few days. Then

I thought about Tez. How many more times would he disappear in and out of my life?

When I felt Chuck stick three fingers inside of me causing a temporary pain all thinking ceased. I winced at how hard he was fingering me, but I was going to take it. It was our normal routine to have rough sex.

"I'm going to make yo ass cum and soon as I do, you're going to clean it up. You hear me, bitch."

Defiantly, I took all that he said with no response. The name calling was something that surprisingly turned me on. We both had gotten a kick out of it.

"So yo ass think you grown today? I gotta remind you who owns this shit."

He flipped me over on the desk to get a good look at my face, and immediately inserted himself inside of me. Chuck was so thick and big. I always had to take a deep breath during the first few moments. The initial pain quickly turned to pleasure. Then he pounded inside me as if it was no tomorrow.

"Oh my God, Chuck! Stop," I pleaded.

"Not until you pay for trying to play me with that bum ass nigga," he responded as he continued to grind inside of me.

"What in the hell is going on?" I heard Shanice scream as she stood in my doorway.

I was so caught up in how good it felt, I hadn't noticed that she had opened my door. I pushed Chuck off of me and hopped off the desk. I tried desperately to pull my skirt back down to save some face.

"When my door is closed, one would think that they should fucking knock before opening it," I angrily said. It was crazy how I sounded like my mother.

"Umm, you told me to interrupt you when the mail came. How was I supposed to know that you would be sleeping with your best friend's husband?"

"Shanice, get the hell out! I'm paying you to do a damn job and I expect you to be doing it!"

She stormed out of the office, slamming the door behind her. I looked at Chuck and he stood there with a wicked grin on his face. "We gone finish or what?" he asked as he tugged at the waist of his jogging pants?

"You need to go. I already told you that I can't continue on like this. Please, just try and work things out with Christian."

"I see what you doing now. I'm not going to keep playing these childish ass games with you. Call me when your ass is ready for the real deal."

He opened the door and walked out. The funny thing was that he wasn't even embarrassed. He was such an asshole and I wished every single moment that I wouldn't have ever let him touch me. It was bad enough that I was sleeping with a married man, but for it to be Christian's husband was worse. The fact that I was the mistress that was causing her so much pain was horrible.

I rushed over to my favorite spot at the window and thought back to how it all began. I'd been distraught about something Mother did and surprisingly *he* was there to comfort me. After several drinks and hours of crying, we went back to *their* house. *How wicked*! That night in *their* bed, Chuck gave me something so special, rough and kinky, I instantly became addicted to it. I'd never experienced love the way he gave it to me.

I took a few steps back then covered my forehead as I thought about Christian almost catching us once. She stopped by my house unannounced and he was lying naked in my bed. It was then that I knew that something was wrong with me. I immediately cut Chuck off after that. I couldn't stand myself for what I had become. That was the weekend before I met Tez. Suddenly, my face became flushed. It dawned on me about the last time I had sex with Chuck. I silently found myself questioning who the father of my child was.

I didn't want it to be Chuck's, but the reality of the situation was that it was a great possibility that my child could be his. We had never used any protection and I hadn't given birth control much thought. It was always quicker to either take the morning after pill or get an abortion. I picked up the phone and dialed out to the receptionist area.

"Shanice, this has been a long and embarrassing day. I want to apologize for what you saw."

"Don't worry about it, Boss. We all got hella secrets, it ain't no business of mine," she said.

"Go on home to your babies. It's almost five o'clock. I have to finish up a few things here but I don't think I'll need you any further tonight."

"Cool, I got a lot of stuff to do tonight anyway. Oh by the way, Christian on the line for you."

A sharp pain zipped through my heart. "Tell her I can't talk right now," I said nervously.

I disconnected the call and poured myself a glass of wine. I quickly swallowed the contents. Was her phone call just a mere coincidence? Or were Chuck's suspicions correct?

Chapter 20

I wasn't sure how long I'd been asleep, but I was awakened by a loud bang on the office door. I hopped off my couch and looked outside my window only to see the moon shining down on the river. I was slightly in a daze but could only guess that it was a little after eight o'clock. I tried to prepare myself for whomever decided to show up at my office unannounced as the banging continued. It was after business hours and no one had said they were stopping by.

I grabbed the stapler and an empty wine bottle off my desk taking my place behind the door. Bad choices for weapons, but all I could think of. I needed something for protection after all the crazy deliveries and unwanted photos that had been taken of me. Who knew what was next. Once the doorknob turned I really freaked out because the only person, besides myself, who had a key was Shanice. I wanted to hide under my desk but I knew that would be the first place my attacker would look.

"Tracey! I know your ass is in here. No need for you to hide now," the voice screamed loudly into the room.

"Christian is that you?" I asked as I slid from behind the door, still a little frightened even though I now knew it was her. Facing Christian was something I didn't want to do.

Startled, she turned around and faced me head on. Her eyes were bloodshot red and accompanied the dried up tears upon her face. Her look had confirmed what Chuck had already told me earlier.

"You've done some really foul things in your life Tracey, but never would I have thought you would stoop this low," Christian said to me pulling her over-sized purse close to her body.

"What are you talking about?" I asked calmly, talking baby steps away from her.

In the back of my mind I knew that she and I would have to have this conversation eventually one day. As bad as I wanted for it to disappear, she was ready for a show down. Her hair was pulled tightly in a ponytail and her face was shiny from the Vaseline she had applied.

"You know, I wanted to kill Megan and all those other women so bad for sleeping with my husband." Christian took huge steps my way causing me to panic more with each of her moves. "Never in a million did I think you would be one of those women on the list, Tracey."

"Christian, I swear I don't know what you're talking about." Guilt began to tear at my insides as I couldn't even keep a straight face. Strangely, it hurt me to see her so upset when I was the one who caused the pain. "Why would I sleep with Chuck? I hate his guts." I had my palms turned upward and my expression seem super plastic.

"That's what I was thinking too. I wanted to believe that for months. I knew you hated him and there was no way possible that you would go for him. But you are your mother's daughter after all," she spat.

"Why are you saying all of this? What would make you think that I would do you that way," I cried, rushing over behind my desk. I need to create a boundary between the two of us since Christian's eyes bled violence.

"Bitch, don't try and make a fool out of me!" Her voice rose to its highest peak. "I already know what's been going on. But I want to hear you admit it."

"I'm sorry, I don't know what else you want me to say." My hands shook uncontrollably.

She threw her head back in laughter. I didn't know if it was a good thing to run or just stand in fear listening to her rant. "Christian, wait…" I started to say, but she immediately cut me off.

"No, you wait, Tracey!" she shouted banging her fist on my desk. "For years I've walked in your shadow, being a loyal friend. For years, I've had to hear how cute I was for a fat girl, or how I should be more like Tracey. Constant comparisons just made me sick. Men only talk to me after you turned them down, Chuck included," she angrily said the words she had been feeling for some time.

"It was only once but I haven't slept with him since," I confessed and lied all at the same time.

"Don't try and bullshit me girl. You think I don't know about you and him? How you wormed your little slutty ass into his heart, I will never know."

"Christian, I don't know where you're getting your information from, but it's incorrect."

"Tracey, just don't say shit! The one thing I want to give him more than anything is a child and I can't. But here's your stank ass, in a position to possibly be carrying his baby," she screamed loudly, then plopped down into one of the chairs which faced my desk. I could see directly into her eyes as tears spilled down to her breast. She rocked back and forth in the chair like a distressed mental patient. I was nervous as hell because I had never seen her so not like herself.

"Christian, I really need you to believe me, it was only once. And you're my best friend so we can make this right." I tried to stall for time. I knew all along, messing with Chuck was a mistake. I never wanted to hurt her. I just needed her to understand that.

"So, you sit here, and try to insult my intelligence, saying only once…like that makes it any better," she grunted through her teeth. "I have his phone records, saw the pictures you sent him through text messages, and his credit card invoice."

My eyes grew to the size of basketballs. There was no denying that she knew.

"I even followed him to your house and sat outside for hours. I wanted so badly for it to not be you," she mumbled getting more and more choked up as she spoke. "And Chuck knew more than anyone, how I hated being compared to you." Suddenly, Christian stood again, throwing all the evidence on my desk with shaking hands.

As my eyes did a quick flip through the images, I saw multiple pictures of myself and Tez, and some with Chuck as well. I didn't even want to pick up the phone records or his credit card invoice, I already knew what I would see. But why pictures of Tez and I?

"I'm so sorry Christian, I swear I didn't mean to hurt you. I went looking for you one night. I had been drinking and he was there and it just happened."

"No, we could just happen to wear the same outfit or

shoes but having sex with a married man does not just happen, bitch," she yelled at me.

"I never meant to hurt you. I hope you realize that," I sobbed.

Christian had been the only good person in my life and I had betrayed her. I knew from that moment forth, we would never be the same, how could we?

"Your definition of hurting someone must be warped. You didn't just hurt me, you ruined my damn life and now I'm about to ruin yours," she said as she pulled a metal object from her purse.

I thought about the razor blade that she tried to use on Megan. I didn't know how good she was with using it, but I was scared that she would practice on me. "Christian, please don't be all dramatic. I don't want your husband. He's all yours."

"That's funny that you think I need permission to be with my own damn husband. Here I am going nuts trying to get pregnant and you're already pregnant by him."

"Christian, I'm pregnant by Tez, not your husband." I was about to hit her with some words to calm her nerves but when she placed the object on the table, I realized that it was a gun, not just a metal object like I'd initially thought. My temperature rose within seconds.

"What, what-what-what- are you doing with that gun, Christian," I stammered over my words.

"Tracey, you know what's crazy?" She leaned over my desk slightly.

"What's with the gun Christian?" I asked again, ignoring her question. We locked eyes.

"At first I thought childish things like sending dead snakes and rats to your office would make you realize that I knew and that I'd get you for it. But then I realized that was dumb, immature on my part. You need something more permanent as your payback."

I had one of those ah ha looks upon my face. I would've never guessed Christian had done those things. I took two steps back but with the big window behind me there was nowhere else for me to go, other than run to my right or left. "Christian, what are you doing with the gun?" I asked with my hands up in surrender mode. Her expression told me that this was my ending. "Let's talk about this," my voice pleaded.

"I'm doing the world a favor and getting rid of a manipulative, conniving slut like you. That bastard ass child will never see the light of day," she said as she raised the .357 in front of her.

The moon glistened off the steel handle as she expertly pointed it towards me. She had her head cocked to the side and the gun was tilted like the gangsters do in the movies. Who was this woman? I fearfully wondered.

"Pleaseeeeee Christian, put the gun down. I swear I'm sorry. I never intended to sleep with your damn husband but I'm not pregnant by him." I pleaded harder than before.

Somehow she had reached the point of snapping and I was afraid she was really going to shoot me. I searched her eyes for any hint of my old friend. But she was gone.

"I don't give a damn who you're pregnant by. I just know that the only thing that will be delivered, is the eulogy at your funeral," she angrily said as she pulled the trigger.

I staggered, then felt my body fall on top of the same desk that I'd sexed Chuck on earlier. At that point I knew my girl had really shot me. As my breaths strenuously left my lungs I could feel her cold eyes watching me until everything went black.

Chapter 21

"Aww man I have some really bad news. Star running back, Chuck Jones, has been arrested for the shooting of Tracey Robbins. For those who don't know, Tracey was found shot three times in her office last week. It's is being reported that Jones and the victim Tracey, had been having an affair. Tracey Robbins, is also the best friend of Chuck's wife, Christian Jones.

At this time we cannot confirm the reason for the shooting, but we are able to confirm that Ms. Robbins was possibly pregnant by Mr. Jones. Whoaaaaaaaaaaaaaaa....he's currently being held with no bond and still declaring his innocence. The police have reported finding Tracey's blood in his car, as well as the gun. Upon further investigation, they found a secret room in his house. Inside, there were pictures of Tracey as well as a tracking and listening device for her car and home.

Something about this story, just doesn't add up for me. You mean to tell me Chuck shot the girl, but was crazy enough to leave this secret hidden room with pictures of her? He had to know the police would come looking for him, right? He was chilling at football practice, instead of getting out of town? Man, I need to see more proof before I start believing what the cops saying.

This looks like a made for T.V. situation right here. Some straight, Jerry Springer stuff for the well off. Or possibly, another situation, where an athlete tries to kill his baby momma. I just hate to see an innocent child suffer in all this. Lord, I just don't understand these men! They piss me off with all this killing the woman stuff. The foolishness needs to stop!

She doesn't want you or you don't want her, then just walk away. Don't be no little punk and kill her because you don't know how to move on. Man what is the world coming to now days? But like I said, I need more evidence. Don't take my word for it be-

cause I don't have a clue about the real deal. So we'll pray for everybody that is involved.

Hit up my line, if you want to weigh in on this real life soap opera. This is Mz. Janee, on the only radio station that provides St. Louis with hip hop and R&B."

Christian laughed loudly as the radio segment went to commercial. She turned down the volume on her iPhone and looked over at my bed. I did the best I could to remain perfectly still. She had no clue that I was listening to her or that I'd gained consciousness. I couldn't believe that the people on the radio thought that Chuck shot me. What the fuck!

Christian had everyone convinced that it was him and not her. I wondered how she was able to pull that off. Her ringing cell phone stopped her laughter. She let out a loud gush of air as she seemed somewhat annoyed by whoever was calling. The phone kept ringing until she stopped it.

"Christian!!! What the hell is wrong with you? You shot her! Then you framed yo husband for it," a voice asked as soon as it walked in the room.

I wanted to turn my head towards it, but I didn't want anyone to know that I was awake, especially not Christian's psycho ass. So I kept my eyes shut tightly.

"And, what's your point?" Christian absently asked.

"My point is, your ass is nuts. Do you not have any remorse?" The woman continued to yell.

Her voice sounded oddly familiar. I barely opened one eye to look at her but all I could see was the table that was filled with cards, balloons, and flowers.

"Oh, so now you have some compassion for the woman who treats you like trash? You knew what the plan was from jump, so don't come at me with that holier than thou attitude," Christian spat.

"You never said anything about shooting her, you just said to work for her, get some dirt on her and ruin her. But you never said anything about shooting her. This is hellas crazy!"

It was Shanice! I couldn't believe it. I almost hopped out of the bed at that revelation. I tried to remain calm but I was beyond pissed. Here I was, shot twice in the abdomen and these two had planned the whole thing out.

"Shanice, I can stay here and console you all day but I

have important shit to do, like get a manicure." I imagined Christian looking down at her hand, grimacing at her chipped polish.

"A manicure? Tracey is lying here fighting for her life! And I don't want to go to jail because of you! That's something that I didn't sign up for. I just want my money and to be done with this whole Beverly Hills 90210 shit."

Christian yawned loudly obviously bored with the conversation. Even though I was mad at Shanice for lying to me, I was kind of happy that she at least felt bad. This soap opera had gotten crazy and had my heart thumping.

"Would you relax, Shanice. Keep your voice down, fool. Damn, you stressing me the hell out," Christian said as she looked my way. I quickly closed the eye that I'd opened slightly and pretended to be comatose again. I wanted to see how much information I could get out of the two of them.

"I have kids that I have to live for and being wrapped up in some conspiracy shit is not where it's at, Christian. Things were cool when you were sending packages, emailing her advertisers bad information and stuff like that, but all this murder stuff, nawl, I'm not down for it."

Damn…they'd gotten me good, I sighed. But Shanice didn't seem afraid of Christian. Her tone let her know that. I silently wished she would slap some sense into her because Christian was out of control and deserved to be brought back to reality. "

"Like I said, I'm done Christian. When can I get the rest of my money?"

"You are far from done Shanice, this is just the beginning for us. For some reason God showed favor upon that bitch, so now we have to go a step further and finish this once and for all."

Goose bumps formed all over my body.

"What do you mean by finish her? I'll tell you what's finished, me! I'm done with this," Shanice blurted with anxiety in her voice.

"Since I'm holding all the trumps, and you have no money, you will continue ruining this chick until I decide I'm through with you. If that isn't good enough, you can always become Tracey's roommate," Christian replied nastily.

Hearing Christian brag about what she had done to me and not being able to do anything about it, was killing me. I prayed silently for strength to keep the charade up. My legs stiffened because I'd been still for so long. Now, I knew what a mummy felt like.

"You can't blackmail me, Christian. I will go to the police, and let them know that it was you, and not your husband who shot her," Shanice announced.

"And how will you explain helping me set Chuck up? With the money my family has, I would never serve a day. Your broke down ass, will probably do something close to life. So dry your eyes and save your tears for someone who cares about a piss poor soul like you."

"I just want this to be over. Just because I come from the ghetto, doesn't mean that this is normal for me. He never told me how crazy you were, nor did he say that I would be involved in a crime," Shanice cried.

"Well *he* hasn't told the truth since the 8th grade, stupid!"

He? Who was this he that they were talking about? Who else could possibly be in on trying to destroy my life?

"Men promise a lot of things all the time, that doesn't mean they will abide by them, Shanice."

"I don't care about any of that, Christian. Like I said, I have kids and they are my only concern."

"And my concern is to make sure you keep your mouth shut and keep pretending to be dumb."

"You are such a psychotic bitch, Christian! I can't believe you don't feel bad for shooting Tracey, or killing an innocent ass child."

I got queasy, fast. For the first time, I realized I'd lost my baby because of the shooting. I wanted to puke. I needed to cry. But I had to be strong and focus on Christian's plan to take me away from everything I've ever loved.

"It wasn't my child, so why should I give a damn?" Christian said as she sat back down in the chair next to my bed. Hearing how she really felt about me, had me mad as hell. I made sure to slow my breathing down so she wouldn't notice I had gotten worked up.

"You shot your best friend. How can you sit there and be so heartless?" Shanice asked tearfully. She was really torn up about what happened. My mama always told me money was the root to all evil. And she wasn't lying either. Y'all rich folks hella crazy and wicked too."

"That same best friend, had to have the cutest boys in high school, wear the best clothes, be great at ballet and piano, the head of cheerleading, valedictorian, have my husband, steal my man's heart, and would've had a child. So forgive me when I say, I should've aimed higher. I'm tired of walking in her shadow."

"It's your fault, Christian. You're the one who brought this all on yourself, with this stupid ass plan," Shanice said.

"This conversation is really boring me. I don't give a damn about anything you're saying."

"You're pathetic, Christian. That's the reason why Tracey always finishes before you."

"Shanice, can you please leave. My best friend is sitting here fighting for her life and you are disturbing me. I'm in mourning." Christian said as she pretended to be heart-broken. I couldn't believe how cocky Christian had gotten. And her Oscar worthy crying session was way over the top.

"I really feel sorry for you Christian. I'd rather be from the hood with a good heart, than rich and miserable like you."

"No, sweetie, you should feel sorry for those who get in my damn way, including yourself," Christian calmly shot back.

The cold callous tone in her voice made my insides shiver. She needed to be stopped, and fast! My options bounced around in my head like ping pong balls. I considered calling the authorities as soon as she left. Then I considered telling my mother. She would know what to do. Then I reverted back to thinking of my child. My baby was gone! My heart melted as Shanice continued to blast Christian.

"I can't imagine being that cold and heartless. You people with money are really ungrateful and crazy as hell." Shanice spoke with anger.

"You want to keep breathing? Then you will continue to do what I say and when I say it. If you ever get out of pocket, those little kids of yours will be swimming in the river. Now, get the fuck out before I have someone throw you out." Christian started humming happily. "leave me and my good friend alone."

I panicked when I felt Christian touch my leg.

I heard Shanice's heels clicking towards the door. Then the sounding of the door closing sent me into panic mode. I felt more afraid than ever. I had the feeling that no matter what, Christian was going to kill me.

Chapter 22

My eyes opened wide to the sight of the white ceiling. The bright lights caused a temporary fog as I tried to shake away the numbing pain that exploded in my brain.

"Well, it looks like my patient is awake," the voice said from the other side of the room. I tried to turn my head towards it but I had no strength left in my body.

"What do you mean patient? Where am I?" I couldn't remember much of anything before this moment. I tried my hardest to figure out how she had gotten me in this position.

"You're my patient. And in very good hands." She walked towards me with a long needle in her hand and a sinister smile on her face. I panicked!

"I swear, if you don't let me up from here."

"If I don't let you up, then what?"

"Then, I'll…"

"You won't be doing a damn thing, sweetie. I'm running this show." Christian laughed at my futile attempt to untie myself.

"This shit isn't funny." I continued to tug at the burlap ropes that had my arms confined to the bottom of the heating pipes.

"This isn't supposed to be funny. Well, maybe it is for me, but I'm sure you won't find any humor in this at all."

"Why are you doing this?"

"Because bitches like you deserve to lose every now and then. Now, open those legs up wide so I can take what belongs to me."

My heart rate accelerated as the liquid in the needle shot through my arm. I wanted to fight but whatever she pumped my veins with had rendered me paralyzed. "Please, stop! I don't have anything of yours. I swear it's not what you think. Please, just let me explain." Tears flew from the corners of my eyes as she continued to laugh at me.

"I'm over wanting to hear an explanation from you. At the end of the day, you did what you did and now you must pay." Her voice took on a stern mother's tone.

"Don't do this! Don't do this! Pleaseeeeee. I'm begging you! I'll do whatever you want, just let me go." My pleas fell on deaf ears as she started to hum a nursery song. She'd changed the lyrics so it seemed more sadistic than anything. *Hush, little baby, don't say a word, Mama's gonna buy you a killing bird. And if that killingbird don't sing, Mama's gonna buy you that shotgun thing. And if that shotgun thing don't work. Mama's just gonna slit Tracey's throat.*

She kept singing in my ear as I began to lose consciousness. "That's right, Tracey, take a deep breath before you die!"

All I could do was cry and hope like hell that someone would save me. As the cramps rapidly shot through my stomach, I realized someone else had entered the room.

"Get the fuck back before I shoot yo ass," someone shouted! I couldn't see his face but I knew that it was Tez.

I opened my eyes just in time to see Tez grab Christian's arm twisting it behind her back. He quickly took the ropes off my arms and tied them around her. Now that she was helpless on the floor, I flew into Tez's arms.

"Tez, oh God! I'm so glad you saved me. I just knew we wouldn't make it. I was so scared, and all I could think about was protecting our baby." Tez grabbed my bleeding body off the ground and carried me to safety.

"I got you Ma, didn't I tell you I wouldn't let anything happen to you. See Tracey baby, you just got to trust me. You and my lil man will always be fine." He looked around making sure that Christian was no longer a threat. He still had his gun drawn and was ready to shoot if he had to.

Suddenly, I jumped. I sat up quickly in the bed breathing like an overheated engine. The sheets were soaking wet and clung tightly to my body. I looked around frantically for a scene of familiarity. The beeping sound of the blood pressure machine reminded me that I was still in the hospital. I had been dreaming once again. When I saw my father sleeping in the chair next to me my nerves calmed slightly. I'd had another nightmare about

Christian trying to kill me.

"Daddy," I called to him hoarsely. My throat was on fire from the tube the doctors removed this morning. Tears formed in the corners of my eyes just knowing my protection had arrived.

"Good, you're awake now. How do you feel? Do you know what day it is? Does anything feel odd about your body?" My father went into doctor mode, shooting off a barrage of health questions and moving close to my face.

"I'm fine Daddy. I actually came to earlier. I just didn't want anyone to know," I quietly said.

"This morning? Why in the hell are you keeping that a secret? There are people out there losing their minds because they thought you wouldn't get better. You were shot three times sweetheart and suffered some serious injuries." He stroked my forehead slightly.

"I know Daddy."

"No, baby, listen. One of the bullets punctured your intestines. And luckily the other two were lodges into your fatty tissue. I'm just so glad you're okay." He paused. "But you lost your baby Tracey. Did you know you were pregnant?"

I hesitated, not sure what he would think of me. "Yes, I knew," I said sounding pretty choked up.

"Don't cry honey."

I'll be fine Daddy," I moaned. "I'm sorry I didn't tell you…just needed some time to think. I didn't want to have to answer a million different questions from people that I didn't really want to talk to."

"Does this have anything to do with why Chuck shot you?"

I swallowed hard the let my fingers slide down beneath the covers. I hoped that fumbling around with my bandages would stop my anxiety. How could I tell my father that Chuck didn't shoot me and that Christian did?

"You and Chuck were having an affair, huh? He was obsessed with you and shot you. I can imagine the kind of questions everyone wants to ask you. Hell, I have some myself," he commented.

"Please, not you too daddy. I can't handle taking judgment from you." I shook my head in disbelief.

"I'll let you rest now, but we will have to talk sooner or later. I know Christian is your friend, but her dad is my boss, so that puts me in a funny situation," he said sternly.

I felt bad because I hadn't taken my dad into consideration when I started messing with Chuck. I now understood how selfish I was. Our affair had indirectly affected everyone around us. "Where is Christian, Daddy?" Has she been here? I knew that she was always lurking, ready to pounce on me in any given moment.

"Oh, you bet she's here...been by your side the whole time you were out. She went down to get some coffee. Christian is a really good friend to you, Tracey. That's why I was surprised to hear that you were sleeping with Chuck. Hell, your mother is so furious, she's refused to come up here."

"I highly doubt she'd come up here," I mumbled under my breath.

"What did you say, Tracey?" His thick eyebrows crinkled at the corners.

"I said I never meant to hurt anyone. It was a mistake, I know that now, Daddy," I sobbed.

I decided not to involve my father with all that had gone on between me and my mother. I would keep it all a secret for now. Little did he know she was now no one to me. He had no idea that I'd been staying at the Four Seasons nor that Mother had changed the locks and left my belongings on the street for common thugs to rummage through. Never in a million years did I want to disappoint my father, but I'd already ended things with a guy that he thought was perfect for me and now this was icing on the cake. Besides, I was certain Christian's pretend cries had everyone thinking that I was the bad guy. I wanted to tell my father the truth but I didn't know how he would handle it. I decided to tuck that little piece of information away until I knew what to do with it.

"We all make mistakes baby. Don't you worry yourself to death thinking about them. Your main concern should be to get better. We can fix everything else later," he said as he patted my hand for comfort. "Plus, we've got some other things to discuss once you get better." Concern showed all over his face.

"Thank you Daddy. I'm so glad I have you in my life. You love me even when I don't deserve it." He pulled my hand to his mouth and softly kissed it."I wish you could stay closer to home more."

"Me too. Its just that things are complicated. We'll discuss later. I just want you to get better, quick. Speaking of which, I've had my new protégé Dr. Scott, looking after your care. He learned from the best so you should expect excellent service. He'll have you back healthy in no time."

A smile seeped through the side of my lips. I'd seen Dr. Scott around in passing over the years. He was very attractive with caramel skin and light brown eyes. He reminded me of Shemar Moore with a slight tan. He had been working with my father since he graduated from Medical School. I was just about to tell him how I remembered who he was when Christian walked through the door. She hadn't a care in the world as she removed her Chanel shades from her face. My skin cringed as I quickly reached for my father's hand.

"Hey now. My friend is up and talking," she said as she tossed her blonde hair over her shoulder. She took a seat in the chair on the opposite side of my bed, directly across from my father and grabbed my hand. I felt my heart beat speed up as she pretended to be happy to see me. Her unstableness had made me uneasy and scared. We looked at one another and the coldness in her eyes sent a chill up my spine. The machine started to beep louder as my nerves continued to race.

My father stood up. "What's wrong baby girl, you in any pain? Let me go grab the Doc," he said with concern. He checked each monitor making sure that I was alright.

"I'm fine, Daddy. I'm just tired all of a sudden." I snatched my hand away from Christian and used both hands to clutch my father's. I held on for dear life. I didn't want him to leave me alone in the room with Christian. I wasn't sure what she would do.

"Don't you go getting sleepy on me and I just got here. You've been sleep long enough. You go ahead and get the doctor, Mr. Robbins. I'll stay right here with my girl," Christian faked excitingly.

"She's been through a lot Christian, you both have. I know you both have a lot of talking to do, but tonight is not the time. Remember, she's lost a baby. Just watch her for me. I'm going to get Dr. Scott now," my father said as he walked towards the door.

I wanted to scream, don't go! He knew that seeing Christian made me nervous, he just didn't know the real reason why. As soon as my father walked in the hallway she turned towards me with an evil smirk on her face. Within seconds, Christian and I were eye to eye as she stood over me.

"This ain't over bitch! If you breathe a word to anyone about me shooting you, I will make sure I kill your ass next time."

"Why are you doing this?" I whined. The loud beeping sounds on my machines and monitors went ballistic. "I already said I was sorry," I whispered back to her.

"I thought if I scared your ass you would stop. But nothing worked. Not my friend on the elevator at your office, or none of my tricks. Nothing! "

I thought back to the incidents that had scared the hell out of me. I never would have thought that it had anything to do with her. "Christian, you really need some help. I'm going to call your mom and let her know what's going on."

"Huh!" She laughed then sat back in the chair, finally allowing me to breathe. "She hates your mother just as much as I fucking hate you. She would do anything to bring the Robbins to their knees." She threw her head back in more laughter.

"What?" I gasped loudly.

"Yes, she told me personally that she despises your mother and father. Besides, this plan has been well thought out. This is just the beginning of what I'm going to do to you, sweetie."

"Get out of my room, Christian!" I tried to yell at her. My heart thumped with excruciating pain as I became ill with nervousness. She laughed again and stood, then leaned over me again, but this time clutching her Michael Kor's bag. My breathing intensified for fear of what she had inside. She attempted to kiss my face as I turned away from her.

"I'll be back and next time, I'll make sure to use this."

She pulled a gun out from her bag and pointed it towards me. I quickly pushed the button to the nurse's station after hearing her say, "Nothing can keep me from killing you, Tracey." Christian laughed evilly again and put the weapon away as she walked out the door.

Chapter 23

"Tracey are you sleeping, its Dr. Scott?" he asked, walking in my room.

Of course, I jumped at first from being paranoid. "No, I'm up. Just sitting here thinking, that's all," I told him. I attempted to sit up but a migraine beat rapidly through my brain. I winced at the pain and groaned slightly. He ran to my side, checking my vitals. I could smell his cologne and I had to admit, his scent was very arousing. I tried to smooth my matted hair down with my hand but he pushed it away.

"Take it easy. You've been through a lot. You should expect some strange feelings that didn't use to occur."

"When do you think I will be able to go home?"

He laughed slightly. "You're healing from gun shot wounds Tracey, and were out for over eighteen hours. I think we should take your recovery a bit slower than you would like." He smiled showing that perfect smile of his. "Realistically, you won't be able to leave for a few days," he said with concern in his voice.

"I was afraid you were going to say that. I need some air," I whined. "I feel so confined."

"How about this? If your vitals are strong later on tonight, I can possibly sneak you up to the rooftop for some fresh air." He hit me with that grin again that warmed my heart.

Damn, Dr. Scott was fine as hell and flirting with me. "Well, I don't have any clothes. I certainly can't go up there in the middle of winter with a hospital gown on."

"You let me worry about that. I know you are a high maintenance kind of woman. I got you covered."

"Would you really do that for me? Why?" I had a hard time believing that people would do things out of the kindness of their heart. I certainly never did.

"The question is, why not? It's not every day that a

woman like you is shot and left for dead. When I heard the story, my heart immediately went out to you. So, what size do you wear?"

Dr. Scott was truly remarkable. He was going out of his way to make me feel better. And it was working. "Seeing as how I hadn't eaten, I'm not sure. I use to be about a six on a good day, so a size four would probably be perfect now." I started to feel self-conscious. I had been in the hospital and hadn't had a facial, pedicure, or manicure. I didn't even want to think about the condition of my hair. I needed someone to work out a makeover for me.

He didn't seem to mind though, because I saw a wide smile as it formed at the corners of his mouth, and it made me smile. He was definitely feeling me, and I had to admit that I was feeling him too. But I knew that we could only be friends because Tez and I were already in love.

"So, it's a date! Well, not a date. I'm sorry I didn't mean to imply," he nervously stammered. "Your father would kill me."

"I know what you meant. What about my hair? It hasn't been combed in a week. You must really feel sorry for me to ask me out on a date," I teased.

"Actually, I think that you are absolutely beautiful the way that you are. You're the perfect woman in every way."

"You only saying that because you don't know me."

"I'm saying it because I mean it. From what I do know, you are a beautiful woman. Just caught up in a superficial life." He held my hand and squeezed it tight.

The gesture was a friendly one, but the look in his eyes said he wanted more than a friendship. But why me? "Dr. Scott, I don't know what to say. You have no idea the kind of mess I'm caught up in. It is beyond superficial, it's actually kind of nuts." I wanted to pour my guts out to him, telling him Christian shot me, and that I'd killed Megan in self defense. But of course I didn't. "My life is so crazy. I don't know what to say."

"The first thing you should say is, Chris. Please leave the, Dr. Scott, to someone who doesn't know me at all. I think we're past the point of either of us being formal with each other."

We didn't really know each other that well. Since my father took him under his wing, we'd only seen each other in a, hi and bye fashion. "Okay, it's just a habit to call you, Dr. Scott. We've never really talked," I explained.

"Well, now we have. You need someone looking out for you, obviously. I happen to think of myself as a ferocious body guard." He flexed what little muscles he had and made a Hulk Hogan face.

I laughed at him and realized that his friendship was something that I wanted in my life. "Okay Chris, but just so we don't get confused, I'm unavailable. All I can offer at this time is friendship. And I really would like that."

"Ahhhh, would that be because of your mystery man, Tez?"

"Yes, how do you know that?"

"I heard you mumble his name this morning when I came to check on you. You've been here a week and I have yet to see him."

"What business is that of yours?" I asked defensively. I had no idea that Tez hadn't stopped by to see me. I assumed when I was out after I initially got shot that he'd come by. That little piece of information had pissed me off.

"All I know is that if you were mine, I would be by your side faithfully."

I could still see the look of doubt in his eyes, as well as genuine concern. He wanted me, and as good as it felt, the last thing that I needed was another man in my life. "I'm not feeling so well. I would like if you leave so that I can rest."

"Tracey, I didn't mean to offend you. All I'm saying is that you need someone to love you the correct way," Chris spoke.

"Who would that be, nigga, yo ass? That's all me right there and the loving don't get no better than this," Tez said as he strolled in like his ass owned the place.

Tez walked right up to Chris ready for a fight. Only in my life did stuff like that happen. Drama was my first, second, and last name.

"Go head and bounce Dr. whatever the hell your name is. Does the board know that you in here hitting on one of your patients?" Tez was pissed as he spoke.

I could see the vein as it popped out of his neck. This scene reminded me of the night that Tez and Chuck were about to fight. My mouth wanted to tell Chris to leave so that I could be with my man, but something in my heart told me to let him stay.

"Oh, so let me guess, you are the infamous boyfriend.

Wow, she must've picked you out of a line up."

Chris was not intimidated at all. The proper doctor talk was gone and a side of him I never saw before had emerged. It turned me on to see him stand up to Tez like that. But my heart still belonged to Tez, a man who hopped in and out of my life every few weeks.

"Whatever the fuck your name is, I suggest yo lil corny ass bounce before yo own peeps have to operate on you." Tez had calmed his tone a little; I guess he noticed that Chris was no sucka.

"Bust a move if you want to. With your little, I-wanna- be-a-gangsta-ass. I've been that b-boy, you trying to be. I just had common sense to educate myself and bust my ass so I could be nothing like you!" Chris spat. "None of this is good for Tracey."

"Man, get yo ass on out of here before something bad happens to you," Tez yelled.

"So you making threats now?" Chris shook his head at Tez and then turned to me with a sorrowful look in his eyes. He never even waited for a response from Tez. "I'm really surprised Tracey that you would stoop this low and call him your man. You're selling yourself short. As soon as you realize that, the happier you will be."

With that said, Chris looked Tez up and down, and then walked out the room. Tez and I stared at each other for a few seconds without any words being spoken. I could feel the anger that surged through his body.

"What the…" he started to say but was interrupted by a knock on the door.

"Come in!" I yelled, relieved that a visitor had come. I would have to deal with Tez another time. As soon as the woman walked in with the cheap, plain business suit and square toed shoes, I knew she was someone that I didn't want to talk to.

"Tracey Robbins?" she asked, pulling up a chair and sitting beside me.

She flashed her badge and a huge smile as she flipped her golden braids to the back. She was here to question me about being shot. I knew that the police would turn up sooner or later.

"Yes, I'm Tracey. That's kind of a given, don't you think?" I made a gesture with my hands doing a virtual tour of the hospital room and my surroundings. "Who else would I be, laid up in a hospital bed assigned to someone else?"

"I just have to ask you a few questions ma'am," she said with the slight frown that had formed upon her lips. "Do you have some time to answer them?"

"Sure, it's not like I'm going anywhere anytime soon," I said, looking over at Tez.

He was still standing there pissed off and almost looked nervous. I wondered if he was carrying anything illegal and now afraid that he would get locked up. That was the downside of falling in love with a thug.

"Ms. Robbins, the night before you were shot, where were you?"

"What does that have to do with anything?" Tez asked before I could even get a chance to.

"We just need to have a little background information before we begin our questioning," the detective replied as she looked Tez up and down.

"Like I was saying, where were you?"

"I was in my room at the Four Seasons. Tez and I had just gone out to dinner," I replied nervously.

I had tried to push that night out of my head. That would go down as one of the worst days of my life.

"Do you know Megan Lewis, Ms. Robbins?"

"Of course I do. We used to go to school together."

"When was the last time you saw her?" The detective fired the question at me as soon as I had finished my last syllable.

"Aye, ain't that ole girl who was doing all that talking that night? Thick lil light skin chick with the fat ass? She was with that lame ass dude Chuck Jones," Tez said.

I looked at him and rolled my eyes. If he was with me, how in the hell did he have time to check out Megan's anatomy.

"Well sir, whoever you are, I don't know about her ass, but I'm assuming you are speaking of the same person. I've heard that she was Mr. Jones' mistress. Is that correct Ms. Robbins?" she asked me with a slight smirk on her face.

How the hell would she know? I wondered. My gut told me that I would be in handcuffs soon.

"What are you trying to say that you are apparently afraid to say?" Tez kept butting in and I wasn't able to get a word in for myself.

"I'm just stating what I've heard. I don't see how three women can run in the same circle and they're all sleeping with the same man."

"First of all Megan has never been in my circle," I meekly replied. "And how would you know any man that I've slept with, Detective…?" I began snapping my fingers. "I didn't catch your name." I was starting to get nervous because I knew that she would eventually ask me about Megan's murder in front of Tez.

"The name is Detective Bailey. And apparently Megan is not in anyone's circle right now. Her mother has been trying to reach her and it seems she can't get her on the line," the detective said as she flipped through her notes.

"Well, I haven't seen her. In case you haven't noticed, I was shot and I'm now in the hospital," I said sarcastically.

Whatever the detective was trying to sniff out, she was not going to get from me.

"Y'all should be talking to that fool Chuck. He shot Tracey. Shit, he probably shot Megan too. Sucka-ass," Tez mumbled.

"We've already talked to Mr. Jones. We were just trying to reach out to some friends of hers to see if they knew anything," she said while standing. "If you can think of anything or hear from her Ms. Robbins, make sure you let me know. And your name is, Sir?"

"Cortez."

"Cortez who?" she replied nastily.

"If I'm not under arrest it doesn't matter," Tez shot back.

She reached out to put her card in my hand but Tez quickly snatched it.

"That won't be necessary, she already told you that they didn't run in the same circle," he angrily said.

Typical black man from the hood in my book, none of them trusted the police.

"It's ok. She's just doing her job. But he is right. I don't talk to her so I doubt she will contact me."

"You folks have a good day. You take care, Tracey, and sorry to hear about you losing your baby," Detective Bailey replied as she walked out the door.

Chapter 24

I sat back on the bed with my eyes as big as watermelons. Finally, I breathed a sigh of relief. I hadn't expected for Megan's mother to check up on her from across the waters. I was thankful that my questioning session was over and that I wasn't about to be taken out in handcuffs. I didn't know what to say or think. That detective had taken me for a loop. So, I opened my arms to invite Tez into a hug since the detective spilled the beans about me losing the baby. I was hoping I would get the chance to tell him myself. Everything just happened so quickly. He seemed to be pissed with me and just stood off to the side. I guess his ego was bruised once again from the detective insinuating that I'd slept with Chuck. Men were fickle like that. Here I was shot and lying in a hospital bed on the brink of death. He hadn't even had the decency to call and see if I was okay, but now he was mad.

"Tez, thanks for looking out for me with that detective. I'm glad you were here."

"Forget the detective. Let's get back to you and that doctor. Yo ass looked like you was real happy when I walked in," he said angrily.

"Yeah, I'm happy that I didn't die. From what I heard, you haven't come to see me anyway." It was a statement but it also was a question of why hadn't he.

"I can't tell you missed me. You all smiling in Doogie Howser's face and shit."

"I was not smiling in his face Tez. We were just talking."

"When you wake up any damn way? Christian said you were in a mini-coma. But I get up here, and you cheesing and a grinning and shit." Tez wouldn't look at me as he talked. He had become extra emotional. "She didn't tell me that mothafucka Chuck killed my seed."

"How did Christian tell you anything? You don't even know

her. Where and when did you see her?" I asked in disbelief. Was Tez in on this plan with Christian and Shanice? After all, I had met him through Shanice. I'd never found the time to introduce Christian and Tez so what kind of game was Christian playing? She must have contacted him personally and confirmed what Megan had told him at the restaurant.

"Umm, she called Shanice, and Shanice gave her my number. Damn, why you asking so many questions anyway? Can a nigga breathe without you sweating him?" He stood at the foot of the bed and looked at me with a scowl on his face.

He had cut his hair low and was wearing the hell out of his jeans that fit just right across the butt. As foul as the words were that flew out of his mouth, he was still looking sexy as hell. Too sexy for me to be paranoid thinking that he was in on some scheme against me. "Tez, baby I'm not sweating you. I was just wondering, how she called you. I didn't even know she knew how to contact Shanice. What did she say?" I asked as if it was no big deal. Really on the inside I was dying to know what he knew.

"I didn't talk to her personally. She left a message, said you was in the hospital. I touch back down and find out yo ass been shot by that nigga Chuck."

I looked at him skeptically, trying to see if I could decipher if he was lying or telling the truth. If Tez was in fact the, *he* that Christian and Shanice were talking about, I didn't know what I would do. I quickly pushed the thought out of my mind because I knew he wouldn't do me like that. We were in love.

"Where in the hell have you been anyway?" I changed the subject quickly. I didn't want to get off into the whole messing with Chuck situation.

"Yo ass foul as hell Tracey. I just can't believe the shit you pulled. You got me looking like a damn fool out here." He slammed his hand down on the window sill.

"Tez, you come in here acting a damn fool without even hearing my side of the story." I folded my arms in frustration.

"I know the truth. You were getting smashed by Christian's husband. She even showed Shanice a few pictures of you and him. From what I hear, the baby may not have been mines anyway," he said.

"Don't you dare stand there and insult me like that." My feelings were hurt." You know damn well that was your baby. Do you know how bad I felt, waking up and realizing that my baby was not inside of me!" I screamed at him. I got shot, Tez! And lost my baby all in the same day!"

He paused for a moment as if he felt the pain of our baby really being dead. As quick as the emotion came, he swiftly replaced it with an angry scowl. "Here I thought I had a classy lady, but you were freaking your best friend's man. Wow! You were so busy with your nose turned up at me, but look at how you living."

"I don't have to justify myself to you, Tez. Especially, not about something that happened before you. I knew I was wrong, so I stopped messing with him."

"Nawl, fuck that. That's why ole boy's chest was on swole at the restaurant. You was his side bitch, out with another man," he screamed at me.

"Who the hell are you to try and judge me? I'm sure you have some foul secrets yourself." I stared at him with the intent to burn a whole through him.

"Look, I just stopped by to make sure you was ok. I have some business to take care of."

He inched closer to the door. He had no intentions on staying here with me. I knew it.

"So that's it? Just like that you turn on me and I'm not classy, let you tell it. I'm the biggest freak you ever met? What in the hell do you know about class anyway? Everybody has a past. My damn baby is dead, and you sit there and try to degrade me." I was in pure disbelief as he continued to act like a jerk.

He thumbed through his Blackberry phone, completely disinterested in the conversation. "Look, I ain't come here to argue. Like I said, I checked on you, you not dead so I can just be about my business now."

His words cut my pride deep, but I wouldn't give him the satisfaction of knowing I was hurt. "That's real low as hell of you to take cheap ass shots at me, Tez. How are we supposed to be together, but yet, you can't even sit up here with me for more than ten damn minutes?"

"None of that shit is my problem."

"Our child is dead damn it! You sitting there like it doesn't bother you is disturbing to me." I started crying.

"Tracey, that's just it, we aren't together at all. We was just fucking. You do too much for me. There is no way I can be with someone whose name is popping like yours."

"Why are you being so cruel? It was a mistake!" My tears flowed like the nile.

"St. Louis is too small for me to try and wife a hoe like you. We can still kick it on the low every now and then, but all that other lovey dovey shit? Nawl! I can't get down with that at all. So I'ma be on my way. I'll holla!"

Tez stormed out the room before I could say anything else. He left me speechless. I wondered, how in the hell our conversation turned into him letting me go? Who in the hell did he think he was? He came in here and tried to judge me when he knew he was beneath me. I was a Robbins. And why was he so defensive about me asking him questions? If there was one thing I knew, a hit dog would holler and I thought I had just run his ass over. Things didn't add up with Tez. Something just wasn't right. Mr. Stevens had a lot of explaining to do.

I grabbed my cell phone and dialed fast. I knew she probably couldn't answer but would at least get the message. "Hey Rayven, this is Tracey. I know you're shocked that I'm able to call. I read your card and thanks for the flowers. Please get back to St. Louis soon. Look, I'm in a little situation; I need you to investigate someone for me..." I continued hoping that my plan worked.

Chapter 25

I felt ridiculous sitting in an Alexander McQueen ballroom gown in a wheelchair with a shawl covering my shoulders as Chris rolled me slowly up the ramp. Each tiny bump caused minor pain in my stomach. I was about to tell him that I'd rather just lay in my hospital bed when he opened the door leading to the roof. It was absolutely beautiful, causing me to gasp slightly.

"Oh, Chris. I don't know what to say," I said feeling like he'd saved me from killing myself.

The edges of the roof was covered with tiny white Christmas lights and green garland. He had set up a small table that was decorated beautifully with white lilies and tea light candles.

"I can't take all the credit for this. The hospital had already decorated for the holiday season but the table was all me," he said while smiling.

"This is the nicest thing anyone has ever done for me. How did you know I liked lilies?" I asked surprisingly.

"Well, seeing as how all the flowers that came here were lilies, I figured it must have been your favorite."

He rolled me to the table and I quickly picked up a flower and placed my nose to it. The aroma coming from it was one of my favorites.

"You really do think of everything. You're the perfect man," I said as I pulled the space heater he had set under the table, closer to me. It was roughly fifty degrees but I ignored the chill spreading through my body until I grimaced as another pain shot up my stomach.

"Are you ok, Tracey? If you're not feeling well, we can finish this in your room." I smiled at him to reassure him that I was fine. He looked at me skeptically as he sat down at the table across from me. "Tracey, I've been dying to ask you a question and I don't want you to get mad," he said.

I sighed heavily and silently hoped that whatever the question was, it wouldn't weigh me down. I nodded my head and he wasted no time continuing.

"Is Tez the man you really want to spend the rest of your life with?"

"I don't want to go there, Dr. Scott. This is supposed to be a happy dinner, not a depressing one." I had been three days and I'd done a pretty good job of erasing Tez from my mind. Once he mentioned him, I had started missing him all over again. Tez had texted me this morning and said that he would have to lay low for a while. I didn't want to get down in the dumps, but couldn't help it.

"I told you to call me Chris. And this is not about you going there, because you think I'm making you. I think you should go there, because you are worth so much more than that loser. Don't you see that?" he asked.

"We're just a complicated story that only I get. You haven't even gotten a chance to know him."

"Tracey, you can't be that naïve and sheltered, that you don't see this guy is on some bull with you." Chris stated facts that I didn't want to hear.

"Not that I have to explain myself to you, but he's the first man I have ever loved willingly. My mother has controlled my life for so long. Demanding that I date such and such, or go on a date with whomever she chose. Tez is the first man that I picked for myself. He's all mine, even if he disappears often. I understand his lifestyle, whatever that may be." I spoke with attitude.

I couldn't believe we were having this conversation again. We barely knew each other. How dare he intrude in my life like that?

"Do you really? I mean seriously, do you know what could happen if you get caught up in his life? I grew up around that lifestyle, and let me be the first to tell you, it isn't as glamorous as it seems."

"If you plan on lecturing me all night, I can go back downstairs to sleep." I released the locks on the wheelchair prepared to leave. I thought about the long journey back to my room and decided against it.

"I'm not trying to lecture you, sweetie. I've seen young women just like you, get used and abused trying to understand this lifestyle. Women who are a lot stronger than you, torn to shreds, by men like Tez." Chris watched me intently as he spoke. He wanted his words to sink into my brain. I just wanted him to shut up.

"So, you think I can't handle myself? You think I need a chaperone or someone's permission in order for me to live? Contrary to popular belief, I'm not some weak little duckling, Chris."

"No, that's not what I'm saying at all. From what I can tell you can handle yourself pretty well. You sure are feisty as hell. But that's part of the reason why I like being around you. I want nothing but the best for you Tracey, and I know in my heart the best is me," Chris confessed.

He stood up then took one step toward me. Before I knew it, the air that once separated us, was completely gone. He kneeled closely beside me. His breath was warm and minty as he slowly exhaled his air around me. I closed my eyes and allowed his Creed cologne to work its way through my being. He was all man and I felt myself wanting to feel him inside me.

I closed my eyes and tried to block the image. I needed some space before I exploded. A man was something I did not want right now. Men had a way of getting me in hard, fast trouble. What were the chances I would find a great man after being shot? Did I have an, I need a man, magnet stuck to me? Even when I wasn't looking, they still found me.

"Chris I can't do this, as much as it seems like it's not a real relationship, I'm involved with someone. Plus, I'm no good for you. I don't want you to get hurt. You've seen what kind of drama follows me. Karma is no friend of mine." I looked at the ground so Chris wouldn't see the tears in my eyes.

"Let me be the judge of your worth, Tracey. I think you are everything that I deserve, everything that I want and need. I want to take care of you, and love you." Chris grabbed my hand and started kissing and nibbling on it. By the time he reached my collar bone, my insides were soaked.

"I want to love these arms, this neck, your eyes, your nose, your mouth and all the way down to your toes. I use to watch you coming and leaving the hospital after talking to your dad, and I would just stare in awe. I'd never seen anything in this world so beautiful."

"I don't know if I should be flattered or nervous that you are a stalker." I laughed to lighten the mood.

"Intrigued by you, yes. But I'm nowhere near a stalker. Let

me be the one who worries about you. Let me be the one who picks up the pieces of your life, and to help place them back together." He stared at me so hard it scared me.

"Chris I..." he placed his fingers over my mouth and silenced me.

"If your answer is, not right now, I'd rather not hear it. I am patient, and I'm sure in time you will realize what I already know. You and I belong together. I plan on doing everything in my power to show you that. For now I want you to get well."

He planted a soft kiss on my lips and hugged me tight. If only he and I would have met a few months earlier things would've been different. He was perfect, a complete gentleman. Why couldn't Tez be like Chris? Why wasn't he the one here comforting me? There was no reason I should have to question if Tez loved me or not. Chris was a good man who was willing to show me. Someone worth something actually thought I was worth fighting for.

"Come here I want to show you something?" Chris broke me out of my thoughts and helped me out of the wheelchair. He walked me slowly across the gravel on the roof with him touching the bandages around my stomach gently. With each step, I leaned more on him than my own two feet.

"This is where I come when I want to think. I love to watch people when they don't know anyone is watching," he said.

"I knew you were a stalker," I teased.

We both laughed causing me to feel the pain of my wounds. I grabbed my stomach, feeling slightly weak from the pain. He gently grabbed me in his arms and lifted me off the ground. I held onto his neck tightly, afraid that he would drop me.

"I got you. I swear I won't let you go," he whispered into my ear. "I promised your father I would take care of you. He's been calling me all day every day." He laughed then turned our bodies towards downtown. Among the lights and buildings, I could see a small glimpse of the Arch. I had never realized how busy the city was at night. Everyone was moving around in a hurry to live their lives. That use to be me, so in a rush to get nowhere. I was finally at a standstill, and in the best moment of my life. ..not worried about money or fame…just being normal and with Chris.

Chapter 26

"Good afternoon, Tracey. My, don't we look well rested and relaxed? You're healing well."

I prayed I was dreaming again. There was no way in hell Christian had come back to see me. I sat up in my hospital bed ready to defend myself. She hadn't been back in over five days. But little did she know I'd gotten stronger and would attempt to fight her if I had to.

"Christian, I don't know what you have going on in your life, but I suggest you get some help." I was livid, but I didn't want to raise my blood pressure. Besides, I didn't know if she would pull out a weapon again, but this time following through.

"Or what? You'll shoot me with the same gun I used to shoot you? Tracey you are laughable at best honey. I guess losing that bastard child, did a number on your little scary ass brain."

Why did she have to bring that up again? I'd silently been dealing with my grief alone, day after day not saying much to others about losing my child. But here she was throwing it in my face.

Smiling.
Grinning.
Wickedly.

It was like I was seeing Christian for who she really was. She seemed to be a different person, far different than the person once considered my good friend. "You wanted to kill me so you'd finally get noticed, huh? How did that turn out for you?" I asked with sarcasm.

"It's working pretty well. Everyone is talking bad about you. They now know what I've known for some time now. That you're a no good slut," she said while leaning back on her heels.

"Funny how I sleep with your husband and yet everyone is

coming here to see me," I said sarcastically. Once again I wanted to hurt her for hurting me. "And just in case you didn't know, your family was here praying by my side the other day, and they are talking about me on all the blogs. Nobody is talking about you still." I wanted my words to cut Christian deep. I couldn't shoot her, but I wanted her to feel some sort of pain.

"If I'm evil and deranged, it's only because you deserve it!" she spat. "Tracey this and Tracey that. All my damn life, I had to hear that. I use to laugh because everyone didn't know the real you like I did. They all thought you were perfect, and they loved you for it. I knew how flawed you were though, and I never betrayed you." Christian threw more evil looks my way than before.

"Look, I never meant to hurt you Christian. And I feel horrible about messing with Chuck." *How many more times would I have to explain that to her?*

"Of all the men in St Louis, why sleep with my husband, Tracey? You just had to have my man, because that was something you didn't have. You wanted to prove to yourself, you still thought you were better than me."

"Christian, it wasn't like that. I swear, I never meant to hurt you. I really don't know why I did it, but it had nothing to do with you. I didn't even consider you while I was doing it."

"What kind of friend are you? All those phony ass conversations about Chuck and who he was messing with; you knew firsthand how he was living foul." Christian moved closer to me causing my nerves to rattle a bit. She seemed sincere as she cried like a newborn, but I didn't trust her at all.

"Believe me when I say, we are over and I would never go down that road again. He's all yours, I swear. Can we just put all of this behind us?"

She didn't seem happy with my answer.

"Wow! Thank you so much for giving me my husband back. See Tracey, the problem with you, is that you can't understand how the real world works. You go from man to man, ruining lives on purpose. People are tired of you taking advantage of them," she screamed loudly and picked up her purse.

"How many times do you have to keep saying it, Christian? If I'm such a bad person, why won't everyone just leave me alone? I won't sit here and let you talk down to me. If you came here to make me feel like shit, you have accomplished that." I pressed the button for the nurse's station. I wanted her out immediately.

"You have all the answers don't you? So riddle me this Batman, tell me why you didn't know that I paid Shanice and Tez to play your dumb ass? Yeah, that was all me. How do you think the paper got that picture of you and Tez?" Christian pulled pictures of her and Tez out of her purse and placed them in front of me.

Oh my God, How could you do that to me? You knew sending that picture of us to the paper would ruin my reputation." I already knew that Shanice was in on the plan, but I had no clue that Tez would do this to me as well. I now knew who the 'he' was that they were talking about in my room the other day. It was confirmed. And to see pictures of Christian and Tez hugged up made me ill. My head began to spin and my mouth was dry as hell. Christian had obviously gotten me good.

"Tracey, Tracey, Tracey," she chanted, shaking her head. Considering the fact, you were sleeping with my husband, me fucking Tez is nothing, right?"

I felt so betrayed. "How could you Christian?" Surely she could see the pain in my eyes.

"Oh and one more thing," she added, stepping away from my bed. "There's also a video circulating out there. Your father should have seen the flick by now, I sent an anonymous package to all the doctors, right here at the hospital. He is sure to die from embarrassment when he sees you."

Christian flipped open a pack of cigarettes and lit one like a pro. Everything about her was different. I didn't even know she knew how to light a cigarette, let alone smoke one.

"Christian, what in the hell is wrong with you? A video? And you sleeping with Tez? Don't you know he loves me?"

"Girl, he's acting, doing exactly what I tell him to do." She laughed victoriously. "I've paid him a nice sum of money, to get some dirt on the great Tracey. And as far as I know, every war has casualties honey. Too bad it was a baby bastard that died." Christian cackled loudly at her own joke.

"Excuse me miss, I'm going to have to ask you to leave this hospital now, before I call the authorities. And smoking is strictly prohibited inside of any hospital," Chris said as he stood in the door way. He looked at Christian with pure hate while I winced in sorrow. He had never seen Christian face to face before, but wasn't pleased with what stood before him.

"Who in the hell died and made you boss?" Christian had her hands on her hips. "In case you didn't know, my daddy runs this hospital. I can do whatever the hell I want to," Christian smugly replied.

"I'm Dr. Scott, and big deal your daddy runs this place. Smoking in here is dangerous and illegal, plus Tracey is my patient and you will either get out on your own, or get thrown the hell out. The choice is yours." Chris was unfazed by Christian.

"Ummm, you sure do seem real comfortable protecting her. Oh let me guess, you have fallen for her spell, too. Well let me give you a piece of advice Dr. Scott, you may want to run fast from her. You wouldn't want to be laughed at for being with the biggest slut ever to walk the streets of St. Louis." Christian continued to flap at the lips.

Before I knew it, I was crying uncontrollably. The realization that Tez had played me, hurt like hell and wouldn't stop flashing in my mind. The shock of being betrayed by so many people was enough to kill me. Chris walked over to me and placed his hand on my shoulder.

"I already asked you to leave Christian. Don't make me throw you out. Clearly your visit is upsetting my patient, so there's no need for you to visit again," Chris spoke in a low tone over my head.

Hearing him speak angrily scared the hell out of me. He wasn't one to play with when he was mad.

"I'll leave for now, but trust and believe, I'll be back. I'll settle the score this time Tracey."

Christian pranced out the room and didn't look back. I could hear her Prada heels clicking on the floor in the hallway. I couldn't even look at Chris as the tears fell from my face. I should've taken that moment to tell Chris that Christian was the one who shot me, but I didn't, I simply cried.

"Tracey, I heard the whole conversation. I wanted to step in earlier, but I wanted to see if you could handle it yourself. Christian is really crazy, and she needs some serious help," he said as he pulled me into his arms. I placed my head on his shoulder and had never felt so safe.

"I'm just in disbelief. How could this be happening to me?

I'm not a bad person," I continued to cry.

"I had a feeling that Tez was a bad guy but for your sake, I didn't want it to be true."

I knew that something was off about Tez, but I never guessed this. How could he do this to me? I gave him my all. I risked everything to be with him, and he played me for a fool. I need to get as far away from those people as possible."

"He's a damn fool, I know that much. There's no way in hell that I would ever let something as good as you, slip through my fingers," he softly replied.

We stared at each other for a few minutes. The sincerity in his eyes caused mine to tear up again. I was tired of crying so I quickly wiped the tears away. I had to become stronger, like my mother would be if she were in this situation. "Chris, is it possible for me to leave here tonight? I have to get out of here, if I stay another moment I will die."

"You won't die Tracey, because I won't let you give up on yourself like that. Where are you going to go anyway? Not trying to be in your business, but your parent's home doesn't seem like a good idea. I've heard about your mother bashing your name around."

"I haven't been staying with them for awhile anyway. I'm staying in the presidential suite at the Four Seasons. But I'm sure my bill is super high by now. I just want to leave and get away from everyone and everything, please release me tonight," I pleaded.

"I know it may be short notice but why don't you come with me for a while. It's cheaper and will be safer. I have the perfect place for you to relax and get your strength back. I promised to take care of you, and I mean that."

Just like that, Chris made the decision. I was more than eager to go with him. He was good for me and I needed him more than what I had first initially realized. I quickly began gathering what little belongings I had at the hospital with me, mostly the items that my dad dropped off when he visited. Chris stepped outside so that he could do his final rounds to finish his shift. I was beyond happy that my life looked like it was about to start taking a turn back in a positive direction. Between Megan's death and being shot, I had all the excitement that I could possibly take.

I sat in the chair and silently thanked God for sending an

angel like Chris into my life. Finally things were back like they should be and nothing and no one would be able to stop my flow.

"How are you today Ms. Robbins?"

Startled by the voice, I almost flipped myself out of the chair. I looked up at the woman and just glared at her. She was the same detective who had visited me before. This time she was also with a fat man in a trench coat, typical detective gear. All that was missing was the donut.

"I'm fine. Wh- wh- what- are- you doing here?" I stammered nervously over my words, then rising out of the chair.

"We found Megan and we thought you'd want to know that personally," Detective Bailey remarked.

The man took out a handkerchief and wiped at the sweat that was profusely pouring from his bald head.

"You did? That's good news. I'm glad to hear that," I replied trying to remain nonchalant.

"Glad to hear it huh? I doubt that seriously," he said as he put the soaking wet handkerchief back into his pocket.

"Why would you doubt that? Megan was my friend."

"I thought you said you two don't run in the same circle," Bailey interjected.

"I mean, we weren't friends but we were cordial to one another," I lied.

"From what we hear, you two weren't friends at all. In fact, you had a fight the night she was last seen," the fat detective replied.

"Megan had tried to embarrass me, but that doesn't mean I wanted to see her dead."

"You did want her dead though, right? She knew your little secret that you thought wouldn't come out. You were also sleeping with your best friend's husband!" he yelled while stepping closer inside my personal space.

I backed up closer into the corner. I was slightly terrified that they knew that I had disposed of her body. How could I get myself out of this? "Well, as you can see, everyone knows about the affair. They have been talking about it on the radio and in the paper. So why would I want her dead because of that."

"Maybe you killed her before you were shot?" the woman suggested.

"You can't prove that. Maybe Chuck shot her just like he

shot me." I felt bad for throwing Chuck under the bus when I knew he hadn't shot either one of us. But it was better him staying in jail versus me going.

"She wasn't shot. She died from blunt force trauma." The male detective continued to scream at me and I was on the brink of tears.

"I don't know what happened to her, all I know is I was just shot. Why are you treating me like a low life ass criminal?" I screamed at them both.

"What the hell is going on in here?" Chris asked as he rushed into the room.

"I don't know, they keep asking me about someone killing Megan. I just want them to leave me alone. Please make them go away," I cried into Chris' chest.

"You heard her. You both need to leave now. You're upsetting my patient," Chris said in a calm, forceful voice. He wrapped his arms tightly around my body.

"We're leaving, no need to get your panties in a bunch. Just remember, Ms. Robbins, we are watching you. Make sure you don't leave town because I have a feeling this is not over," the male detective said as he winked at me and walked out the door.

"What was that all about?" Chris asked me as soon as the door closed.

"I have no clue. I don't even see how they could assume that I could kill someone."

"It's ok. I'll make sure they never bother you again. I know that you could never do something like that," Chris reassured me.

I smiled at him but on the inside I felt horrible for lying. There was no way I could ever tell him or anyone else that I really did kill Megan.

Chapter 27

As soon as I left the hospital life got one hundred percent better. I kept thanking Chris for saving me over and over again as we stood in the foyer of his home. I breathed a sigh of relief while taking in the decor. Chris would make someone a great husband, but I kept reminding myself about his promise to me, "No strings attached," is what he said. He just wanted to make sure I got back in good health.

"Wow, this place is awesome. It's so peaceful and serene here."

I stared at the house in awe. True, I grew up in a mansion. But it was not as beautiful and homely as his small cabin style home.

"My father and his brothers built this house for my mom back in the 60's. She loved the backyard because she could plant almost anything back there. I keep it up in memory of her," he said.

Chris stood with a proud look on his face as he continued to show me around. He was dressed down from his normal suit or white jacket attire. I could really appreciate looking at him in jogging pants, a tee shirt, and a pair of Jordans. "There are so many different sides to you Chris, it's like you are almost too good to be true. I don't deserve someone like you to look after me. I just want to thank you."

"You deserve everything good that could possibly come your way. You just have to realize and accept that into your life. How many times do I have to tell you that? No matter what anyone else says, you are a special woman," he said lovingly.

He didn't say who, but I knew he was thinking about my mother. She'd showed up at the hospital just a day before and made it clear that I was not welcomed in her home. She told me right in front of Chris and two nurses that I had embarrassed the family to no end. The video that Christian sent out was the nail in the coffin. Not only had the hospital staff received it, but it was sent to the local papers and blogs as well. Mother quickly had every item that I had left at her house, including my dishes, boxed up and sent to the hospital in boxes, which Chris immediately put into storage for me.

Unbeknownst to me that was why Chris offered to take me home with him. The word traveled quickly around the hospital that my mother was furious and ashamed of me. Chris' generosity could have been love, but I knew it was probably more like pity. I was a little reluctant at first, but he assured me that I wouldn't have to do anything that I wasn't ready for. No commitments, I kept reiterating.

"Tracey, I think it would be a good idea if you took a nap for a while. You've had a rather long day, don't you think? You look tired."

I could tell he was still in doctor mode. He felt my head for a fever and looked into my eyes for weariness, I assumed. Then out of the blue, he kissed my forehead. "Are you trying to say, I look ugly Dr. Scott.?" I laughed it off, but my insecurities started to kick in.

"You know I would never tell you anything like that," he replied.

I tried to smooth down my nappy hair but he removed my hand and kissed it, just as he had in the hospital. "I'm going to go and get my hair done tomorrow," I announced. "This is the first time in life that I've gone this long without seeing my hair stylist."

"Are you sure you're ready for that, Tracey?"

"It's just the beauty shop. What's the worst that can happen?"

"I'm not saying it like that, you just need to get a lot of rest. Your body has been through the fire, it needs to restore itself. Besides, you've been living a life where the outside appearance counts. I like the real Tracey, where it's what's on the inside."

I smiled. He had a point. I did need to change my way of thinking. "You're right Chris. I know I probably should lie down, but I really can't sleep now. I didn't want to tell you, but I constantly have nightmares about the night I was shot."

"You should have told me that before now Tracey. I'll prescribe you something to help you sleep. You can take it until we get you to a counselor, or someone to talk to. And you know that you are never ugly in my eyes. So stop fidgeting with that bird's nest on top of your head." He laughed hard at his own joke, and I couldn't help but smile as well.

"You're so not funny! Seriously though, you have done enough for me. I couldn't ask you to do anything else. And I don't want you to leave and go pick up a prescription. Let's just spend the rest of the day in this beautiful back yard." I stared ahead at the huge gazebo.

I was nervous to be alone with him. My nerves always kicked into overdrive around him, simply because I didn't want to fall for him. I was normally super confident around men, but Chris had some kind of power over me. Kryptonite is what I called his aura. I was always powerless around him.

"Tracey baby, you really don't have an idea how much more I want to do for you. I watched you in that hospital bed faithfully for a week straight thinking, who could do something like that, to someone so beautiful? I would kill Chuck with my bare hands if given the chance.

I blushed. "Thanks for wanting to protect me. I don't know what else to say." My shoulders shrugged.

"I'm not expecting you to say anything. I want to be everything to you, if you just let me. As a doctor I'm normally chasing women away, but you won't budge with me."

"I can't, I don't deserve to be loved. I've done so many people wrong in life. I've slept with my best friend's husband, and slept with other guys just based on their status. I don't know how to give love, nor receive it properly. Everything I touch becomes jaded, and I would die if that happened to you, especially since you've been so nice to me." I was being honest when I told Chris my true feelings. He was one person that I didn't want to hurt.

"If it is your love that taints my soul, then so be it. I have to have it."

I blushed again.

"You want it too, so just open your heart and receive it. I know we haven't known each other long, but it doesn't take months to know when you've found your soul mate." He paused to look me straight in the eye. "If I didn't feel so strongly about our connection, Tracey, I would've given up hope by now." He placed his arms around my waist and pushed his nose against mine. For several seconds we stood there and inhaled each other's breath.

"Tracey, can I have you? I know I said no strings attached, but I want you so bad I feel my insides about to burst. If you can't right now, I have no choice but to understand. But I want you to know, I want you in the worst way possible." Chris spoke so softly, I had to strain to hear him.

I stared deep into his eyes. I couldn't see anything but love behind the initial look of lust. I was always quick to jump into bed with men without thinking, but this time I was certain that it was right. I removed the straps on my dress and decided to let my inhibitions free. I walked towards the mahogany gazebo and positioned my naked body on the soft cushion. Chris immediately pulled me into a bear hug and laid me on the floor. He slowly removed my bra and panties while I squirmed under his scrutiny and closed my eyes from embarrassment. The bandages from the shooting were visible and caused me to feel uncomfortable. I tried to place my hand over my left side; but it was useless.

"Open your eyes and look at me, Tracey. I want you to see that your bruises and scars mean nothing to me. You have nothing to be embarrassed about, when it comes to me. And I really want you to see my eyes," he said as he winked at me.

He took his time as he kissed and licked my mid-section causing my temperature to rise. The moment Chris removed his shirt showing his washboard abs I really got hot. I wasn't sure how he'd magically pulled a condom from his pants but before I knew it Chris was naked, strapped-up and climbing on top of me with ease. I couldn't wait to feel him inside of me. I pushed my hips up toward him letting him know my body was ready.

He moaned and talked in a slow, seductive tone. I had no clue what he was saying since my mind had slipped off into la la land. It felt so good having someone to hold me, knowing they really cared for me. Although I wanted to prolong the feeling, I could feel my hormones raging. My pussy had become soaking wet. "Oh my God, make love to me, Chris."

Chris didn't waste any time following my instructions. He said nothing, only springing into action. He inserted himself inside of me at the perfect pace, making sure he handled me tenderly. That shit felt so good, he almost made me cry. "Mmmmm," I moaned as he thrust into me, stroke after stroke. My body jerked a little, but he wouldn't let me go. Tonight was all about pleasing me, and he continued to do so. Even when I felt a sharp pain shoot throughout my body, he kept going and I did too. I kept moving my hips back and forth as Chris let out moans of pleasure. I knew he was about to cum when he pushed deeper inside of me and hollered like someone was about to kill him. I began stroking him as hard as I could until I felt my legs shake and my clit tightened. Us cumming together was just what the doctor ordered. It was just what I needed. No one, not even Tez, had ever touched me so tenderly before.

Once again I let my sexual desires get in the way of rationale thinking. I wanted to take things slow this time. For once, I wanted a relationship not based on sex. I hoped I hadn't ruined a good thing.

Chapter 28

"Tracey, I've been calling you for a few days now. Yo phone keep going to voicemail. I thought you had blocked me or something."

"What do you want Tez?" My tone should've told him that I was done with him. "Why are you calling me?" I asked. I hadn't heard from him since the hospital I was truly surprised that he had the nerve to call. He was good at disappearing and I wanted it to stay that way.

"Truthfully, Tracey, I'm on some confession type shit. I feel real bad for some foul shit that I've done. I gotta clear my mind from all this bullshit," he said.

"Go ahead. I'm listening, but you only have two minutes before I hang up."

"Now you know I ain't never been no two minute brother," he jokingly replied, attempting to lighten our mood.

I didn't laugh at all. And I waited about ten seconds before I told him, "I don't see anything funny. Speak before you get the dial tone."

"Ok, calm down. It's about Christian. I ain't got a lot of time cuz she'll be back any minute now."

"What about her? Back where?" I stopped myself. "nevermind, I don't even want to know."

"Look, Christian and I met almost a year ago." Tez revealed that info like it had killed him to do so.

"Oh, really," I replied letting him know that I was already on to him.

"Shortly after, she came to me asking me if I wanted to make a few dollars. Of course I said yes, after she told me twenty thousand. She kept talking about some chick that she wanted to bring down."

"So, what's your point Tez?" Is this where you explain to me how you could set me up like that? Christian has ruined my business!"

"I swear I didn't mean for things to go the way they did. I was supposed to make you fall for me, but I fell for you too. Then Christian wanted me, sexually." He paused. "I sexed her plenty of times, no lie, but I was never feeling her. But she just kept paying me more and more. She knew after I met you that I wanted you. And you know what else Tracey?"

"What?" I snapped.

"I'm still feeling you. These feelings are real girl, no lie."

"Tez, is that it? Because you can go fuck Christian some more as far as I'm concerned."

"Listen, I just want you to know the truth about Shanice. Christian knew you were looking for a new assistant, and I suggested her hiring my cousin Shanice."

"Tez, that's enough. I know about Shanice already. And I'm not about to sit on the phone while you reveal all your lies. I have a lot on my mind and I just don't have time for this today. You have a few seconds left," I replied while looking at the time on my watch.

"Damn, you rushing me all fast and shit. Like I was saying, the only thing she didn't plan was me falling in love with you. And I just needed to call you today because I realize Christian is over the top crazy. It's bad. Tracey, you need to watch yourself. She is really obsessed with doing something bad to you."

I rolled my eyes as he continued to drag out the story. I'd already heard enough and didn't want to hear anymore. Those people were now obsolete in my life. I wouldn't miss them at all.

"I shoulda known this was a bad idea the moment she drugged your drink at the club that night. Me and her put you in the bed naked. And as bad as I wanted to have you at that time, I knew I wanted it to be at your own will."

"Damn," I sighed. He finally told me something I didn't know. "You know this is all fucked up, Tez, right? I'll never forgive you."

"I'm sorry baby. I never wanted to hurt you, and I hope you can find it in your heart to forgive me for the pain I caused you. Listen Tracey, the girl is off though…it's getting worse. I need to let you know that Christian is planning on…."

"Hello? Hello, Tez?" I hollered frantically in the phone. "Tez, Tez...you there?"

I immediately called him back.

No answer.

I tried unsuccessfully two more times, each time I got voicemail. Had she done something to Tez? Or was this just another one of his disappearing acts? Fear built up inside of me. It wasn't like I could call Chuck. He was locked up. Christian had gone insane and I needed to know what her next move was. I had to stay ahead of her. She obviously would not rest unless she had completely finished me off. I wasn't about to let that happen. She'd gotten the best of me before, but next time things would be very different, I told myself deceitfully. Quickly, I picked up the phone ready to confess one of my many secrets but as soon as I began to dial, I heard a voice.

"Hello."

"Hello," the other voice chimed.

"Rayven, is that you?"

"Yes, girl. Since when have you been answering on the first ring?" she joked.

"Oh my God! I'm so glad you finally called back. Did you find out the info I asked for? And girl, shit got worse!" I kept firing off one question after another. "Did you know Christian was screwing my man?"

"No, but I knew you were screwing hers."

Everything went silent. It was an embarrassing moment for me.

"I've known for a while Tracey. Of course I think it was a bad call, but all this stuff that you've been telling me that Christian has done is horrible."

"It gets worse. I spent the next twenty minutes filling her in on what Tez told me and how the line went dead. Rayven was shocked but told me not to worry; she knew somebody who knew somebody at the police station. I thought about telling her what I'd done to Megan, but a funny feeling in my gut said keep it to yourself.

Chapter 29

Of all the days that I'd chosen to go with Chris to his office, this was a bad one. When the woman pranced inside and closed the door fear filled my eyes. Quickly, I darted beneath the desk hoping she hadn't seen me. I knew Christian had come to kill me. Chris simply stared at her never even leaving his seat, behind his huge oak desk. I could tell he wasn't afraid.

"Good evening, Dr. Scott. Chris, right?"

"For you, we'll just leave it as Dr. Scott. What can I do for you Christain? Must you keep showing up, ruining lives. You need medication, bad." Chris leaned back in his chair, not the least bit bothered by Christian's visit.

"Oh cocky, I like that in a man. Prescribe me some medicine? No, I'd rather have you prescribe me some of you. I'm ready and everything, completely naked under this coat."

Christian stood in front of his desk with a short trench coat on. I could see her Jimmy Choos from the slit below the desk.

"You know you should do standup comedy, Christian. You are really disturbed, you know that," he said while laughing. "Now, what do you want?"

"Shut up! You shut the fuck up now. Don't call me disturbed!" she screamed causing goose bumps to form all over my body. I wrapped my body with my own arms searching for comfort. I prayed she wouldn't whip out a gun and pop Chris just as she'd done to me. Unstable was her middle name and Chris' rejection had struck a nerve.

"I've decided that your little girlfriend Tracey will die tonight and you're going to help me."

"I will not help you do anything to harm Tracey, so you might as well get the hell out now!"

I tried not to move but a part of me said make a run for it!

I could hear Chris lifting the receiver off the large phone on his desk. "I'm calling security," he told her.

"You know Chris, you turn me on. Put that phone down and let's chat. We don't have to be enemies just because me and Tracey are. We can be so much more than that. I really hate that Tracey swept you in her web, because I would suck you off so good right here on the spot." She made a snort and shouted out a dry laugh.

"Get the hell out!" Chris shouted! I could feel his legs touching my body as he stood up and backing away from the desk.

"Oh sweetie, I'll leave soon, but please know my threat is real. If you know what's good for you, you will do exactly what I say. And because you been such a sport, and a cute one at that, I'll give you a peep at all you are missing."

I wasn't sure what Christian was doing but from Chris' next comment, I assumed she had unbuttoned her coat.

Christian, close your coat. I'm not interested in seeing you naked. He took two steps around the desk making contact with Christian. My heart rate sped a mile a minute listening to the two of them tussle. By the time that I'd peeped my head out from under the desk I could see that Chris had grabbed her arm and twisted it behind her back. Her tits were completely exposed and the hairs down below resembled a bush.

"I asked you to leave, please don't make me hurt you. Tracey has had enough. You pretty much ruined her reputation, why won't you just let it go?"

"Stop...please help! Please...someone help me...hurry! Stop Dr. Scott. I don't want to do this!"

Christian grabbed at his arms and pinched at his skin. They began to tussle harder, back and forth as Christian continued to scream loudly as if she were being murdered.

"Christian, what the hell is wrong with you? I haven't touched you." Chris tried to remove Christian's grip on his arms as she dug her nail further in his skin.

"Help somebody! He's trying to rape me!"

"What's going on in here?" The door was kicked open by an orderly who had walked by. Behind him stood Dr. Miller, an older surgeon who had worked with both of our fathers for a long time.

"Dr. Miller, this young lady is crazy and disturbed, she

came in here naked," Chris tried to explain.

"She threatened Dr. Robbins' daughter, and when I would-n't take the bait, she started attacking herself and yelling like I was doing it." Chris was out of breath and in disbelief about the whole ordeal.

"He's lying! He attacked me and said that if I didn't have sex with him, he would show everyone at the hospital this tape of Dr. Robbins' daughter having sex." Christian was an expert at lying.

"I honestly don't know who to believe," Dr. Miller said as he shook his head.

"Dr. Miller please, you know me. You know I would not make this up. I want him arrested now!" Christian cried out, of course a stream of fake tears.

"I'm sorry Chris, but I'm gonna have to contact the police. There has to be a thorough investigation with allegations like this."

"Hell no! She's lying and I'm leaving!"

I jumped up from beneath just in time to tell Dr. Miller what I saw. Somehow I'd gotten the courage to get out my first word when Christian stared at me defiantly. Simultaneously the orderly grabbed Chris around his arms in an attempt to keep him from leaving.

"I love a good love triangle. Don't you, Tracey?" Christian asked me with a devilish smirk.

I turned angrily to face her, but the gun that she had pointed to my head stopped my movements. She pulled the weapon so quickly from her coat I had no time to run for cover. Her eyes were vacant, completely void of emotion. Her lips had turned upward into a smile and my heart sank as she pulled the trigger. I felt the bullet penetrate my brain and it only took a few seconds for my heart to stop. She had finally finished her mission.

Chapter 30

"Tracey! Tracey, wake up! Tracey, please wake up!"

I felt someone shake me, so I fought back, kicking, scratching and screaming like hell. I assumed it was Christian. I wasn't about to let her win this time.

"Tracey, please calm down, baby it's me," the voice called into the darkness.

"Chris? Is that you?"

I rubbed his face, just to get some type of familiarity in the dark. We'd fallen asleep earlier watching television in his bedroom.

"Yes, baby I'm here," Chris said as he hugged and rocked me like a child.

He tried his hardest to console me. He leaned over my body and turned on the lamp on his nightstand. "Oh God, I had a dream that Christian framed you, and you were going to jail. And-and-and-and she killed me," I cried.

"It's ok Tracey. I'm here and I promise I won't ever leave you. I mean that. How many times do I have to tell you the same thing? I'm not afraid of Christian."

He rubbed my hair and continued to rock me until my crying stopped. I removed my arms from around his waist and wiped the tears with the sleeve of my shirt. "It was just so real. I was so scared. I'm fine now, just a stupid nightmare." I didn't want Chris to see me as some needy chick. I loved him for wanting to help me, but despised the fact I was playing the damsel in distress role. In my opinion, there was nothing worse than a needy chick.

"It's perfectly normal to be scared Tracey. You've been through a whole lot. I'm surprised you haven't broken all the way down already."

Chris gave me a reassuring squeeze. I pretended to feel

better but silently I wondered why I had that dream. It seemed so real that I almost felt as if it was a premonition. I truly believed she'd done something to Tez but couldn't prove it yet. His phone continued to go to voicemail whenever I tried to reach out to him. Between Christian shooting me, Tez being a total fraud, and me killing Megan, I had become a total wreck.

My phone rang, shaking me from my thoughts.

"Tracey, your mom is calling again," Chris said as he held my phone in his hand.

As usual, he played my protector. He knew that whenever she called I wound up being upset. I looked down at her name and number, and everything was a blur. I pressed answer and braced myself for our latest conversation.

"Hello," I said wearily into the phone. I gave Chris a *why did I answer* look.

"I'm leaving your father," Mother sung into the phone.

"What? Why? He's going to be devastated!"

"Who gives a damn about him? He's old now and is never home anyway. I have no use for him. Besides, I'm going to help Anthony become a politician," she replied.

"You can't possibly be serious? What do you think everyone will say about you when they find out you are with my former fiancé?"

"Personally, I don't give a damn what all these no good people say about me. I have my eyes set on the White House."

"Mother, you must be drunk. Do you not hear yourself?" I tried to reason with her.

"Don't you worry about what the hell I'm doing. I fully expect you to support me and Anthony."

"Mother, you need some professional help. I can help you with that." I tried my hardest to take the weariness out my voice. The last thing I wanted to do was give her ammunition against me.

"Help me? You can never help me Tracey. I have been helping you, by telling anyone in the circle who will listen, Chuck seduced you by getting you drunk. If you should ever come back around, you should go with that." My mother's voice was slurred, which meant she was home drinking alone. Lots of drinks.

"Mother, he didn't seduce me, I knew exactly what I was doing. How many times do I have to tell you that? I've realized my mistakes, and I'm trying to be a different person now."

"A different person? Is that what they call it nowadays. You certainly weren't a different person when you fucked Chuck. Or what about when you moved in with Dr. Scott, a man you barely know?" Mother laughed hoarsely in the phone.

"Anyway, now is not a good time to talk. I'll call you back." I wanted to end the call immediately. She and I had nothing positive to speak about.

"So have you fucked the good doctor yet? At least later you can say you're pregnant if he tries to leave you."

"Ughhhhhhh. He and I are just friends, Mother," I responded.

"A man does not need a woman to just be his friend," Mother stated as if it were a fact.

I felt Chris touch my knee slightly for support. "I'm grown Mother, which is why I need to make my own choices.

"Yeah, like fucking Chuck." She laughed heartily. "But you know when I saw Chuck leaving the guest house I was ecstatic. The Santanas always thought their daughter was better than you. I couldn't wait to call over there and let that bitch, Sophia know what was going on," she slurred worse than before.

"You did what, Mother?" My mind couldn't even begin to grab hold of the information being given.

"Yeah. She was so shocked, completely devastated. She thought her daughter had finally beaten you by getting a husband first. I interrupted that bullshit. Her own husband can't keep his hands off me, and now her son-in-law was doing the same thing with you."

"You told on me, Mother? You're the reason all of this is happening to me?"

I was shocked, but not that surprised. She had been locked in a fierce competition with their family for years. Although telling on me was something that I never imagined she would stoop so low and do. "I can't believe you drug me into your petty ass competition," I hollered at her. "Mrs. Santana likes me mother. She sends me stuff all the time."

"That's fake, stupid! "And I'll I tell you another thing darling," she continued like a deranged woman, "it just drove me nuts to hear about Christian and Chuck every day. I threw plenty of women Chuck's way to ruin their marriage. But Chuck sleeping with you, that was the perfect revenge."

I could barely speak after hearing what was being said to me.

"You sacrificed me and my happiness, just to settle revenge with someone? I was doing fine in my life without you butting in. I can forgive you for Anthony. But this, ruining my life? I can never forgive you for that." I spoke the words out loud because had I left them in my head, they would have driven me insane. Hell, they still did not make sense out loud.

"Silly child, I don't need your forgiveness. You say your life was perfect, but we both know that is a complete lie. What you were doing, is being a slut and ruining our family's good name. I told your father a long time ago, we made a mistake welcoming you in our home. You will be just like your real mother, nothing more than common, Tracey."

Her words stung but I didn't want to let her know that. She and I were never going to be able to reconcile. I had become tired of hearing her throw that up in my face.

"Or I can always be like you Mother, a regular whore. You talk about how you made a mistake picking me, maybe you did. You should have just left me where I was, and your little infertile ass could just keep explaining to everyone why you couldn't get pregnant.

"Tracey, why can't you see, I'm only trying to do what's right for you? That's all I have ever done, since day one. Make all your decisions and tell you right from wrong, so you wouldn't be placed with the ugly choices that life brings."

"Mother, I'm capable of taking care of myself."

She laughed again, cutting off my declaration of independence. She was a cold hearted bitch and the main reason that I was as well.

"Well, that's good. So, I guess this is the perfect time to tell you that I will be dissolving your trust fund this week. You really don't deserve to have the Robbins family money."

"I don't need or want that money in my life, Mother." I couldn't believe my next set of words. "Money doesn't make me who I am. I'll earn my own future. And I don't need you in my life to do it!" I told her firmly.

"You sleeping with Chuck is proof, you need me to still be in your life. I've slept with plenty men and have never had one shoot me. Was the pussy that bad?" She momentarily paused as if a new idea popped into her mind.

I stopped her and blurted out what I shouldn't have. "Chuck didn't shoot me!" I shouted.

"What?" Her voice trembled.

I breathed heavily mostly because of the way Chris was now staring me down.

"What did you just say?" he asked getting up close in my face.

"You heard me."

"So, who shot you, Tracey?" Chris grabbed me by my shoulders as I held the phone to my ear, not listening to anything my mother said.

"I can't say."

"C'mon baby, we can get through this together. Just tell me."

I wasn't sure when Mother hung up, but the dial tone blared in my ear let me know she was gone. I hated her so much, but at least I'd told her the truth about Chuck.

"Tracey, hang up the phone. I'm sorry I even gave it to you. I seriously had no idea how your mother was. I heard stories at the hospital, but to say things like that to you is so unnecessary. I'm so sorry baby, don't cry," Chris said as he removed the phone from my hands.

How many more times would he be there to pick up the pieces? He had become my new Christian, always saving me.

"I'm not crying over her. Believe me, my tears dried years ago. She couldn't make me cry if she wanted to. I'm shocked she would stoop so low, just to play petty games."

Mother had proven, nothing or no one was off limits, when it came to her pursuit of shallow happiness and wealth. I was amazed that Chris still wanted to be anywhere near me. My family was a dysfunctional embarrassment.

"Tracey, you gotta tell me what's going on. I will always be here with you Tracey." Chris reassured me of his love. I was glad that he was so patient with me.

"Thank you, Tez. I love you so much, I need you in my life. I don't think I could make it without you," I said.

His arms stiffened around my neck and he backed away from me.

"Tracey?" Chris had a blank look on his face, and I was scared that he realized he actually didn't want this drama.

"Yes, baby." He'd made me nervous.

"Do you still love Tez?" He could barely ask the question. I looked in his eyes and saw his uncertainty.

"No, Chris! Why would you ask me that, when I'm here with you? This is exactly where I want to be." I grabbed his face so that we could look into each other's eyes.

"Because you just confessed your love, but you called me Tez." The flash of anger that washed over his eyes had somewhat surprised me. "Just let me know that all this isn't in vain. My heart is out here on the line, Tracey. If I'm not what you really want, be honest and tell me." Chris yelled at me.

Chris was angry, and I couldn't say I blamed him. He'd been more than patient with me and I was messing it up. I didn't want to lose what I had with him. "Of course you're what I really want. I'm sorry if I hurt you by calling you his name. My mind is a mess. I didn't mean it; I swear I don't love him." I was beginning to think that maybe Christian put a curse on me. I cringed at the prospect of never being happy again.

"Come here, I don't want you to ever hurt when you're with me. I hate seeing you like this. You have to stop playing the victim Tracey, and fight back. But you won't beat the devil, not until you let God take over as captain. You can't fight this alone, even I can't. You need a higher power baby."

He always spoke of a higher power, and I really wasn't trying to hear that. "God obviously doesn't know that I exist. I've been suffering like crazy these past few months, and God hasn't done anything about it," I told him wearily. All the God talk made me uncomfortable. I had a feeling Chris was a religious nut, when I saw all the bibles and crosses around his house.

"That's not true baby. He is there. You just have to reach out to Him. Confess your sins, ask for forgiveness, and leave your burdens there." Chris was on his knees with his hands together. I knew he didn't think I was going to pray also.

"I don't even know how to really pray, baby. I'm embarrassed to say that, but I always felt rather silly talking to the air like that. I don't want to be one of those holy rollers, who look down on everybody else either." I tried to get him to drop the subject, but he pursued it anyway.

"Not all people are like that, true genuine Christians don't look down on the lost. We can pray together until you get used to it. I just want you to be happy. I know that finding Him first, will be the only way you and I can stand a chance. Give me your hand, Tracey."

I placed my hand into his and released my trust into his heart. He wanted to save me and I was willing to let him. At least for now. I had gotten so use to doing life on my own and that had gotten me nowhere. As he began to pray for my peace of mind, the tears started flowing.

For once, the tears didn't seem to weigh me down. With each tear I washed away my feelings of hurt, anger and resentment. I had no idea, praying could feel so good. I could really see myself getting use to it. Or at least, I would try. Something had to give and I didn't want that something to be my life. I knew that I would have to be strong for my father in the coming weeks. Once my mother told him that she was leaving him he would be a complete mess. Something new never sounded so good. I was willing to try anything. Then I paused. This was the perfect time to start being honest.

"Chris, honey, there's something I need to tell you."

He grabbed my hand. "I'm here Tracey," he said genuinely. "I hope you're ready to tell me who shot you."

My initial thought was to tell the truth about what I'd done to Megan, but just that quickly I'd reverted back to the old Tracey. I just couldn't go through with it. I decided to hold out until our next prayer session.

Chapter 31————————

I pulled in the driveway of my parent's home. The normally bright house looked dark and dull. Almost as if someone had sucked the life out of it. I was more than convinced that, the someone, was my mother. For years she had that effect on me and now that I was gone, I knew she would do it to the closest thing around her. Maybe that was the reason my father had called and asked me to come over.

I sat in the truck for a moment to gather my thoughts. I hadn't spoken to her since she had drunkenly revealed that she would be leaving my father. I hoped like hell that she hadn't told him of her plans yet. I knew that it would hurt him to be alone. The confrontation that she and I was about to have was inevitable. It had been a long time coming and I was ready to pay the dues.

I stepped out of the truck and quickly made my way to the front door. I could hear music playing loudly in the house. It sounded like the blues which meant that my father was home alone. Mother hated the blues, saying that it sounded like slave music. I tried to open the door but realized it was locked so I pounded on the door waiting for the butler or the maid to answer. No one came to the door so I made my way around to the side of the house where the help entered. I turned the knob realizing it was unlocked. The servant's door was never locked. It was even darker inside of the house than it was on the outside. Everything was out of place and it looked like no one had cleaned in days, maybe even weeks. This was very unusual for our house. We often had surprise visitors stop by, so the house was always im-maculately kept.

"Daddy!" I yelled out. "Daddy, you in here?"

I walked into his den and saw him sleeping on the leather lounge chair. He looked as if he hadn't shaved in days and the smell of bourbon was strong in the air. I shook his arm, waking him from his slumber. "Daddy. What's wrong? Where is every-one?" I kept looking around wondering what the hell had hap-pened to the place. He had the curtains drawn tightly and the room was void of all light. I leaned over to the coffee table and clicked on his side lamp.

"She took em all with her," he said inaudibly as he cradled himself tighter into the couch.

I looked around the room and noticed that all of the pic-tures with him and Mother were inside of the fire place. He hadn't even bothered to burn them. They were just inside with broken glass everywhere.

"What happened, Daddy?"

"That bitch. She left me. I gave her everything she wanted and she still left me," he mumbled as he turned his face away from me.

I hung my head as his pain translated to my body. Obvi-ously Mother had gone through with her plan to leave him for An-thony. I didn't believe that she would actually do it.

"You have to get up Daddy. It's not the end of the world. Mother is just plain evil."

"She's with Anthony. Can you believe that shit? I gave her every stupid ass thing she wanted, even when she didn't deserve it and she left me for a kid I damn near raised. She ruined my life."

His sobs were louder than his voice. I guess he must've really loved her. All this time I thought that their marriage was an arranged one, with no love. However, he was devastated.

"Yeah, I know, Daddy. I caught them together. I wanted to tell you but I didn't want to hurt you. I'm so sorry."

"Caught them?"

"Yeah. Having sex." I swallowed hard, embarrassed to even say it. "She didn't deserve you."

"You damn right she didn't. Slut!" he added with deceit. "She took all the happiness up out of me. Always jealous of you, you know. She did everything in her power to make sure our life was a living hell. Guess that's my fault. I should've told you the truth years ago."

"Told me what?" I asked. I wanted to know the answer but I had a feeling that Pandora's Box was about to be wide open. His face showed guilt, more than I'd seen from him ever before.

"She's not your real mother," he said softly grabbing my arm with his wrinkled hand.

I sat there for a second waiting on the other shoe to drop when I realized that he didn't know that I already knew. I stared into his face and saw the overwhelming sadness of a very un-happy man. I hadn't noticed how old he had looked when we were in the hospital. Had Mother's departure aged him in such lit-tle time? I wondered.

"I've always known that. She told me that I was adopted whenever she had a chance to rub it in my face. That's not your fault though. You did the best you could do and you were a great father to me."

"No I didn't. I should've protected you more. She was just so damn jealous that I had gotten Sophia pregnant."

My face bawled up instantly. *Did he just say he'd gotten Sophia Santana pregnant?*

"Tracey, forgive me, honey. When Sophia decided that she couldn't have a baby out of wedlock and wanted to give you up, I decided to get full custody of you. Gertrude resented you before you were even born."

My head started to spin as I took in the information. He had to be drunk and just speaking incoherently. No way was Sophia Santana my real mother. That would make Christian and I *sisters*.

"Daddy, you are drunk. You don't know what you're saying. Mother said you both adopted me from some city out of town," I said while trying to decipher what was real and what was just drunk talk.

My father sat up on the couch and looked at me with a sorrowful face. He rubbed my cheek and then pulled an old, tat-tered picture from his jacket pocket. He handed it to me and my hands shook out of fear. It was a picture of him and Mrs. Santana, kissing next to a tree. They both looked so young I barely recog-nized them. However, she looked exactly like me now.

"Sophia and I were high school sweethearts. Everyone just knew that we would get married and have kids, that was the plan but I was two years older than her. I went off to college and left her here, pregnant. I had no idea that her folks sent her away to a small town until she had you. Then, I met your mother at a college party that she had crashed. It all happened so quickly."

"Wait, Daddy, that doesn't make sense. Mother said the two of you were together since high school. How could you have possibly been in love with Mrs. Santana?" I eagerly asked.

"Your mother was always great at pretending to be something that she's not. I didn't meet her until I was in my first year of college. I got drunk at a frat party and woke up the next morning with her in my bed. I couldn't get rid of her after that. She kept popping up wherever I was. She found out that I came from money and she showed up one day saying she was pregnant. My own momma almost died from shame."

I sat down on the floor next to him in disbelief. The story made no sense to me. I was always told another story and I had believed it. What was being told to me now was something that I couldn't wrap my brain around.

"I'm not understanding what you're saying, Daddy."

"You were adopted, just not by me. You're my biological child; mine and Sophia's. That lying heffa, Gertrude wasn't really pregnant when she lied to my parents. She just used that lie to get into our family. Plus, when she found out Sophia had a baby by me and was giving the baby up for adoption, she somehow twisted my arm and we adopted you as our own. Sophia didn't like it one bit, but she knew Gertrude would make her life a living hell. She was determined to marry me at all cost."

"No, no…no… no," I kept repeating, "this is all too much."

My father walked over to his bar and poured himself another glass of bourbon. He quickly swallowed it and then looked at me with tearful eyes. "I just wanted everyone to be happy, especially my parents. I couldn't cause a lot of shame on the family so I married Gertrude; and the three of us became a family. Sophia came to me a month after the wedding saying she wanted you back. She told me she was pregnant again but not by me. She said she wanted to raise her two girls together but Gertrude wasn't having it. She told her she would expose the fact that she'd gotten pregnant so young and out of wedlock."

"Daddy, are you saying what I think you are saying?" I asked incredulously.

"I'm saying that Sophia is your real momma and Christian is your biological sister," he replied matter of factly.

"But that's not possible. We're the same age. We've been raised together since birth. We don't even look alike."

"It's true, baby. You were born a year and a half before Christian. Gertrude never wanted the secret to come out so she forged your birth certificate. You don't look like Christian because her father is Hispanic. Sophia met the bastard when I left for college." He walked towards me and handed me a shot of his bourbon. I downed it and then held the glass out for another. My stomach did flips as I thought about how horribly Mother had treated me over the years and her secret hatred for Mrs. Santana. She was a complete fraud.

"I don't know what to say. I mean, I don't even know how to comprehend any of this. Why are you just now telling me this?" I angrily asked.

"What difference would it have made? By the time you were old enough to know the truth, you had started to act so much like Gertrude, I couldn't reprogram you if I wanted to."

"Christian is my sister? How could you raise us so close together and not say anything. Do you know what you have done? Christian was the one who shot me, Daddy!" I yelled at him.

"What? I thought Chuck shot you. You don't know what you're saying. He became flustered and paced back and forth holding his head. "There's no way Christian did that," he said, slurring over his words.

"It was Christian! She's jealous of me. Did they tell her the truth? Is that why she is so damn crazy now?" I asked questions that I knew my father didn't have the answers to.

"Hell, I need another drink. I didn't think things would turn out like this. I had no clue that our lives would be so intertwined. I'm so sorry. I've already lost Gertrude, I couldn't handle losing you too," he cried.

I thought back to how many times I had ever seen him drop tears and today was the first time ever. I walked towards him and placed my arms around his neck. I kissed his cheek and tried my hardest to comfort him.

"It's alright Daddy, we will figure it out. I don't know how but, we will. I promise you on my life I will make this better for the both of us," I said, hugging him tightly.

He held on tighter and for the first time, I felt a bond with a family member that I knew would only make me stronger.

Chapter 32

It had been exactly two weeks since Chris and I started praying. The chaotic lifestyle that I once lived had completely disappeared. I spent most of my days in Chris' green house trying to learn how to plant and grow things. It may sound boring, but for me it was better than fake smiles and pretend friendships.

Christian had still kept a low profile. It almost made me nervous that I hadn't heard anything from her. But I was grateful for the peace. Rayven told me that she spoke to her and that there were no signs of any craziness. She even told Rayven to tell me that she still loved me and was sorry for what she'd done. Maybe she was trying to move on with her life just as I was.

When Chuck had been released from jail, due to lack of concrete evidence and my letter to the judge, I just knew she would pop up again. But she didn't. Even though he was a reckless low life, I was happy he wasn't spending the rest of his life behind bars. My father and Chris had advised me to make sure Chuck was a free man. Of course my father urged me not to tell the authorities that Christian had attempted to kill me. I still couldn't wrap my brain around the secret that Christian and I were really sisters. I didn't know what revealing the truth would disclose so I decided to just leave it be for the time being.

Rayven called me with some new information on Tez's disappearance that she thought I needed to know immediately. She agreed to meet me in my office so she could let me in on what she found out. I was a little afraid because she wouldn't tell me over the phone. That meant that she had discovered some heavy information. Maybe he was dead.

As I stood in the hallway, I couldn't help but feel saddened. I could still see tiny little speckles of the yellow caution tape that was placed over the door. I pushed it open and stared at the blood that was still in the carpet. It looked as if it had been cleaned, but you could still see the remnants. I felt a pain in my stomach like never before.

The spirit of my baby still mourned inside me. It knew that this was the place where its life was taken. I sat in the chair and just took it all in. It had been a long time since the night of the shooting. I'd tried to push it out of my mind but sitting in my chair shook the memories back up.

"Tracey, can I talk to you for a moment please?"

I didn't hear the office door open, but there was Christian standing before me. She looked great, maybe twenty pounds smaller. Her hair was now cut short and colored exactly like mine. It was creepy because we almost looked exactly alike. I don't know how we hadn't noticed before that we were really sisters.

"Christian, what are you doing here?" I asked feeling like coming to the office was a bad move.

I was scared as hell. The only way out of there was where she stood.

"My life is a mess. I'm so depressed; I can't believe I acted this way. Most of all I can't believe I shot you. I don't know how to make it right, and it is eating me up at night."

I didn't interrupt her as she talked. My mind was too busy thinking of an escape plan.

"I just snapped when I found out about you and Chuck. I tried for months to get you to tell me the truth and you wouldn't," she spoke in a low tone.

I didn't know if it was done on purpose, but it freaked me out. She sounded like she was possessed.

"Christian, I forgive you."

"You should. You were the one person who was supposed to understand how I felt." She looked at me with pain in her eyes then quickly removed any emotions out of them.

If I could have one do over in life, sleeping with Chuck would be it. I wanted nothing more than to have the old Christian back in my life. Had I not slept with him things would be different.

"I know what I did to you was foul. I have never acted so stupidly in my life. I could've killed you and went to jail." She fidgeted with her hands and stared at the floor. "Thank you for never turning me in," she added.

"Your actions have been hard for me to swallow, Christian. You really tried to ruin me. I think it was a little too extreme," I said sternly.

"I just want you to forgive me, be my friend again. We can talk and shop just like we use to. Let's just forget about all this. I miss you and want to have you back in my life," she said calmly. But she had a wild crazed look in her eyes as she tried to explain the last couple of months. Strangely, it was the same wild look she had the night she shot me.

"Sure Christian that sounds like a good idea. We need to discuss some things anyway." I needed to get out of her presence immediately. I discreetly pulled my cell phone off my side and dialed Chris's number under my desk. I should've listened to him and never came back to the office. This was one of the times I wished I wasn't so damn independent. I never wanted to let people think for me. Now, I was in a position that I didn't want to be in.

"Let's hug it out, just like when we were little. I really miss those times. Fun times, when you and I were against the world," she said as she walked over to me, slowly.

I quickly let the phone drop on the floor.

"I would like that too. We have embarrassed our family enough."

I needed help and there was no way to get it. The meeting time with Raven was at least another thirty minutes away. I didn't want to hug Christian and I felt that I needed to make a run for it. Against my better judgment I got up and opened my arms for a hug. Christian suddenly grabbed my face and started to kiss me on the lips. I tried to shove her off and run, when I felt the barrel of a gun in my side. I couldn't believe I let her get me in the same spot again.

"I knew that you wouldn't be willing to let bygones be bygones, so I brought my friend here to help you decide." She smiled at me through clenched teeth.

"Christian, please don't do this," I begged.

My heart fought to remain calm. I didn't want to send my body into any stress considering the damage it had been in for the past few months.

"You either play my way, or your Mother and Father will be in all black crying at your funeral," she spat in my face.

I wanted to punch the hell out of her, but the gun she placed in my side kept me from reacting.

"You see, I'm pregnant with Tez's baby now Tracey. And I'm going to have me a happy ending,"

I had to gather my thoughts before I talked. I didn't want to say the wrong thing.

"The first few months have been rough as hell. I've been throwing up and carrying on, but I'm so happy." she said as she rubbed her stomach and poked it out further.

"Congratulations, Christian. I'm really happy for you and Tez," I nervously said. I put on a fake smile but nothing could have been further from the truth. However, I was willing to say whatever in order to keep her calm.

"I really wish Tez could've been here to enjoy this. He wanted your baby so bad. Feel my stomach, put your hand on it and feel that love that he and I had for each other."

She forced my hand on her stomach and I couldn't feel anything other than a great sense of hate for her. I noticed that she kept speaking of Tez in past tense. It bothered me to the core.

"Where's Tez, Christian?" I had a feeling she'd done something bad.

"He's really of no concern to you sweet pea, well maybe a little. After all, you were the last person he contacted," she responded.

I frowned. "I haven't talked to Tez in forever, I'm happy with Chris,"

"You always land on your feet, don't you? A real life feline with nine lives," Christian angrily spewed at me.

She raised the gun and pointed at me. I didn't want to die so I told her what I'd promised I wouldn't say. "Christian, we're sisters, you can't do this," I exclaimed.

"Fuck that fake ass, blood sister stuff. I'm tired of walking in your shadow and I am going to solve this little problem, today," she replied.

"No, we are really sisters. Your mother is my real mother. I just found out."

She laughed loudly at me and wouldn't take in the words that I was saying to her.

"You really are stupid Tracey. You'll say any damn thing to save your life. How are we sisters when we have different mothers and different fathers?"

"It's a long story, but we are," I explained.

"You'll do anything to try and save your measly ass life. I don't believe you!"

"I swear I'm not lying to you. Call your mother and ask her if you don't believe me. This is the truth."

"No, the truth will be me blowing a bullet through your head!"

"Christian, I'm walking away from all the lies and the deceit. I just want to be happy." I held up my hands while I talked. I wanted to show her that I was not about to fight her.

"I didn't win Tracey. I lost because I still don't have you in my life. That's all I ever really wanted was you. We could raise this baby together." She rubbed my face lovingly with her free hand.

"Then don't do this, Christian. Please put the gun down and let's just walk out of here."

"No Tracey, you don't get it. I really want you. I've been in love with you since we were ten. I wanted so many times to kiss you and hold you," she said.

She kissed me again and I physically felt my skin crawl. I had just told her psycho ass that we were sisters. How in the hell did I not see this years ago? I thought she just looked at me as her sister and best friend not someone she wanted to be with romantically.

"Christian I'm sorry, but I'm not gay. And I swear on my life that you are my little sister. I'm going to walk out of here now and I really want you to get some help. You have to save yourself from whatever seems to have its hold on you." I spoke slowly and made sure my voice remained flat. I didn't want to give her a reason to use that gun.

"I knew you wouldn't get it Tracey. I'm sorry it had to come to this. I can't live without you, and I won't allow you to live without me."

She laughed really hard and put the gun to my chest, at that moment I knew it was do or die. I fought like hell to get that gun out her hands. I knew that it was either Christian or me. I planned to live and get back to Chris and the happy life that I deserved. She could rot in the eternal pits of hell as far as I was concerned.

We wrestled around for the gun. Christian was a lot

stronger than I thought. She quickly took control of the situation. She hit me repeatedly with the butt of the gun in my face. I felt the blood as it flew out of my nose.

"Did you really think that you were stronger than me, you stupid whore!" she yelled as she continued to hit me with the gun.

I felt myself getting woozy and I thought of Chris and his promise of a happy life. That gave me a newfound burst of energy to keep pushing and not give up. She almost killed me the first time, and I would die trying to prevent that from happening again.

"Christian! Oh my God you are going to kill her. I'm calling the police," Rayven screamed. I silently thanked God for sending me help.

Christian turned towards the voice just as I grabbed the Swarovski vase off my desk and hit her with all my might. She looked at me with a confused look and slumped on top of me. I was out of breath as it took everything in my body to push her off me. My head was spinning as I crawled on the floor, trying to get off the ground. By the time I stood up shivers took over my body. I realized what had just happened. Not again I told myself as the room began to spin. "I've killed someone again!" I shouted while Rayven attempted to calm me down.

"Who did you kill, Tracey? What are you talking about?"

Her voice had deep concern. Even Rayven was now afraid of me as she looked down at Christian's limp body.

"Nooooooooooooo!" I screamed clutching the sides of my head between my hands.

I think she's dead, Tracey. She's not moving."

My heart beat nearly stopped. Had I killed my own sister?

Chapter 33

Life couldn't get any worse. While Rayven sat on the floor next to Christian listening to the paramedics' instructions, I noticed Shanice at the doorway. Her appearance seemed to be totally opposite of what I'd been used to. "Why are you here?" I shouted.

She quickly developed a mortified look on her face after coming to her own conclusions about what went down. I wanted to kill her for even being there. She had been in on this from the jump. I knelt swiftly, then reached over Christian's body to assist Rayven. I checked her pulse realizing it was barely there. My brain had gone haywire. My next move was uncertain. Suddenly, I picked up the gun, stood ferociously, and pointed it at Shanice.

"Get out! Get the fuck out of my office, and forever out of my life. I was nothing but nice to you, and you ruined my life. How dare you even show your face here?" I yelled like a lion ready to attack. My insides were jumping, but I steadied my hand to keep the gun pointed Shanice's way.

"Tracey, I swear I didn't know that she was gone do all this. Had I known I would've never agreed? I was only here to give her information about you," she stammered.

"You had no right to invade my life like that!"

"That was before I got to know you, Tracey. I tried to call it off, but Christian threatened to take my babies from me," Shanice sobbed.

It was now her turn to beg for her life just like I had done. She was the one who deserved a life like that, not me. I felt powerful as she looked towards me for mercy. I wrapped my finger tightly around the trigger ignoring Rayven's pleas to drop the gun. I'd had enough being a victim and it was time I took back my life. I was meant to be on top, not wallowing in the bottom all desperate and shattered.

"Do you know what kind of hell I have been living in, bitch? You thought you would just ruin my shit and then walk away? You never sent the December issue of my magazine to the printer like you said you did! That shit made me lose thousands of dollars and advertisers. You're the reason for my downfall!" I screamed.

Shanice cried and covered her face with her hands. "That was all Christian!" she sobbed uncontrollably. "She took the files and there was nothing I could do about it."

"Tracey, you don't want to shoot her girl. You don't want to go to jail. Just put the gun down," Rayven pleaded with me again. This time she touched my arm.

"You don't understand Rayven…you've missed so much." I angrily wiped the spit that flew out the corners of my mouth.

"I get all that, I swear I do. But the police and paramedics are right outside the door. You better put that gun down before they walk in." She took another step towards me and looked for a sign that I would not shoot.

"I can't believe that someone like this had the nerve to try and take me down. She's nothing, comes from the hood, and will never be anything! She deserves to die, and is no better than Christian," I said, trying to convince Rayven that killing Shanice would be a good thing.

"Trust me, she knows she is foul as hell and I know Christian did some messed up things, but I can't take losing the both of you. She's going to jail but you don't have to join her. You didn't do anything wrong, Tracey, so just put the gun down."

Rayven was the voice of reason that I did not want to hear. Christian, Shanice, and Tez had all planned to take me down. Tez was possibly dead and now Christian was on the floor about to join him. I was pissed that Shanice wanted to make herself the innocent one in all of this. She pursued me, and pretended to work for me. She could have said no to Christian. Who gets bullied this day and age into doing something so reckless and stupid? In my book, she was anything but innocent, and she should have to pay just like the rest of us. The gun was level with her eyes and I could see the fear behind them.

"Put the gun down now!"

The cops rushed in the room, and caused further confusion to the already tense standoff. I could see at least five uniformed officers, all with their guns drawn out at me. They were yelling, shouting, and all planning to attack me. The two detectives who had been harassing me about Megan walked in. Detective Bailey looked as if she felt sorry for me while her fat partner looked as if he was seconds from breaking out into a cheer.

"You have two seconds to drop that gun now Ms. Robbins!" He screamed at me while making his way further into the room. "Let me handle this," he told the others, smiling at me.

He dangled a pair of handcuffs in front of him as I contemplated taking Shanice out once more. But I knew that all I had worked for would be buried next to her, if I took that route. I lowered the gun and the cops rushed me and roughly knocked me to the ground. Before I could explain to them what happened, I was handcuffed and placed under arrest.

"What are you doing, get your damn hands off of me?" I screamed as I wrestled with the knee that was now placed in my back.

"Tracey Robbins, you're under arrest for the murder of Megan Lewis. You have the right to remain silent…." As he continued on with his arresting mumbo jumbo, I could only focus on the word murder.

"Murdered Megan? What in the hell is going on?" Rayven yelled in the face of the detectives.

"That's right! Your lil' friend here murdered her in cold blood and dropped her into the Mississippi River," the detective screamed loud enough for everyone to hear.

"I didn't kill her! Let me go before I sue your ass," I hollered as I wrestled to no avail. The detectives grip on my arm was solid as he pushed me towards the door.

I saw a tear drop from the corner of Rayven's eye as her eyes boomeranged between the paramedic's chest compressions on Christian and me being arrested. I was completely embarrassed as the cameras went off, while I was escorted by the detective from the building. Once again, I would make the papers. Gossip was what the city thrived off of. I saw the construction workers that I had previously turned down with my nose in the air and the random females in the building that I dismissed because their outfits were cheap and tacky. They all gawked and openly laughed at me. Even the old security guard, Kurt, stood and watched with a sly smirk on his face.

"Don't worry Tracey, I'm going to follow you guys down to Central Booking. They have to process you first but don't you say a word," Rayven said, rushing from behind.

"Call Chris and let him know what happened. Call my dad too. Oh my God, I'm so scared," I cried loudly. I had never been in jail before and I wasn't sure what would happen.

"Don't worry friend, I got you. I swear you won't be in there long," she told me walking alongside the male detective.

Suddenly, he tightened the cuffs purposely. I rolled my eyes at him as he smirked in my face.

"Please hurry, Rayven. You know I can't handle this."

"Calm down. When you get in there, wipe your face and make sure you take a fabulous ass mug shot." She smiled hoping to ease my fears. "You know these vultures are going to try and get a copy of it," Rayven said as she turned towards Shanice.

"Shanice, ride with Christian to the hospital. I know she's bat shit crazy, but just in case she dies, I don't want her to be alone."

Rayven was excellent with taking charge in chaotic situations. Shanice locked eyes with me as she got in the ambulance with Christian. Her pathetic ass really had no clue that my life was not one to envy, but definitely not one for someone to try and take away from me. She would have to pay for her part in this bullshit one way or the other. I preferred to give her the other.

Chapter 34

I sat staring at the dingy white walls. I tried to count how many dots were marked on the brick concrete. The room was cold and desolate, except for the desk, the chair I was sitting in, and the one across from me. Nothing about the room said you were welcomed here. I wasn't sure anyone would want to feel comfortable in this place. I felt dirty and just tried my hardest not to touch anything.

I'd been waiting for several hours. Rayven said it wouldn't be long, but that had turned into a lie. The detectives took turns trying to break me, but I wouldn't budge. The man was talking in a hushed tone with the woman in the farthest corner. I couldn't hear them, but I was certain that it was me, and not the Chinese food he devoured, they were discussing.

The fat greasy male detective made it his business to stare at me intently. He was paper bag brown, near bald, and laced with a heavy scent of pastrami. The neck of his shirt was wet; an unhealthy dose of obesity was my reasoning. His stomach stuck out further than his chest and completely covered his pelvic area. No way was any woman getting worked by this slop bucket. That explained why he was so uptight, lack of vagina caused stupidity in men.

He grabbed the chair and pushed it close to mine. We were so close I could see the yellow specks of tartar on his cigarette stained teeth. He sat there for several minutes staring at me with a mean scowl on his face. I looked behind him at the glass mirror, and shook my head. Did they really think people didn't know the purpose of it? Nevertheless, I was scared as hell, and knew nothing good would come of the situation.

"Where were you the night of November 22nd, Ms. Robbins?" the detective asked nastily.

He asked me the same question over and over, slightly changing the wording each time. My mouth instantly started to dry. I imagined a thousand tiny cotton balls gathering on the roof and sides forming a collage. Even my sweat beads were nervous, I could feel them racing down my back and straight to the top of my underwear.

"Where was I the night of November 22nd?" I asked.

I knew where I was, but I also knew that this detective had already made up his mind that I wasn't there without even hearing my answer.

"Yes, Ms. Robbins, that's exactly what I said. Where were you?"

He traced my hand with his fat, slimy fingers. I guess that was his attempt at being nice. I snatched my hand away from him and we stared at each other. Even though he was disgustingly bald and fat, I could see the remnants of a once handsome man. Either time or the job had been hell on his appearance and life.

He was rude and cut throat. When he threw the cuffs on my wrists at the office, he tightened them harder than necessary. When I complained coming into the jail, he twisted my arm harder. He began interrogating me as soon as I was dumped in this room.

"I was at home watching T.V. I have already given my statement to the nice detective lady. I'm not sure what the purpose of talking to you again is," I rudely responded. I was trying to not have an attitude, but he was making it really hard for me. I wanted nothing more than to go home and sleep. The medicine that I was given by the paramedics for the pain in my nose had started to make me tired. They wouldn't even let me wash my face and the now dry blood was starting to crack.

"Home? That's really strange, seeing as how your mother and neighbors have said they haven't seen you there in weeks. Pardon us poor people, Ms. Robbins, but I was not aware that you have more than one home? And where exactly was this home located? The Four Seasons right?" he asked as he rolled his eyes far into his head.

"Yes, that is correct. I'd been living there for a couple of weeks. Is that a crime or something?" I rolled my eyes back at him because I didn't appreciate his sarcasm at all.

"What I understand is that a murder was committed. And

all of the evidence that I have points directly at you." He leaned back in his chair and chuckled slightly.

"Your evidence is nothing more than bullshit. I didn't murder anyone."

I leaned back in my chair also. If he wanted a standoff he was going to get exactly what he wanted. He grabbed the folder that was on the table and pulled out several pictures of a decomposed Megan. I quickly turned my head and tried not to cry. I didn't want to give him any sign of weakness on my part. Rayven told me that this would possibly happen.

"Isn't this your luggage, Ms. Robbins? Not too many people around here with expensive luggage like that. I have a witness who knows for a fact that they saw you with it," he said, throwing more pictures on the table.

"You may not know a lot of people with that bag but I know several. We run in two different circles, sir, you couldn't fathom such a life. I mean, with all due respect, I've had bags that cost more than your yearly salary," I replied smugly.

I could tell that I'd pissed him off as his eye began to twitch. He cleared his throat and then snarled at me.

"You little bitch. I hope they give your ass the death penalty."

"Easy detective, you don't want to cause some of that fat around your heart to swell. You know, that could possibly cause a heart attack." I turned my nose up at him so he would know that I was disgusted. He stared at me until his breathing had returned to a normal pace.

"Why did you kill Megan, Tracey? I have a witness who says you were jealous of her."

"Is my lawyer here yet?" I asked angrily.

I had to stop myself from blurting out how much of an unnecessary pointless problem Megan was for me. I could never be jealous of an afterthought like her.

"I see I struck a nerve. So, you were jealous of Megan?" he replied as he continued to antagonize me.

"I didn't kill Megan. Are we done yet?"

"I'm asking all the questions around here," he yelled as he banged on the table.

I didn't even flinch because this guy was a joke to me. I was no longer scared of these people. If they had enough evidence, I wouldn't still be sitting in this room.

"Have you ever heard of police brutality, sir?" I asked him coolly.

"Have you ever mashed someone's head in and then stuffed them in a bag in the river?"

"I have never killed anyone before. How many damn times do I have to say the same thing?"

"Look at these pictures! How can you sit there and pretend you didn't have a hand in this?"

He placed the photos close to my face. I tried to turn my head but he grabbed my jaw and placed the photo on my face.

"Look at this! This is what you did to her. Just dropped her in the river like a piece of trash."

I tried to shake the image from my mind but her eyes staring so lifeless would not go anywhere. My stomach lurched and I emptied the contents that I had eaten earlier onto the floor.

"Now will be the time to confess Tracey. We're here to help you," Detective Bailey said as she rubbed my back gently.

Before I could respond the door opened and Anthony and Rayven walked in. I wiped my mouth and tried to wipe away the tears that flew out the corner of my eyes.

"We are here representing Ms. Robbins. Any questions you have for her should come to me first," Anthony said loudly.

I raised my eyebrow wondering why in the hell would he of all people show up here. He knew that I did not want to see him. I wanted to kill him for the pain that he caused my father. Not to mention that he was once my fiancé who was now sleeping with my mother as well as one of my former guy friends.

"Is that a fact? You come in here with your shiny, expensive suit and your Italian leather shoes and you think that I'm going to cut her some slack. Well, prepare to bill the hell out of your client. With the evidence that I got, she'll be looking at trial," the detective said as he stood up fast and hard, causing the chair to fall on the ground and scare me.

He walked towards the door and slammed it. He had issues and I couldn't figure out why.

"What are you doing here Anthony?" I asked as soon as the detective walked out the door. I knew that I was in a lot of trouble but I didn't want his help at all. Even if he was a brilliant attorney, I still didn't want or need his help.

"I'm obviously here to save your ass. I'm sitting at home minding my business when breaking news of you being arrested flies across the screen," he responded with an attitude.

"I told you that I was done with you. So, you can leave the same way you came in," I said while folding my arms across my chest defiantly.

"This is not the time for you to get ghetto on me. You're in more trouble than you can imagine. Now we use to be close friends, I at least owe you this favor."

He gave me a meaningful look and I stared at the ground. We both knew that him helping me was going to put him in the middle of the ongoing war that I had with my mother.

"What will Mother say?" I asked the question just to get the elephant out the room.

"I know how to handle Gertrude, it was her wild ass daughter that got away. But I seriously want to repay you for not telling my secret," he said genuinely.

I looked at him and smiled. Mother still had no clue that he was sexing Kensington on the side and I would continue to keep my word as long as I walked away from this whole mess un-scathed.

"Deal, but you better get me off, asshole, or I will call her and tell," I said with a smile on my face.

"You do know that is blackmail right? You're in enough trouble as it is." We both looked at each other and laughed.

"Now let's see if we can get you out of here immediately. I told you a long time ago, you lay down with gutter rats and you will come up with rabies," he rambled on.

I looked at Rayven and we both rolled our eyes. I was somewhat confident in my defense team and knew that I would get off. I'd been very careful to make sure no one saw me leaving the hotel that night.

Chapter 35

I sat up on the hard mattress when I heard my name being called. I grabbed my jacket that I had used to protect my body from some unknown disease that the cell carried. I looked around the dirty place and thanked God that this ordeal was finally over. As hard as Anthony and Rayven tried, I had not been released the night before as promised. Even though it had only been nine hours, I spent every hour crying and counting down until my arraignment this morning.

I smiled at the young guard as he opened the door to my cell. He smiled back showing a set of perfectly white teeth and a dimple in his chin that was kind of sexy. The thought of being locked up and being at his mercy caused me to smile a little harder.

"Your chariot awaits you Ms. Robbins," he said as he slightly bowed.

My constant crying had caused all of the guards to tease me when they made their round every hour. I didn't find it funny but it did help pass the time a little faster.

"Thank you. You have been very nice. We should have met under different circumstances," I replied back as I rubbed my hip against him.

"I'm sure we'll see each other again," he breathed in my ear hoarsely.

The attraction between the two of us was something that I knew we both felt. I stopped walking and turned towards him. He stopped in his tracks and touched the gun that was on his side.

"I'm not about to try to escape. I just want you to look me in my eyes when I tell you, I will never see you in here again. This life isn't for me."

Attractive or not, I didn't want to see him inside of this

place. The conditions in jails were way worse than I could have ever imagined.

"I hear that all the time. But yeah, you look like you may have a little something going on for yourself. Did you really kill that girl like people saying?" he asked as we continued to walk.

"Trumped up charges, the police are convinced that I'm a cold blooded killer because we didn't get along. I didn't do it but she didn't deserve to have a life anyway," I said, turning my nose up at the thought of Megan and how she was still causing me problems while dead.

"How can you say that about someone who is dead? You really are cold hearted like they saying," he said as he grabbed my arm roughly and dragged me towards the courtroom.

I could barely keep my balance as he yanked the door open and pushed me inside. I smiled at my father who was sitting in the front of the courtroom. His eyes still held a distant vacant look, but him supporting me was appreciated. I don't know why, but I looked around hoping to see my mother there as well. I wasn't surprised that she wasn't present, but Chris was there. He waved towards me and I stopped to speak to him when the guard flung me towards my seat.

"Ouch, you hurt my arm, asshole," I angrily yelled as I sat next to Rayven and Anthony.

The guard didn't say another word as he undid the handcuffs and quickly walked away. What his problem was, I hadn't a clue but I would be sure to get his ass fired for the way he just handled me.

"Hey girl, sorry we couldn't get you out. I hope you were okay in there," Rayven said genuinely.

"It was horrible. I'm just ready to get this over with. Did you guys find out anything about who could've killed Megan?" I asked.

"No. But you will be free, don't worry."

"And how's Christian?" I directed my question to Rayven.

"Christian is still alive. Her baby didn't survive though. I hear she isn't doing that well," Rayven replied.

"Good morning to you as well, Tracey," Anthony said as he cleared his throat. "We were able to collect quite a bit of information in so little of time. Trust me, you will be walking free in no time."

"Thanks again, Anthony. I can't tell you how happy this

makes me," I said as the judge walked in. Chills bumps rose up on my arms the moment that I got one look at the judge. She intimidated me instantly. But as soon as all were seated, Anthony immediately sprang into action.

"Your honor, with all due respect, the state has built a case all based on circumstance, rumors and fabrications. We're asking that all charges against, Ms. Robbins, be dropped and she immediately get released," he said.

"Your honor, the suspect, has committed a callous and calculated murder. Her family has a great deal of money and influence in the community, which would place her high on the list as a flight risk. We're asking that she be held without bond," the D.A. said as he stood tall and confidently against the wooden desk.

I couldn't think of his name but this same bastard had eaten at our house on several occasions and now he was trying to have me convicted. I glared at him and silently wished that he would disappear.

"We have several witnesses that can vouch for Ms. Robbins whereabouts on the night that the murder was committed. As well as a sworn statement from one of the participants who had conspired to ruin her life," Rayven chimed in as she handed the bailiff as well as the prosecution a stack of papers.

The judge took her time reading over each one carefully. The silence in the courtroom was driving me madder with each second. I prayed that whatever Rayven and Anthony came up with was enough to convince her that I was innocent.

"After carefully reviewing the information I have decided to drop all charges against Ms. Robbins until you have some reliable evidence. It seems that there is more to this story than what you realize," the judge said to the prosecution as she looked sternly over the brim of her glasses.

I wasn't sure what was said after that as I started to scream and cry. I grabbed Rayven and Anthony and hugged them both at the same time. The judge banged loudly with her gravel and Rayven placed her hand over my mouth to quiet me. She gave my arm a slight squeeze and we both silently continued to celebrate.

"Quiet! I understand you're happy Ms. Robbins, but you're not all the way innocent in any of this. If more evidence should arise, I'm sure you will be indicted and back in court. Karma knows the unknown and there is no way to escape it," the judge lectured me as I continued to nod my head.

She could have called me an evil bitch, as far as I cared. I was just glad that I was a free evil bitch. I turned towards my father and smiled widely at both him and Chris. They both looked as if they couldn't wait to wrap their arms around me.

"Your honor, the death of Megan Lewis was caused by Tracey Robbins. Clearly she and Ms. Robbins had some animosity towards one another. The last time she was seen was at the same hotel that Ms Robbins was living in," the D.A. screamed anxiously.

"There's no proof and nothing that points towards Ms. Robbins as her murderer. We convict people based on evidence in this good state. As I was saying, you are free to go Ms. Robbins and make sure I never see you inside this courtroom again. Bailiff, please take Detective Smith here into custody. It seems he has had a part in all of this mess and nothing makes me madder than dirty cops."

I turned my head towards the fat detective that had questioned me so hard and looked at him with shocked eyes. He quietly put his hands behind his back and hung his head low. His partner looked just as shocked as I did as he was taken into custody. How was he involved in this mess?

"Cliff notes version, Christian hired him to help in all this mess. He was knee deep in the shit. He took those pictures of you and Tez at that orgy party and everything. I'll have to explain it to you over drinks tonight," Rayven whispered in my ear as we walked towards the door.

Anthony stopped me and held me by the shoulders. "I'm glad you're out of this mess Tracey. And I'm sorry for hurting you. I was wrong," he told me.

I smiled at my ex. "Everyone deserves to be happy. So, whether it's Kensington or my mother, I'm fine with that."

"Well just so you know, I'm running for state Senate and my advisor told me your mother doesn't fit the profile. Plus she's bad for the campaign, too chatty and interfering in my affairs already so I'm leaving her soon." He leaned to kiss me on my cheek then walked out the courtroom leaving me speechless.

Karma, I thought to myself. I kept feeling a pair of eyes on me so I finally turned my back slightly. The guard who escorted me down was standing in the doorway with a scowl on his face. He almost seemed angry that I had gotten off. "I told you, you will never see me in here again. Maybe next lifetime, baby," I said, making my way past him.

"Sooner than you think boo," he replied with a wink.

I looked at him as he closed the courtroom door. His grin looked more evil than happy. I shook off the eerie feeling that he was right and walked towards my father and Chris who had already walked out ahead of me. In my haste I bumped into Mrs. Santana and almost knocked her over.

Her face was stained with tears and she quickly wiped them with her silky handkerchief. She gave me a tight lipped smile right before she turned and glared at my father.

"Tracey, why don't you watch where you are going," she said, smoothing the invisible wrinkles from her skirt.

"Is it true?" I asked.

"Is what true, dear?" she asked coyly. I could tell that she already knew what I was talking about.

"Are you really my mother? Like, did you have me and just give me up to Gertrude?"

She stared at me lovingly and I saw so much of myself in her eyes. I wanted to reach out and hug her. She was what I was looking for all my life. She was a wonderful mother to Christian, loyal and devoted. I wanted that in my life and had always missed it. The tears that tugged at the corners of her eyes spilled past her water proof mascara and I knew that what my father told me was true.

"It's okay mother, you don't have to cry. I'm sure you did what was best for you at the time," I told her as I placed her face into my hands.

As quick as the moment of sincerity came she took it away. Her eyes flashed anger. Mrs. Santana had become cold. She pushed my hands away from her face and looked at me with disdain.

"Don't you ever call me that again? I have only one daughter and because of you, she is on her way to the crazy house. I may have birthed you, but you are nothing more than a whore, just like that psychotic bitch that raised you," she yelled at me.

"You act as if I asked for her to raise me. I never asked to be born. I never asked for any of this! You should have thought of

the consequences when you spread your legs and got pregnant!"
I screamed back.

"How dare you, you little slut!"

"Oh, I'm the slut?" I asked in a calm tone. "Should I tell everyone why we're both sluts?" I moved closer so I could talk softly in her ear. "You asked me to never tell anyone that you were at the orgy party. I kept my word, and made sure you kept your perfect life. But know I'm the slut?"

The slap that came next was something that I was not ready for. My face swung around slightly and the sting was almost unbearable. As she drew her hand back to hit me again my father stepped in and grabbed her arm.

"It's me and Gertrude that you are angry at Sophia. Don't you dare take this out on our child," he said as he spoke with authority.

"That bitch is not my child. She's no product of mine. She may not have conspired to ruin Christian's life, but she is just as guilty. The day she decided to spread her legs and fuck her husband and the day she signed the papers to send my baby away made her guilty. I will never forgive her for that and I will never forgive you," she replied meekly.

Her words stung harder than the slap but I could see that she was still hurting from losing my father all those years ago. I thought of all the times I caught her looking at me oddly over the years. I'd always thought that she didn't like me but it was really the hurting behind not being able to have her child with the man that she loved.

"Let her go Daddy. She's hurting just like us and all we can offer are prayers." I turned towards Mrs. Santana and looked at her with pity. "I'm sorry about Christian. I really loved her like a sister before I even had a clue that we really were related. Hopefully one day, we'll be able to have a relationship together," I said.

I grabbed my daddy's hand and then placed my free one into Chris.' We walked towards the doors and I smiled at everyone who passed me by. I was a free woman and nothing and no one would be able to take that from me.

"You'll have to pay for your mistakes just like everyone else, little girl. Gertrude has you believing that you can get away with anything but mark my words, you will pay," she continued to yell after me until I walked through the revolving doors.

Chapter 36

"Guess what fashionista rocked thigh high Dior boots out of the court room after being exonerated on murder charges? None other than, Tracey Robbins, that's who. I don't know about you guys, but I'm getting sick and tired of this chick. She needs to sign an endorsement deal with us, we talk about her so much.

"MURDER? Girl you are lying to me," Mz. Janee chimed in.

"Yes, people, murder. Her and her best friend Christian Jones, finally had the big pow wow that we had all been waiting for. It looks like Tracey is the last woman standing, as Christian was carried away in an ambulance. Of course our spies thought that was the reason for her arrest, but we got down to the nitty gritty and found out it was actually for murder," Staci Static said.

"I can't believe it, this story just keeps getting bigger," Mz. Janee continued to co-sign.

"This story is just sad. But you Tracey Robbins fans, don't count your girl out yet. She hasn't murdered anyone, she was actually innocent. But here is the crazy part," Staci paused for the dramatic effect that she knew everyone was expecting.

"If Tracey didn't commit the murder, then who did? I know there isn't a killer on the loose, prowling around in these here streets. It just sounds to flaky, I'm thinking that money may have influenced some people."

"What?" Mz.Janee screamed to the top of her lungs. "I don't think so. Just because you have money doesn't mean you can pay your way out of anything. I think Tracey is innocent and she needs to take a vacation after all of that. You can't help but feel bad for the girl. She has really gone through some drama."

"I don't know about feeling bad for her, after all, she ain't no angel. But she most definitely needs to take a break, a long one at that. Go somewhere warm and just mind your business for *a while. This is what happens when we butt our noses into some-one else's mess, you quickly get tired of them. She's a true testa-ment that everything that glitters isn't gold. I'm team Christian!"*

"Whatever, I sure wouldn't mind having some of that gold. Help a sista pay some of these bills off. My question is, who will now be St. Louis' it girl. I'm not counting my girl Tracey out though, she'll be back! I guess we are now watching the throne. As always STL, we will keep you all informed when the next heir steps up. As for you Tracey, be careful what you continue to do because you know the streets will still be watching you. Team Tracey over here," Mz Janee said as they ended their segment.

I cut the radio off and sat back on the blanket. The cool air was all around me but the frozen pond was one of my favorite spots to sit and think. This spot was one of the fonder moments in my life, ice skating with my father. I smiled thinking of how grateful I was that I wasn't in jail.

Rayven and I never got that drink but we spent hours on the phone as she brought me up to speed with everything that she had found out for me. The part with the detective was the where I was really bugging out. He had been under Christian's payroll for quite some time. He was the one who took the pictures of me and Tez at the party along with Christian. He also had done all the surveillance on Chuck and me. To keep a low profile they barely met in public and were smart to destroy all evidence. However, they forgot to clean up the most important detail. The gun that the police caught in my hand was the weapon that Christian used to shoot me.

After bumping into Mrs. Santana after court I really wanted to contact Christian. She needed to know that the two of us really were sisters. No man and nothing else would be able to come in between that.

I pulled my legs close to my body and hugged them for some sort of warmth. Being in jail for hours, I didn't want to miss a single second of air, even if it was freezing. Shaking, I grabbed my thermal and took a warm sip of the cider I had made. I closed my eyes as I allowed the liquid to comfort me. It wasn't until I heard the earth crunching close behind me that I opened them.

"Tracey," the man said as he touched my shoulder.

I jumped and quickly turned to face him. I blinked several times just to make sure I wasn't inside of a dream.

"Tez?" I asked in disbelief.

"It's me, baby. Told you I was going to come back for you when I got my shit together."

He smiled down at me and I felt as if the sun had moved through my soul. I was beyond warm. Even after all of the things he done to me, I still felt love for him.

"What are you doing here, Tez? Where have you been all this time?"

I sat up on my elbows in disbelief. I could not believe that he was standing before me. I reached out my arm and touched his leg just to make sure he was indeed real.

"I'm here for you, baby," he said.

"Is it really you?" I stupidly asked. I was still in a state of shock. No one knew what happened to him the night that he hung up on me. I really thought Christian had murdered him.

"Yeah, fool. Who else would it be?"

He threw his head back in a sexy laugh and then sat down beside me. He knocked the snow off his Ugg Carnero boots. I tried not to stare at the diamonds shining on his Bulgari watch. Wherever he was, he had been living well.

"Everybody thought that you were dead. Where have you been all this time?"

"You know me, Ms. Bougie, sometimes I shake the situation. Needed to regroup. After that crazy bitch Christian cut loose I had to leave for a while."

I cringed at him calling me that name. I was no longer that person. Hearing him say Christian's name felt even crazier. I pondered on whether I should tell him that she and I were really sisters. I wondered if he knew that Christian had been pregnant with his child? That was so nasty, having sex with two sisters. Ugh!

"I'm not Ms. Bougie anymore. I don't even live around those people. I had to regroup more than anybody, considering all the things that were done to me."

"Yeah, I know. Shit was foul. If I could take it all back I would. That wasn't me at all. I was just trying to get a quick buck," he said as he looked at me with a need for understanding.

I felt my emotions flare. The fact that he had been a part of the drama still hurt me. I wasn't sure I would ever be able to understand that. "I don't know what you want me to say. I can't say that I forgive you, at least not yet. I'm just trying to remove any and every thing negative out of my life," I replied as I took another sip of cider. The heat that I felt when I first saw him had started to ice up again.

"I know what you been up to. I kept tabs on you. You've done good for yourself. I always knew you were better than that role you put on." He stared intently at me causing me to become nervous.

"You've been keeping tabs on me, but why?"

I wondered if his interest in me was still malicious. He'd proved that he didn't love me. Everything I thought that we had was a total lie.

"Girl, you crazier than I thought if you can't see I love you. All bullshit aside, you the one," he said while pushing my hair from my face.

I closed my eyes under his touch. It had been so long since I had that feeling. I loved Chris' touch, but this was something that I could not explain. Too bad it couldn't excuse him for what he had done to me. I had started to form what I thought were relationships with him and Shanice both. The events of the past few months had caused me to really take a look at my life and how I had been living it. My attitude was horrible and it was all because I had always felt entitled. I thought everyone owed me everything because I had the money and the power that they longed for.

"I called Shanice this morning and told her that she could have the magazine if she wants it. I'm going to take a little break," I told him as I opened my eyes.

Shanice had really turned into a nice girl as I got to know her. I would have never thought we had anything in common because she was ghetto as hell but she proved me wrong.

"Oh word? I'm happy for her, she deserves a break like that. But umm, how you just gone ignore what I just said to you. Why you avoiding me?" he asked lovingly.

"Tez, I'm happy you are okay. I really am. However, I'm a different person now. I don't think or act the same."

"Nobody is asking you to. All I'm asking is that you give the real me a chance. I'm not a saint but I ain't the same person I use to be either," he hollered a little louder than he needed to.

He was trying to get his point across and I was not feeling it. I'd gotten used to being treated gently by Chris. "No, I can't go backwards and if you love me like you say you do, you would respect that." Now it was my eyes that pleaded for understanding. The last thing I needed to be was confused

"So what, that's just it? You can't lie and say you didn't miss me. I know like hell you did. I sure missed you and those lips and them hips." He ran his hand softly up my leg.

My phone rang on the blanket and startled the both of us. We both looked down and saw that it was Chris calling. I silently thanked God for stopping what was about to happen.

"What you gone do, Tracey? I'm right here and he on the phone," Tez stated the obvious.

I wrestled with the idea of whether I should answer the phone or not. This was the exact confusion that I wanted to avoid. I knew that being with Chris had brought out the best side of me. As I reached for the phone my screen went blank. I had waited too long and now he was probably worrying about me. Chris didn't deserve for me to be dishonest with him.

"See, he hung up. Even he knows that your choice should be me. Just let me back in. So many things I want to do to your lil sexy ass."

He pulled me close to him again and kissed me on the lips. It took exactly one second for me to kiss him back. As our tongues moved in and out of each other's mouth effortlessly, I saw images of Chris and me praying together. His smile flashed before me and I knew that he was the one I wanted.

"I have to go, Tez. I'm in love with Chris. He completes me in ways I didn't even know was possible. He believes in me enough that I feel powerful and confident in myself." I pushed my way out of his arms and stood up.

"That's cool, but listen to me when I tell you this, the way I just made you feel ain't no damn lie. Go ahead and feel all empowered and shit, but I'll get you back." He momentarily flashed an angry frown upon his face. Just as quick as it appeared he wiped it away with a smile.

"I'm sorry Tez, but I can't go back down this path getting back with you is a setback. I'm truly glad you're alive and well though." I didn't give him a chance to respond as I grabbed my blanket from under him, grabbed my cup and hurried towards my truck. It felt good to be able to walk away from the lust that I felt for him. That was the only thing that he and I had in common. The fact that I recognized that put a huge smile on my face. My recovery was finally finished.

The past couple of months, had been a complete hell on earth for me. However, it caused me to realize, life did exist outside of my Mother's circle. And I was a lot stronger than I initially thought I was. So, my Oprah dream had been deferred, but I knew I would bounce back. I never really considered that being a woman, meant being the co-pilot while God ordered my steps. I had grown a lot closer to Him, and was waiting patiently on the next season he would bring me into. I was over that old me, and had let go of everyone in that life. Money didn't make me nor would I let losing some of it break me!

I sat in my truck still smiling at how I had come a long way. I knew that Chris would eventually become my husband because he was sent to me at the perfect time in my life. I put my hand in my pocket to call him back when I realized that my phone was not in it. Frantically, I looked inside the blanket I had for my picnic. It wasn't in there either. I had dropped it somewhere on the ground in my escape from Tez.

Tez pulled up on the side of me holding the phone in his hand.

"Hey baby, you left your phone down by the pond. I must still make you nervous," he said as I rolled my window down.

"Thank you Tez. I thought I lost it and no comment on the other stuff."

He was cocky if nothing else. He just didn't know when to give up. The flirting back and forth was fun, but I didn't want to start a fire off dimming sparks.

"I told you I got you boo. You need to put more faith in a brother."

"I can't lie and say I'm not a little tempted, but please don't make it hard for me. I'm really trying to get myself together."

I attempted to roll the window up, still on my mission to leave. He placed his hand on it so it wouldn't budge any further.

"Seriously though, I got a room down at the Lumiere. I'll be living there for a little while. Whenever you get bored with your new life, come and holla at me. No strings attached. I'ma give you the key just in case."

As he stuck his hand into his pocket to grab the key a black Mercedes with dark tinted windows pulled up on the side of my truck. Tez turned around to see who was behind us when the window rolled down. I saw the look of panic wash over his eyes as he screamed at me.

"Pull off Tracey," he yelled loudly. "I've seen them with Christian!"

I tried to turn the key but my shaking hands caused them to fall out the ignition. I reached down to grab them when I heard a loud popping noise. Tez's body hit the ground and his motorcycle fell to its side.

The masked man smiled at me and I noticed how perfectly white his teeth were. As he pulled up his black ski mask my eyes immediately darted to the dimple in his chin. He was the guard from the Justice Center. My heart skipped several beats as I thought of his warning to see me sooner than later.

"I don't have any money on me, just take me to an ATM and I swear I will give you all that I have. You don't have to kill me," I reasoned with him.

He must've read up on my life while I was in jail. He wanted to rob me. These kind of people always were looking for a quick come up.

"This isn't about business honey, this is principle and loyalty right here," the voice on the side of him said.

As soon as I heard her icy voice, I knew that no matter what I did, I was now about to pay the devil with my soul. Sophia sat up in the car and looked at me with a wicked grin on her face. The pearl handled gun in her hand was leveled with my face.

"You remind me of everything that I hate. May your soul rest wherever in the hell it sees fit," she said as she pulled the trigger.

I closed my eyes and braced myself for death.

CHECK OUT THESE LCB SEQUELS

V.I.P.

CONFESSIONS OF A Groupie

A NOVEL BY AZAREL

ORDER FORM

MAIL TO:
PO Box 423
Brandywine, MD 20613
301-362-6508

FAX TO:
301-579-9913

Ship to:
Address:

Date: Phone:

Email:

City & State: Zip:

Make all money orders and cashiers checks payable to: **Life Changing Books**

Qty.	ISBN	Title	Release Date	Price
	0-9741394-2-4	Bruised by Azarel	Jul-05	$ 15.00
	0-9741394-7-5	Bruised 2: The Ultimate Revenge by Azarel	Oct-06	$ 15.00
	0-9741394-3-2	Secrets of a Housewife by J. Tremble	Feb-06	$ 15.00
	0-9741394-6-7	The Millionaire Mistress by Tiphani	Nov-06	$ 15.00
	1-934230-99-5	More Secrets More Lies by J. Tremble	Feb-07	$ 15.00
	1-934230-95-2	A Private Affair by Mike Warren	May-07	$ 15.00
	1-934230-93-6	Deep by Danette Majette	Jul-07	$ 15.00
	1-934230-96-0	Flexin & Sexin Volume 1	Jun-07	$ 15.00
	1-934230-89-8	Still a Mistress by Tiphani	Nov-07	$ 15.00
	1-934230-91-X	Daddy's House by Azarel	Nov-07	$ 15.00
	1-934230-88-X	Naughty Little Angel by J. Tremble	Feb-08	$ 15.00
	1-934230847	In Those Jeans by Chantel Jolie	Jun-08	$ 15.00
	1-934230820	Rich Girls by Kendall Banks	Oct-08	$ 15.00
	1-934230839	Expensive Taste by Tiphani	Nov-08	$ 15.00
	1-934230782	Brooklyn Brothel by C. Stecko	Jan-09	$ 15.00
	1-934230669	Good Girl Gone bad by Danette Majette	Mar-09	$ 15.00
	1-934230804	From Hood to Hollywood by Sasha Raye	Mar-09	$ 15.00
	1-934230707	Sweet Swagger by Mike Warren	Jun-09	$ 15.00
	1-934230677	Carbon Copy by Azarel	Jul-09	$ 15.00
	1-934230723	Millionaire Mistress 3 by Tiphani	Nov-09	$ 15.00
	1-934230715	A Woman Scorned by Ericka Williams	Nov-09	$ 15.00
	1-934230685	My Man Her Son by J. Tremble	Feb-10	$ 15.00
	1-924230731	Love Heist by Jackie D.	Mar-10	$ 15.00
	1-934230812	Flexin & Sexin Volume 2	Apr-10	$ 15.00
	1-934230748	The Dirty Divorce by Miss KP	May-10	$ 15.00
	1-934230758	Chedda Boyz by CJ Hudson	Jul-10	$ 15.00
	1-934230766	Snitch by VegasClarke	Oct-10	$ 15.00
	1-934230693	Money Maker by Tonya Ridley	Oct-10	$ 15.00
	1-934230774	The Dirty Divorce Part 2 by Miss KP	Nov-10	$ 15.00
	1-934230170	The Available Wife by Carla Pennington	Jan-11	$ 15.00
	1-934230774	One Night Stand by Kendall Banks	Feb-11	$ 15.00
	1-934230278	Bitter by Danette Majette	Feb-11	$ 15.00
	1-934230299	Married to a Balla by Jackie D.	May-11	$ 15.00
	1-934230308	The Dirty Divorce Part 3 by Miss KP	Jun-11	$ 15.00
	1-934230316	Next Door Nympho By CJ Hudson	Jun-11	$ 15.00
	1-934230286	Bedroom Gangsta by J. Tremble	Sep-11	$ 15.00
	1-934230340	Another One Night Stand by Kendall Banks	Oct-11	$ 15.00
	1-934230359	The Available Wife Part 2 by Carla Pennington	Nov-11	$ 15.00

Total for Books $

Shipping Charges (add $4.95 for 1-4 books*) $

Total Enclosed (add lines) $

* Prison Orders- Please allow up to three (3) weeks for delivery.

Please Note: We are not held responsible for returned prison orders. Make sure the facility will receive books before ordering.

*Shipping and Handling of 5-10 books is $6.95, please contact us if your order is more than 10 books. (301)362-6508